REVIEWS FOR J.T. FLEMING'S
Tracks of a Pigeon-toed Horse & The Obsidian Serpent

Fleming writes his characters off the page and into your heart.... With just a touch of mysticism, great descriptions of these lands and the people on them, Fleming combines all this to create one very good story after another. Anyone who loves westerns will really appreciate these books, and it is refreshing to have women characters just as interesting as the men....

Western fans will love this true balance of dialogue, descriptive prose and action. The historical information is skillfully woven into these stories which are filled with humor, sudden fast paced action scenes and a clear love of nature and the out-of-doors. I highly recommend these books and those yet to be written....

Author LINDA DUNNING

(Ghost Lights; Lost Landscapes; Restless Spirits; Specters in Doorways)

I bought this on a chance—one of those 'pick-it-out as you look'. It pulled me in and kept me up late into the night reading. Kept the suspense until the end. A great mystery in the main plot and a secondary plot that had me buying his second book before I finished the first!

cinderpf; Utah

Being an avid reader of all types of books, from J.K. Rowling, to James Patterson, and everything in-between, I began this book with high hopes of many evenings of entertainment. I was not disappointed. Mr. Fleming's knowledge of the Utah area I grew up in was evident, and it was obvious he had done his homework.

This book covers the very controversial area of Mormonism in the 1800's, and examines the pro's and con's of plural marriage, and a people who were not saints, but very much wanted to be.

I was impressed with the way I was pulled into the story, from page one. I give this a definite thumbs up, and also recommend "The Obsidian Serpent" which continues the story of Collin Mitchell and makes you want for more.

nana211 Oregon

MOURIEL

Secret of the Lost Crow

Also by J.T. Fleming

Tracks of a Pigeon-toed Horse

The Obsidian Serpent

Mouriel
Secret of the Lost Crow

MOURIEL

Secret of the Lost Crow

BY

J. T. Fleming

Mouriel: Secret of the Lost Crow

Library of Congress # TXU001897363

ISBN:978-0-9832461-6-9 (PBK)

This novel is a work of fiction. Names, characters, places, and incidents are the product of the author's imagination or are used fictitiously. Any resemblance to actual events, locales, organizations or their doctrines, or persons, living or dead, is entirely coincidental and beyond the intent of either the author or publisher.

FORTRESS PUBLISHING, LLC
Clearfield , Utah

*Dedicated to my wife, Gail,
proofreader, critic, typist, and
best friend.*

With special thanks to all those who took the time to read and comment on this project while it was in progress.

Mouriel

Secret of the Lost Crow

PROLOGUE

The War

Mouriel watched as a pattern of brilliant white lights flashed across the dark matter and surrounded a whirling vortex of angry crimson light. The seething vortex surged outward, expanding in a red hot blaze, illuminating the space around it in a searing conflagration.

Time meant nothing as the two forces collided. The force of the attack struck the white with a power that threatened to break through the containment barrier. The barrier strained, struggling to restrain the seething crimson maelstrom.

Mouriel caught the signal from his leader and moved swiftly to confront an even greater mass of scarlet lights strung out across the dark matter in a long sinuous shape. The scarlet shape twisted, coiling about itself like a snake ready to strike and waited, its nearest prominence gaping like fanged jaws. Mouriel and the lights that followed him drove like a spear into the heart of the enemy, the jaws snapped closed, devouring the white within a boiling sea of crimson.

Beyond the edges of the pulsating cloud that was the enemy, a greater gathering of lights waited… anticipating. Suddenly, a brilliant white incandescence flared from within the enemy, lancing outward like the explosion of a white hot star, shredding the crimson cloud into a tattered lacework of drifting tendrils.

Oceans of Time

Mouriel stood watch patiently. Time had no meaning. The plan was moving forward.

Below, the watery blue world beckoned unceasingly, promising wonders beyond his experience and comprehension. Oceans lapped at sandy coastlines, forests carpeted the hills, grass rolled across valleys and plains, snow capped the tallest peaks. Yet, none of it could he touch. None of it could he taste or feel. It was as far from his experience as anything he had known. Yet he knew what it was. He knew what it meant. It was the doorway into eternity. And it beckoned…. How it beckoned….

Still, Mouriel kept his post, a lone watchman holding firm against the savage rage of the enemy—the madness that fought to break the boundaries and escape its prison.

And the war raged on.

Time moved on the world below, and something changed. Suddenly, the beckoning of the blue world surged up to engulf him with an unrelenting intensity. Mouriel felt himself wrenched from his post—drifting at first, then speeding toward the blue world, speeding downward, into the voracious maw of the crimson enemy and into the heart of the war.

Argonne Forest—October 1918

The old man dropped the horse's reins and slid over the edge of the trench and into the water soaked muck below. Overhead, the sizzling glare of a star shell slashed the darkness, illuminating a shadowland of torn earth, scattered weapons, and concertina wire draped with the faceless dead—hanging like discarded puppets in the tangles of coiled razor wire or half sunk in the mud.

The old man turned to the right, sloshing through mud, working his way along the sagging boardwalks of the trench. With every step, his trousers grew heavier as the homespun cloth sucked water from the floor of the trench like a man half dead from thirst.

At a crossing of the trenches, the old man paused and glanced upward. Overhead, the flare sizzled strongly for a moment; then, as though the old man's glance had shriven the life from it, the flare sputtered and died, leaving the trench shrouded in the final moments of darkness before sunrise.

For a moment, the old man waited, sensing movement and the muffled sound of troops moving like wraiths toward him. When the troop appeared, it came as a long line of hump-backed shadows flowing like a dark fog through the dimness of the intersecting trenches. Their feet plowed through muddy water, and each man kept his eyes on his feet as though sight alone could keep him from slipping into the waist deep water. They moved like men already banished to the depths of hell—banished with no hope of release.

Minutes passed as the old man waited silently in the shadows, while the soldiers dissipated one by one, until nothing moved in the silence of the morning.

Suddenly, the silence shattered. Cannons thundered and pounded the earth. Machine guns rattled death across barren, pockmarked fields, and the enemy came. The old man could feel them as they neared… through the trenches… four of them filled with power… each one filled with a lust for murder.

Hatred filled the atmosphere with an almost tangible stench. The four turned a corner. And in the dimness of the predawn, they stood face to face with the old man—a foe older than time, and their weapons sprang upward, firing.

Mouriel's hand sped downward to the pistol tucked in his belt, and the trench erupted in thunder and flame.

MOURIEL

Chapter 1

Utah Territory
Deep Creek Mountains—June 1869

The mountain shuddered with the deep, hard *thump* of seven closely spaced explosions, and for a moment, all life paused as if stunned to motionless silence. Mule deer froze in mid-step, ears tilted like compasses pointing directly toward the epicenter of the offending event. A chipmunk halted its work on a grounded pine cone and stared intently in the same direction. Birds severed all conversation, and the mountain was suddenly and completely silent.

No echoing reverberation followed, for the whole of the event had taken place deep in the ore-bearing strata of the mountain, and only that one solid *thump* of vibration had escaped to signify the presence of men in the depths of the earth.

Deep within the mountain, shattered rock clattered to an uneasy rest on the tunnel floor. Dust and the smoke of burnt blasting powder rushed up the throat of the tunnel until it burst upon the outside world in a chaotic cloud of tumbling gas and dust.

Three-hundred feet below, and a quarter of a mile into the mountain, two miners raised their candles and peered cautiously from the niche where they had taken refuge from the violence of the explosion. The dust settled, and the air slowly cleared until the tunnel walls became visible in the dim light of the two candles. Silently, they made the long trip back down the tunnel until they reached the rubble littered floor and the face they had just blasted.

"What in the hell!" The first miner raised his lamp higher and frowned. "That was only the seven charges; wasn't it, Mike?"

Mike Deagan lifted a candle and peered into the gloom. "Just seven… an' that upper reliever was only half a charge 'cause we thought it was drilled a little shallow."

Art Williams eased forward, shuffling toward the shattered face of the tunnel and the strange sight that lay before them. "Must have cut into a pocket of some kind," he suggested.

Deagan shrugged. "We seen plenty of 'em before."

Williams stooped and thrust his candle beyond the shattered remains of the face and into the pocket. "Bet you ain't seen the likes of that before."

Deagan edged up beside the older man and bent to peer into the pocket. "Good lord! How'd he get in there?"

* * *

An hour later, the County's only deputy sheriff glared at the corpse and shifted his feet uneasily. "This ain't funny," he growled. "I could throw the both of you in jail for movin' that body and wastin' my time with your stupid jokes!"

"We didn't do nothin'!" Deagan wailed. "We blew the face, and when the dust cleared, there he was! We never touched nothin'!"

Williams, the elder of the two, nervously rolled a cigarette and shoved it between his lips. "The kid's tellin' the truth," he growled at the deputy as the mine foreman took his turn to view the remains.

"Don't make no sense," the foreman muttered. "There ain't no way that body could get in there before you blew the face. That pocket is in solid rock."

"Them bones didn't walk in there by themselves," Williams snarled. "We never put 'em there, and nobody else could have done it neither… not with Deagan and me standin' back there waitin' for the dust to settle. It wasn't that thick, an' we would have seen somebody!"

"Somebody put that fellow there," growled the deputy. "Either it was the two of you, or somebody else. You say you didn't do it, so maybe you shot that face and then took a little nap while the candles was blown out. Nobody comes down here after a shot like that, until you call it *clear*. Maybe you just sat there in the dark all comfortable like while somebody came in here real quiet and put that fellow in that hole."

"We wasn't sleepin'!" Deagan wailed, knowing his job could be gone in an instant if Jack Ramsay thought they had slacked in their duties for even a minute.

"You got no call to say something like that," Williams snapped defensively. "We called for help not more than five minutes after the dust cleared, and there're twenty men up top that can back us up on that. So there weren't no time for sleepin'."

Ramsay shrugged in the constantly shifting light of the candles. "That's true," he admitted reluctantly. "We all felt the charges go off, and it wasn't more than ten minutes before half the crew was spreading tales about a corpse buried in solid rock."

Williams lifted his candle so the light played directly in the deputy's eyes. "That's right," he intoned stubbornly. "Nobody could get in or out with that thing without at least half a dozen fellows watchin'. The night crew drilled for those charges before we came in this morning. Deagan an' me went in soon as we come on shift. Half the crew watched us go in and waited for us to drop the charges an' set 'em off. We ain't that deep yet, so the crew waits up top 'til the dust settles. We do that every morning. Soon as we call it clear, the muckers come down with the ore carts an' everybody starts loadin' 'em up."

Ramsay nodded in agreement. "It's exactly as he says, Deputy. I have to agree that there is no way they could have brought that corpse down here without half the crew knowing about it."

Ramsay pointed toward the pocket. "How long before you can get that thing out of here?" He demanded abruptly. "I've got twenty men standing around, doing nothing, while we debate how that fellow got down here. I really don't care how it happened. I just want it out of here and my crew back to work."

The deputy shrugged. "An hour…maybe two," he answered unhappily, knowing that the inevitable push for instant results was about to make life miserable. "I need some time to look things over real good. This ain't normal, and I need to make some good notes on everything I can find. The Sheriff ain't gonna be happy if I don't."

Ramsay shook his head. "Make it thirty minutes," he said tersely. "Mister Gromley wants those men back to work."

"Thirty minutes ain't enough," squawked the deputy. "Mister Forestall told me I could have enough time to do whatever I needed."

Ramsay planted himself directly in front of the deputy. "Listen, Simmons. Mister Forestall may be the biggest stock holder, but Mister Gromley runs the shipments, and I'm the whip that keeps the wagons rolling." Ramsay lowered his voice to a murmur only the deputy could hear. "I'm sending the crew down to load the ore carts. Deagan and Williams will be drilling for the next hour. I'll give you that long. Once the charges are set, you had better be finished, because there won't be anything left to look at after that."

"You ain't being very cooperative," Simmons protested. "In fact, you're coming close to obstruction."

Ramsay raised an eyebrow. "Now, Deputy Simmons, you know I would never do anything to obstruct you in your duties, but we both know there is little or nothing to be gained by spending a lot of time fussing around down here. Obviously, the man didn't die here, so any evidence related to his death will be somewhere else entirely."

Simmons shook his head as if unconvinced. "I'm not so sure..."

"Do you really expect to find anything helpful?"

"Probably not..."

"Exactly!"

"I suppose an hour would be enough," Simmons admitted grudgingly. "As long as those two don't trample anything while they're drilling."

Ramsay put a friendly hand on the deputy's shoulder. "I'll instruct them to walk lightly and keep out of your way as much as possible," he agreed smoothly. "You boys heard that!" he called over his shoulder.

At the niche where they had waited out the blast that had opened the pocket, both miners stooped to retrieve tool bags loaded with single-jacks and bits.

"Deagan! Williams!"

"We heard!" The pair snapped in unison.

Ramsay lifted his candle until the pair was dimly illuminated. In the dead air of the tunnel, the candle flame barely flickered. "We've lost more than an hour already," he snarled. "If I thought for a minute the two of you had anything to do with that thing, I'd dock your pay until every bit of the cost was paid back. Then I'd fire the both of you."

Ramsay took one last look at the open cyst and the rotting corpse within then hurried up the tunnel toward fresh air and light. Simmons was close on his heels.

"Jackass," Williams grumbled when Ramsay's light had disappeared beyond the curve of the tunnel. "You an' me are in for it now, Deagan."

"What are you talkin' about?"

"I'm talking about Ramsay stabbin' us in the back."

"Why would he do that? He knows we ain't done nothin'."

"You're still a little green, ain't you?" Williams tossed his tool bag near the mouth of the cyst, ignoring the dried-up corpse within. "Think about it, kid. Gromley has been pushin' this crew like a man possessed. Six weeks ago, we was working sixteen and eighteen hour days, seven days a week. Now we got a night crew and we're still workin' twelve hour shifts. All 'cause we hit a vein of silver over in tunnel number one. Strange thing though… soon as that new night crew struck that vein, Ramsay fired every one of 'em and brought in a bunch of fellows nobody ever seen before.

"O'Neil was one of them that was fired. He told me Ramsay gave 'em no warning and offered no reasons for replacing the crew. Now Ramsay says he's got his eye on you and me. You can bet we'll be out of a job right soon, and I'll give you odds that it won't be long before all of the old crew is fired and no one is left but these new fellows."

Deagan dropped his tools near the opening of the cyst and sat down on the bag. "I can't afford to lose this job," he groaned. "Why would Ramsay replace everyone? We ain't slowed down none; we've actually been doin' better than ever. Mr. Gromley told us that no more than a week ago!"

Williams dropped down beside the boy and fished the makings out of his tool bag. In the dimness of the candle light, he loaded tobacco onto a small rectangle of paper. When the cigarette was rolled and lit, he leaned back against the tunnel wall and stared at the ragged roof.

"Somethin' fishy is goin' on," he mused thoughtfully. "O'Neil claims there's ore shipments goin' out of here at two or three in the morning. He says he asked Gromley about it, but Gromley denied it and told him all shipments go to Tooele under guard at first light—never earlier. Safer that way... so he says."

"What's that got to do with firing everyone?"

"Don't know," Williams admitted, "but it's a bit coincidental, don't you think?"

"So you think something sneaky is going on and we're gonna get fired because of it?"

Williams glanced toward the tunnel entrance. "Take a look up there and tell me what you see," he instructed.

"Nothing. It's black as pitch."

"Exactly."

"I don't get it."

"Listen kid. We started this tunnel by driving straight into the mountain. That was before Gromley bought in last year. Forestall was runnin' the whole show by himself back then, and we were following a skimpy little vein. We never saw enough silver to pay the crew let alone pay for the whole operation. Forestall was losin' his shirt. All of a sudden, Gromley shows up and buys up half the operation. Two weeks later, Ramsay hires on.

"By then we had punched six-hundred feet into the mountain. Now, for all that time, we ran straight as an arrow, hoppin' and skippin' right on that little vein. All of a sudden, Ramsay says the vein is bearing to the northwest. Now, you and me been workin' this face for two months, and I sure ain't seen a trace of that vein since we started drifting northwest."

For a moment Deagan sat silently, breathing slowly in the darkness, inhaling the scent of damp earth mixed with the sharp tang of blasting powder. "You shouldn't be smokin' so close to that powder," he muttered.

"I talked with Andy Hawkins over at the Ophir mine," he confided after a moment. "He says they're getting' some good stuff, but they ain't got a real vein. He says it's like some kind of underground placer deposit…real fine too."

Williams threw up his hands. "That's just what I've been sayin'! If we're getting' any color out of this ore, it's too fine to see. And we ain't got the equipment to extract it. All I've seen is a little galena.

"Some of that stuff they're talkin' about up to Park City is like silver wires runnin' through the rock. You can make money with ore like that, but this stuff… Gromley would have to run every bit of it through a crusher and then through some kind of sluice to wash out the silver. I ain't seen any special equipment. Have you?"

"We got a small crusher," Deagan responded.

"But we ain't usin' it much, and even if we did, we ain't got anything to extract the really fine stuff. Do we?"

"I reckon not."

"So where is Gromley getting the money to keep this operation running?"

"Folks say he's rich," Deagan suggested.

Williams shook his head. "He won't be for long if things keep goin' like this."

"So Ramsay's gonna fire you and me?" Deagan squawked. "Why us?"

Williams shrugged. "I don't know what's gonna happen, kid. I just got this feeling, and I don't see you and me surviving, if there's funny business going on."

Deagan frowned unhappily and got to his feet. He took a single-jack and a drill from his bag. "Guess I better put out some feelers for another job," he muttered unhappily.

"You and me both," Williams responded tiredly.

* * *

Several hours later, the two miners stood at the gate leading to the outside world. Williams hunched down in his coat and stared at the boot heels of the man preceding him in the long line of miners waiting to be searched before leaving the Emma compound. Deagan stood close behind Williams, fidgeting nervously as he did every day. It was a half-hearted and haphazard search at best, but Deagan never changed, and the fidgeting served only as a provocation for one of the guards who seemed to take pleasure in terrorizing the nervous Deagan.

Williams glanced toward the younger man then suddenly jabbed an elbow in Deagan's ribs. "Calm down, you idiot," he hissed.

Deagan slapped a hand to the offended ribs. "What's that for!"

"We go through this every day!"

"Just makes me nervous!"

"Well knock it off!"

The exchange caught the attention of Deagan's nemesis, and the guard moved down the line until he stood beside the pair.

"You two are up to something."

"The kid's just nervous," Williams grumbled.

The guard frowned. "You oughta be used to this by now," he growled.

"I ain't never gonna get used to bein' searched like some kind of criminal," Deagan snapped.

The guard shifted his shotgun until the twin muzzles of the ten-gauge rested against Deagan's right knee.

"Turn out your pockets, criminal."

Deagan danced to one side. "Are you crazy?" He yelped. "That thing might go off!"

"Just turn out your pockets, boy."

"Okay…okay… Just point that thing somewhere else!"

The guard grinned and pointed the gun at Deagan's left knee.

"How's that?"

"Imbecile," Deagan muttered as he made a show of turning out the pockets of his coat.

"Pants too," the guard ordered.

"Don't got none," Deagan snapped. "But I got a big ol' pocket in the flap of my long johns. You want to see that? Maybe catch a look at my bare butt while you're at it!"

"Just get out of here," hissed the guard. "Get him out of here, Williams!"

Williams grabbed Deagan by the arm. "Come on kid."

Deagan yanked his arm free and stomped off through the gate and down the road toward town. Williams shrugged and followed close on the younger man's heels. Deagan slowed his shuffle-footed rush and let Williams catch up.

"You shouldn't have told him about that pocket," Williams grumbled.

Chapter 2

Utah Territory
Uintah Mountains—June 1869

The old man reined his pigeon-toed horse to a stop and quietly surveyed the small clearing and the carnage that lay before him—two men dead and a third hard hit, but alive. Forty feet away, a man lay on his back, his open eyes staring sightlessly into a fluttering canopy of aspen and pine that blotted out the sky overhead. A second man lay crumpled among the trees at the edge of the clearing, nearly invisible amid a tiny field of bright blue flowers. It was too soon for the putrid smell of death, and the old man was grateful for the clean scent of pine and the hint of sage drifting on a light breeze.

The third man lay face down on the hard-packed mountain soil. Blood soaked his hair and the collar of his shirt, and it was only the slight movement of one hand that gave any indication that he still lived. The old man muttered something under his breath as he dismounted and knelt beside the man. Almost tenderly, he rolled the man over and inspected the damage.

The wounded man groaned and opened his eyes. For a moment, he lay quietly, as though dazed. When he spoke, the words came with an effort.

"I know you," he said hoarsely.

"I reckon you do," the old man responded, feeding water from his canteen between the dry lips of the younger man.

After a time, the younger man struggled to his feet, and for a moment, stood swaying like a small tree caught in a brisk wind. "I feel like my head is about to explode," he complained.

The old man shook his head in exasperation. "Dang near did," he grumbled. "You been shot. I was followin' along your back trail an' heard the shootin' commence, but I was too far down the mountain to be any help. All I could do was come along as quick as I could an' pick up the pieces."

"I remember the shooting," the younger man responded, "but it was just a dream…a nightmare really…like a war with hundreds of cannons firing so fast I couldn't tell them apart—guns that fired forever and never ran out of ammunition… and thousands of men dead in a tangle of mud and razor wire."

"Sounded like a war up here," the old man conceded, ignoring the wet mud and the blood staining the legs of the younger man's trousers. "Your womenfolk sent me lookin' for you. You're a week overdue, an' they been worried sick. I told 'em there weren't no reason to worry, 'cause only God himself could keep you away from two fine lookin' women, an' then *He'd* have to drag you away kickin' and screamin'."

The younger man looked blankly at the old man and struggled to make sense of what he was hearing. He felt caught between two worlds—one consumed by death and the incessant roar of gunfire, and one filled with silence and the scent of pines and sage. Yet in his mind, he could almost see two tall, slender women who were somehow connected to him in a way he could not explain.

"Two women," he said quietly. "Mort!" he blurted suddenly.

"Don't be an idiot," growled the old man. "I'm Mort. Sarah and Susan sent me to find you and bring you home. Seems they're kind of fond of you."

The sandy haired man bent and scooped up his empty revolver. He broke the Smith & Wesson .44 American, ejecting the empty cases and reloaded. Quietly, he shoved the pistol into a worn holster. Suddenly, he remembered home and the women who made life bearable.

"I remember. Although I ain't so sure what's going on inside my head now days," he muttered unhappily. "Sometimes, I don't even feel like myself. It's like I'm another person entirely."

"Are you pullin' my leg, Mitchell?"

Gingerly, Mitchell touched the sore spot on his skull.

"I hurt too badly to pull anyone's leg," he grumbled.

The old man shrugged. "I reckon most folks would feel a bit strange after takin' a knock on the head like that, but there ain't nothin' wrong with you. You're the same as you always been."

"I don't feel the same."

Suddenly, the old man snorted. "You an' me been partners since before the watchers fell," he growled. "Before the war even began... 'course things are a bit different now, an' you don't remember, but we're both the same where it counts."

"Partners?"

"A long time," the old man replied.

"Ever feel like you're living a dream?" Mitchell asked bleakly.

The old man shrugged. "Every day... makes me feel old sometimes. Then I remember how things was before the war, when life was good... an' I remember how good it will be when the war is done.

"I remember friends... I remember you, Mitchell; but I can never think of you by that name. When I see you, I remember the war, an' your name burns like fire across the sky."

Gently, Mitchell shook his head. "I never fought any war," he said uncomfortably. "Closest I ever come to war was fighting Black Hawk and his renegades back in these mountains."

The old man grunted humorlessly. "Sometimes, you make my head ache, Mitchell. I ain't talkin' about no Indian war. You know there ain't but one war; an' it ain't never done 'til the end."

* * *

Two days later, Collin Mitchell reined the plow horse to a halt and dropped the reins over the cross beam of an old single bladed plow. The horse was one of a matched pair… a gypsy cob and a good, strong plow horse.

Quietly, he removed his hat and wiped the sweat from his forehead with a dusty sleeve. It was mid-June, and the days were already hot and dry. The rock-hard mountain soil had never seen a plow, and it was almost too late in the season for planting a garden of any kind so high in the Wasatch Mountains. But Sarah and Susan were both hopeful that something would come of the effort, and Mitchell found it difficult to deny either of the women anything they asked. They asked little enough as it was, and when it came right down to it, he had a few hopes himself, and two sacks of potatoes ready to have their eyes popped out and planted as soon as the field was ready.

Mitchell sighed and replaced his hat, knowing that a late planting had been inevitable. The last three months had been a mad rush of activity, leaving little time for anything other than the most essential needs.

Three weeks had been lost moving sheep through fifty miles of rugged mountain terrain. Another month had been expended buying one-hundred head of cattle and herding them to a wide mountain valley near the Strawberry River.

Now, two miles of barbed wire blocked the entrance to the valley, holding both herds on a range five miles wide and fifteen miles long—a range lush with mountain grasses, sagebrush, and cottonwoods, all watered by a cold mountain stream and trapped within the steep slopes of the Wasatch Mountains.

Mitchell watched as Daniel Pratt waded his horse through the icy waters of the creek separating the Kid's property from that held by Mitchell and his family. The foundation for the Kid's house lay nearly a mile to the west, nestled amid a random stand of pines and a scattering of aspen. The location was every bit as good as the one Mitchell had chosen for his own family, and from Mitchell's point of view, both places held promise.

For Mitchell, the long, wide valley and the land along the edge of the Strawberry River was a haven far from any city and the humans who thronged together like ants in an anthill—humans who always found someone else's business more interesting than their own.

The Pratt kid dismounted and ground-hitched his horse. "Looks like we're makin' some headway," he offered as he joined Mitchell.

Mitchell nodded, realizing that the Pratt kid was no longer just an employee. In fact, that relationship had ended before it had hardly begun, and the Kid had simply become a partner and a friend who could be relied upon, even in the worst of situations.

"Think we have enough help?" Mitchell asked.

The Kid shrugged. "We've got eight good workers buildin' the foundations, and two more herdin' the cattle and sheep. More than that and we'll just have 'em trippin' over each other."

Mitchell nodded in agreement. The five men working on the east house were working well together and seemed to be progressing swiftly toward setting the rock for the walls. At their present rate, the house would be finished in a few weeks, and they could begin work on the west house.

"I think we should leave things as they are," he observed. "I put that Hansen fellow in charge. They say he was a carpenter and stone worker before he came out here. He seems to know what he's doing, and the others were following his directions anyway."

"Whatever you think," the kid agreed. "He's been coming over and taking charge of the crew at my place too. At this rate, my place should be finished soon. The barn shouldn't take more than a week or two after that."

The Pratt kid glanced toward the tightly packed wagons near the stream. "Your womenfolk don't seem too put out," he suggested.

Mitchell shrugged. "They don't show it, but they're both ready to get free of those wagons. They drew straws yesterday to see who got the east house and who got the west."

The Pratt kid shook his head. "With all the trouble folks are kickin' up over plural marriage, I think I'll just keep the one."

Mitchell glanced toward the wagons, where Lynne Campbell worked beside Sarah and Susan preparing lunch. "You ain't even asked her yet," he pointed out. "Ain't much chance of you getting' a plural wife when you can't even get up the nerve to ask one."

The Pratt kid grinned. "I got the nerve; I just ain't had the right opportunity."

Mitchell let his eyes rove the mountainside. He felt a strong sense of wariness and the uneasy pressure of eyes watching from deep within the shadows of the surrounding trees.

Utes. He thought, suddenly mindful of how isolated the valley was...how far from help, should the remnants of Black Hawk's renegades decide to attack.

Mitchell sighed unhappily. He had lost all desire to fight the Utes. After a year of fighting—a year of chasing Black Hawk and his raiders through the mountains of Central Utah—he understood just how damaging Mormon settlements had been to the Ute way of life. Mormons had finally found a place where they could live in relative peace, but for the Utes, ancestral fishing grounds had soon turned into fenced farmland, and areas that had once provided needed resources had suddenly become inaccessible. It seemed inevitable that the Utes now went hungry and were often reduced to begging food from the very people who had overrun the land.

"Utes?" asked the kid.

Mitchell shook his head. "Just the feeling we're being watched."

"Utes," the kid concluded sourly. "They're all over the place. I saw three of 'em prowlin' around the upper end of the valley two days ago. They watched the cattle for a while and talked a bit. Then they just turned around and rode off. I thought I was in for a fight over them cows, but them Utes... they just rode off."

Mitchell looked across the Strawberry River and let his gaze travel up the length of the valley until the grassy meadows were lost amid the trees in the distance. "Those fellows could be part of Chief Tabby's bunch," he replied. "And most of Black Hawk's renegades have made peace. I heard that the few who haven't made peace are down south or over to Elk Mountain."

"Hope they stay there," the kid muttered.

Mitchell shrugged. "If they don't, we'll just have to deal with it." He nodded toward the valley on the opposite side of the Strawberry. "In the meantime, you could take one of those cows and run her clear to the north end of the valley. Tie her to a tree and leave her."

"You want me to give one of our cows to them Utes?"

"That's the idea."

"I don't get it. Not more than a year ago, you was out with the Legion killin' 'em."

Mitchell looked at the younger man and frowned. "Things change," he said quietly. "Black Hawk had his reasons, but most of the Utes ain't bad—just hungry. Put a cow out there for 'em the same time every month. We got plenty. By spring, we'll have fifty or sixty new calves anyway. Two years down the road, we'll have more cows and sheep than we can handle."

"Reckon so," the kid replied.

For a moment, the Pratt kid stood quietly, looking into the distance where jagged cliffs broke through the treetops, stabbing into clouds that lay like a gray blanket over the mountains to the north.

"Lynne says a letter came from Tooele," he advised.

"Must have come with that load of supplies this morning," Mitchell responded. "I haven't seen it though."

"It ain't good news," the kid confided. "I guess your womenfolk opened it. They gave me the gist of it and sent it along."

Mitchell took the offered letter and read its contents quickly.

"Not good?" asked the kid.

"Not good," Mitchell replied, handing the missive back to the kid.

When the Pratt kid had finished reading, Mitchell nodded back toward the wagons. "They'll insist on coming along," he advised grimly.

Chapter 3

Utah Territory
Deep Creek Mountains—June 1869

Two weeks later, a dust covered carriage, followed closely by an equally dusty wagon, rolled down the ruts some folks were calling a *road* leading into the mining camp of Silver Creek. Few people gave the road much thought, unless they were immediately concerned with the exposed rocks and potholes that seemed to have formed some demoniacal compact to destroy any piece of equipment that rolled along the rutted surface of the road.

When wet, the road turned into a slippery, clinging kind of mud that adhered to everything it touched and grew with each new contact. A man on foot would slip and slide with every step while the mud clinging to his boots grew thicker and heavier until it broke away under its own weight and began the process anew. Wagons fared no better, and a team of horses soon became exhausted as wheels slid from side to side in the ruts, battering themselves against the rocks hidden beneath the surface of the mire.

When dry, the passing of teams and wagons crushed the hardened mud into a bone dry dust that flew up from the ground to engulf anything that moved in a choking cloud of rust red powder.

In general, travelers on the road and most settlers along the Wasatch Front knew little or nothing of the fact that their new-found home had once been the bed of a gigantic lake with waters nearly a thousand feet deep—a lake that had cycled from full to empty more than a dozen times in its lifetime.

Those facts were generally unknown, and the people of the valley simply went about their business in blissful ignorance, while those who had any knowledge of Great Basin geology lived with the hope that God and geologic time moved slowly and the lake would never refill in their lifetime.

Sarah Mitchell snapped the reins on the backs of the team pulling the carriage and turned her head stiffly from side to side.

"How about taking over for a while," she suggested, offering the reins to her younger sister. "My neck has a crick in it."

Susan Mitchell took the reins and watched as Sarah stretched and shifted uncomfortably.

"I offered more than an hour ago," she advised. "If you have a crick in your neck, you have no one to blame but yourself."

Sarah shot a sidewise glance at her sister, then shrugged and eased her aching back muscles against the back of the seat. There was no sense starting a fight over Susan's ephemeral offer. Susan had been more interested in seeing new country and had only offered halfheartedly. Sarah had kept the reins only to keep the peace.

Moments later, Collin rode up beside them.

"You gals doing okay?"

"Fine," Sarah responded, feeling the pain of stiffened muscles with every jolt of the wagon.

"She's all stiffened up from driving the team," Susan offered. "I should have taken over a lot sooner," she admitted.

Mitchell took a hard look at both women. There was a kind of grim competition between the Flitton girls—a competitive nature that went far back into their childhood. Mitchell had never seen a head to head brawl between the two women, but every now and then he saw signs of impending doom for a man irrational enough to interfere. Now seemed like one of those times.

Susan was a tall green-eyed brunette who loved the outdoors. She was a woman completely secure in her sense of self-worth, and though two years younger than her sister, she was so much like Sarah they could have been twins. Susan was as beautiful as her sister; and while she was an active, vibrant young woman, she was the kind of woman who drew a man's eye.

Sarah was a tall, blue-eyed redhead—a strawberry blond in the summertime when the summer sun had time to bleach the color from her hair, and at five-feet seven inches, she had grown from a tall, lanky girl into a stunningly beautiful woman—a woman who knew her own mind and was not afraid to let anyone know what she thought.

Sarah had a temper—a temper that could flash as suddenly as lightning from a stormy sky. Susan was a slow burner, like blasting powder on a slow fuse. Yet both women had depth and a kindness that generally overcame the occasional flash of temper, and smiles that could charm the meanest of souls.

Sarah loved books and good literature. Susan preferred the outdoors. But both women loved the mountains and deserts of the Great Basin, and nothing could have tempted either of them into any other part of the country. But six months in the mountains had them all crazy with cabin fever, and both women had insisted on coming to Silver Creek.

"Let's stop and rest," Mitchell proposed. "There's a small spring about a mile up the road. You can see a couple of trees off to the right a little. The spring is near the trees. We can get some shade and have something to eat. Daniel and I can water the animals, and we can all rest up for a bit."

* * *

Late that afternoon, the mining camp finally came into view. Sarah sighed in relief—not because the camp itself was anything special, but because ninety miles of wagon rutted road was more than any woman should have to bear, and suspecting now that she was more than a month into her third pregnancy, the return trip promised to be even more unbearable.

Ellen Wells' boarding house was a two story frame building that looked like nothing more than a large box with clapboard siding. It was one of seven wooden structures in the would-be town, and like the others, the building was in drastic need of paint and repairs, and the roof alone seemed in good condition. Two of the upstairs windows had been cracked sometime in the past, and a third was boarded over, awaiting a replacement that might never reach Salt Lake City let alone a place so far off the map as Silver Creek.

The weathered gray slats gave the house the look of something far older than its five years of existence, and when the buggy finally stopped near the sun faded front door, the three women were convinced they were about to spend several weeks in quarters squalid, miserable, and uncomfortable.

"I hope they have beds," Susan moaned as they climbed down from the buggy. "I don't think I could stand sleeping on a cot for even one night."

Sarah stood quietly near the buggy and stretched her aching muscles. The house looked as though it had seen plenty of use, and she could only hope for something better on the inside.

"We'll have to make do," she said. "We're not very well prepared, and living out of the wagon is out of the question.

"Maybe it's better inside," the Campbell girl chimed in.

Sarah smiled at the younger woman and laid a hand on the girl's shoulder. "It may be," she replied. "In any case, we *will* make do."

The three women had hardly stepped away from the buggy when the faded door seemed to fling itself with a violent shudder against the outer wall of the house. The cause of the sudden commotion made a swift exit through the open doorway, leaping from the rickety porch to the dusty yard in a bound that left her skirts fluttering about her knees. The girl came to a sudden stop less than two strides from the arriving party.

"Who are you?" She demanded without the hint of a smile. "You must be those rich people who talked dad into selling out half of his mining claims."

Susan stared into the dark eyes of the young woman, noting the crow black hair and the immaculate dress of the most modern style. Though she had barely turned twenty, Miranda Barrett was a girl with the full figure of a woman and the air of someone who classed herself well above the common sort of folk surrounding her.

"You must be Miranda Barrett," Susan responded. "I don't think we talked your father into anything... In fact, *he* came asking if we would be interested in buying half of his mining operations. I believe he told Collin he needed capital to acquire a crusher and other necessary equipment."

The girl frowned. "Why would he do that?" she demanded. "We had plenty of money, until dad disappeared. But I own those claims now, and you won't cheat me like you cheated him."

"Miranda!"

The girl flinched at the stern voice, and the woman who had been standing in the open doorway crossed the yard and took her by the arm. "That was rude and unladylike. You know better."

The girl frowned and stared at the ground. "I apologize," she grumbled.

"You know nothing of your father's arrangement with the Mitchells," the older woman advised.

"It's alright, Mrs. Wells," Sarah assured the woman. "No one would expect you to be happy with things the way they are. Have you heard anything from your father?" She asked the girl.

"Nothing," the girl admitted sullenly.

"We should talk inside," Ellen Wells suggested quietly. "You've had a long trip. And I'm sure it was an uncomfortable one. You must be tired."

She glanced toward the wagon, where the Pratt kid was trying to walk off the stiffness of a four day ride on a hard wooden seat. After a moment, she turned and led the women into the house. No one spoke until she had guided them into a small parlor.

When they were all seated, Ellen Wells looked at each of them in turn, as though trying to absorb everything about them. She delayed only a few seconds before rushing out of the room and calling the threat of "tea" over her shoulder.

Sarah sat quietly, listening to the soft *clink* of spoons and china cups as the woman hurried about her kitchen searching for her best service. It was a ritual Sarah had experienced often, and one she had performed herself more than once. In fact, her own last effort had been in response to an unannounced visit from Brother Brigham himself, and Sarah had stumbled all over the house in her efforts to be the good hostess. She had never expected such a reaction to any visit *she* might make, and it made her extremely self-conscious.

"Please…"

The sound of Sarah's voice caught Ellen Wells in mid-stride. The woman nearly threw her tray of cups and saucers on the floor in her effort to spin and focus her attentions on Sarah.

"You don't need to go to any extra effort for us," Sarah cautioned. But she knew the admonition had fallen on deaf ears as soon as Ellen Wells had set her tray on the small table and waved one hand in dismissal.

"It's no effort," she responded. "We saw the dust from your wagons more than an hour ago. Your letter said you would arrive today if everything went well, so I figured the dust was yours and put on some tea and coffee."

Sarah started to decline the refreshment, but the Wells woman raised her hand again.

"It's alright," she defended. "James told me you folks are Mormons. The coffee is for me. The tea is just some yarrow. We heard your Brother Brigham wanted you all to stop using tea, and coffee, and tobacco." She filled the cups all around, talking steadily, hardly stopping for breath.

"I don't see the harm in a little tea or coffee," she offered, "but I surely get tired of the smell of bad cigars. And these miners tend to spit their cud anywhere they please….."

Susan smiled. "Thank you," she said quietly. "Have you heard from James?" She asked.

Ellen Wells glanced toward her young niece and shook her head. "We haven't seen him since last November. He went out one morning… said he was going to one of his claims and never came home."

Sarah placed her cup on the table and leaned forward as Ellen Wells seated herself beside her dark haired niece. "Was that something he did often?" she asked.

"Not often," Mrs. Wells replied, "but often enough. I didn't worry until a day or two had passed. Then I began to feel uneasy. I said as much to some of the fellows boarding here. Two or three of them were between jobs and offered to go out looking for James. They searched for several days, but never found anything."

Sarah knitted her eyebrows in thought. "Were many of the miners out of work when you brother disappeared?" she asked.

Ellen Wells shrugged. "There are always a few. They come and go for a number of reasons. There could have been ten or twenty back then… There are only three small operations here, but the real work is ten miles north of here at Gold Hill. I think the fellows who are looking for work just move about the county until they find a place that will take them on."

Sarah frowned. "Did any of those men seem desperate for money at the time?"

Slowly, Mrs. Wells shook her head. "No…. I don't know. Some of them might have been, but men are so close-mouthed about things like that. I don't think I would have known if they were. The fellows who searched for James certainly seemed grateful for the week of free room and board I paid them for their efforts. Grady Cannon took the lead of them. Grady organized the searches and kept the men on track. He and Miranda seem to have an understanding of sorts."

Ellen Wells sighed unhappily and glanced toward her niece. "Miranda and I believe her father met with foul play."

"Is there someone you suspect?" Susan asked casually. "Someone who might profit in some way?"

Ellen Wells shrugged. "No one in particular.... Just a feeling, but there was nothing to suggest anyone would harm James... until that business at the Emma mine. The county sheriff ordered the body to be held for a few days while Deputy Simmons finished his investigation. I forced myself and insisted on seeing the remains."

Ellen Wells looked at her niece as though judging the girl's ability to handle the grisly details of the viewing.

"It was James," she said finally. "It was difficult to tell, but I'm certain it was James."

Susan frowned. "It must have been an awful shock," she observed.

"It was! At first, I couldn't believe it. James was such a strong man... And how did he end up in that mine? I just can't understand it at all!"

Suddenly Susan left her chair and stepped to the room's only window. From one corner, she peered on an angle through the glass panes towards Silver Creek's dusty main street. The town was still in the early stages of its growth, and as yet sported few buildings along its slightly serpentine Main Street, and of those now standing, few of them were worth bragging about, and all of them in desperate need of paint.

It was an ugly little town, and Susan was already acutely aware of how pinched their lives would be for the next few days. The prospect was unexciting, and she wondered how a young woman like Miranda Barrett could stand the isolation.

"It's a dreary place," the girl observed as she came to Susan's side and studied the dusty street and the sun weathered structures scattered down its length. "There isn't a day goes by that I don't wish I was somewhere else."

Chapter 4

Utah Territory
Deep Creek Mountains—June 1869

The Emma mine lay nearly one hundred and twenty miles west of Great Salt Lake City near the base of the eastern slopes of the Deep Creek Mountains. The mine was a flurry of activity, and for nearly six months, the owners, Henry Forestall and Frank Gromley, had been running crews night and day. Rumor had it that the Emma was producing sustainable amounts of silver mixed with traces of gold, copper, lead, and zinc. Sustainable, it was said, meant only a meager profit, which rumor again asserted had been no more than five-thousand dollars a month—a figure that caused some miners at the Emma to scratch their heads and wonder that any profit could be made from ore that showed so little evidence of the minerals it supposedly carried.

Yet work at the mine continued day after day. Wagons filled with ore made their way to the smelters east of Tooele, and the miners were paid week after week. And that was all anyone in the camp really cared about, because a miner's pay was all that kept the little town and its shops alive.

It was early morning. The sun had just broached the peaks of the Onaqui Mountains to the east, and the dividing line of light and shadow worked its way swiftly down the face of the Deep Creek Mountains until the entire range was awash in the morning light.

The dun gelding shifted uneasily. Mitchell tugged gently on the reins, reminding the animal to behave. For a moment, the dun trembled, legs shaking as though the animal fought an overwhelming fear.

Mitchell reached out, patting the animal's neck. Deliberately, he uncased a new pair of field glasses, focusing the view on the mine entrance nearly half a mile up the canyon. At the moment, there was little activity at the entrance—a single ore cart dumping its load from the end of a narrow gage track to the top of a huge and ever growing mountain of tailings. As he watched, a second cart rolled out of the mine, turned and followed an alternate track along the face of the mountain. The slight downward incline of the track made it possible for the two men pushing the cart to maintain a slow pace with little effort until the cart reached the end of the track on a trestle six feet above the roadbed.

Mitchell watched as one of the men pulled a lever and the cart tipped forward, discharging its load into the wagon parked below. The wagon, now fully loaded, remained motionless for a moment as the driver waited for the dust to settle. When the air was clear of dust, the driver climbed onto the seat. With a snap of the whip, the team lurched into the harness, and the wagon rolled away from the trestle and down the rutted roadbed leading to the Emma's warehouse.

On the trestle, the two miners watched as the wagon jounced along the roadbed. Finally, when the wagon rounded a bend and disappeared from view, each of the miners reached into a hidden pocket and surreptitiously dropped its contents to the ground at the base of one trestle leg.

"Now, that's interesting," Mitchell muttered quietly. He looked down at the motley colored dog panting and grinning beside the dun. "Think those fellows are hijacking a little high grade ore?" He asked the dog.

The dog barked once, tossed its head, gave a little side wise hop, and came to rest sitting just a little closer to the dun's right foreleg. The dog looked back over her shoulder expectantly. Mitchell smiled and tossed a small piece of jerky in the dog's general direction. The dog exploded from the ground like a contortionist in a twisting leap, snapping the treat from the air.

"You are a strange mutt," Mitchell told the grinning animal. "That was a very good trick."

Mitchell dropped the field glasses into his saddlebags and nudged the dun into a walk. "Let's go up and take a closer look at that mine," he told the dog.

For a moment, the motley colored animal stood watching as horse and rider wandered up the trail toward the Emma mine. Then, as though suddenly seeking prey, the beast snapped her jaws closed and launched herself into the olive green forest of sagebrush encompassing the trail.

By the time they reached the fence spanning the mouth of the canyon, a sense of foreboding brought Mitchell to a halt beside the open gate and the trail leading to the mine offices.

"I'd like to talk to the owners," he told one of the guards standing beside the gate.

The guard shifted his shotgun and shook his head. "Owners ain't here today. Ramsay might talk with you though."

"Who's Ramsay?"

"Mine Superintendent. He pretty much runs the whole show."

"Then I can see him?"

"You can wait here. We'll tell him what you want. If he wants to talk, we'll send you up to his office."

"I see."

"Want to tell us why you're here?"

"I'd like to take a look at that pocket where that body was found."

The guard grunted out a humorless laugh. "Don't see that happenin'," he grumbled, "but we'll let Ramsay know what you want."

Twenty minutes later, Mitchell stepped into the sweltering heat of Ramsay's office. "Name's Mitchell," he offered. Ramsay ignored Mitchell's hand and pointed to a chair. "Nothing to see," he declared. "We blasted that pocket out of existence ten minutes after Simmons removed the body. There's nothing left of it."

Mitchell shrugged. "Even so, I'd like to take a look at the area."

Ramsay shook his head. "Ain't gonna happen," he grumbled. "I got men and equipment down there, and I ain't takin' any more chances lettin' outsiders down there. Simmons did nothing but get in our way."

Mitchell sat quietly, repelled by Ramsay's animosity. The man's words were innocuous enough, yet the emotions behind the words blew like a hot desert wind, scouring everything in its path.

"Ellen Wells thinks the body was that of her brother, James Barrett," Mitchell said finally. "I don't see how that could be possible, but I told her I'd look into it."

"It's not possible," Ramsay interrupted with a growl. "It's impossible. Deagan and Williams are responsible. I don't know how they managed it, but when I figure it out, I'll take it out of their hides. We were shut down for more than two hours. I had over twenty men standing around doing nothing the whole time. Deagan and Williams couldn't pay back those wages in a month if they worked for nothing. That doesn't even account for the ore we didn't bring up. The whole thing was a damned mess, and I won't compound the problem by letting anyone down there but the crew that belongs there."

Mitchell shrugged. "Deagan and Williams might be able to help. They could describe what they found."

Ramsay's face tightened. "Talk to them all you want!" He snapped. "Just do it on their time, not mine!"

Mitchell scowled. Ramsay eased back in his chair, his hand dropping to the open drawer of his desk.

"You don't seem much interested in the fact that a dead man was found imbedded in solid rock nearly six-hundred feet underground," Mitchell observed coldly. "The whole camp is talking about it, and nobody has a hypothesis that makes any sense."

"I'm *not* interested," Ramsay contended. "I think it was Deagan and Williams, and that's all there is to it."

Mitchell felt himself grow angry at the man's indifference.

"You won't change your mind?"

"Not a chance."

"Then I'd best leave. I've taken enough of your time."

Ramsay slid his chair back and stood behind the desk.

"You'd be better off beating some answers out of Deagan and Williams."

"They may be quite innocent," Mitchell advised.

"Think that if you like," Ramsay growled. "I find the idea absurd."

Mitchell left the office highly irritated. Ramsay's attitude and pig-headed insistence that the whole affair should be blamed on Deagan and Williams seemed unreasonable. Deagan and Williams were obviously the most likely culprits for placing the body in the deepest bowels of the Emma mine. But what spurred Mitchell's curiosity was the question of *why* they had done it.

It seemed ridiculous that they would kill the man and months later retrieve the corpse and orchestrate its discovery. In the process, they were sure to bring themselves under suspicion for a crime that most certainly would have been considered just another disappearance in the vastness of the western wilderness.

By the time Mitchell was half way back to town, his anger had dissipated as though it had never existed. He was feeling in a much better mood when a rider came from between two buildings on the edge of town and rode purposefully toward him.

Mitchell reined in the dun and waited. He studied the rider, as the man drew closer and halted his mount.

"Are you Mitchell?" The man asked congenially.

"I am."

"They said you rode out toward the Emma."

The man removed his hat and wiped his forehead with a large blue bandanna. My name is Simmons. I'm a deputy sheriff for the county.

Mitchell nodded his head in acknowledgment and took the deputy's proffered hand.

Simmons was a tall, lean red-head with a sun weathered face, brown eyes bracketed by the tracks of crow's feet, and a bristling mustache of a slightly darker shade of red than the hair on his head.

Simmons swung his horse around. "I heard you had some kind of partnership going with old Barrett," he said. "Ellen Wells told me you were coming and wanted to know what happened to Barrett."

Mitchell shrugged. "Not much I can do, if Barrett is dead."

"Won't help Barrett any," Simmons agreed. "But you might get yourself into a fix if you aren't careful."

Mitchell frowned. "That sounds like you suspect something other than a simple disappearance."

"Maybe," Simmons responded. "Obviously, you know about the corpse found in the Emma mine."

"I do."

"Ellen Wells identified the remains as those of her brother."

"She mentioned it," Mitchell replied.

Simmons shook his head. "I don't know how she could be as sure as she lets on," he said firmly. "There wasn't much to go on, as far as I'm concerned. But if she's right, then we have a problem."

"How so?" Mitchell asked.

"The fellow was shot," Simmons replied. "Right through the head."

"Murder?"

"Bullet went in the top of the head and came out down near the back of the neck."

"Hard to do that to yourself," Mitchell offered.

Simmons nodded. "Bad enough finding the fellow in that mine. Might have just ignored that and called it an accidental death with no explanation of how the corpse came to be six-hundred feet underground... But murder...that's another can of worms altogether."

"So, you think it was Barrett?" Mitchell asked.

"I have no idea," Simmons responded. "The clothing was pretty rotted. I think that's what convinced the Wells woman.

"It was strange though. The fellow looked like he had collapsed right on the spot. He was sitting with his back to the wall. One leg was stretched out and the other was bent back underneath him. Doctor Mills, over in Tooele, says one leg was broken, but no other trauma other than the bullet hole."

"Someone must have moved the body," Mitchell concluded.

"What?"

"You said the body was sitting with its back to the wall… pretty hard to shoot someone in the top of the head when they're sitting in a little niche with their back against solid rock. And it ain't likely he crawled in there with a broken leg and a bullet through his head. Seems pretty certain he was put in that pocket somehow."

Simmons frowned. "That sure makes Deagan and Williams look guilty as sin."

"Not of murder," Mitchell offered.

"Why not?"

"It's possible," Mitchell admitted, "but that fellow has been dead for a while… almost a year if it's Barrett. The only thing Deagan and Williams could have done was put a decomposed corpse in that pocket after they blasted it open."

"They could have killed him months ago then brought the remains into the mine," Simmons argued.

Mitchell shrugged. "That's what Ramsay thinks."

Simmons shook his head. "Doctor Mills thought it would be nearly impossible to move the corpse without it coming to pieces. It pretty much came apart before we got it out of the mine. We handled it pretty carefully, but it didn't help much."

"Just one more oddity," Mitchell grumbled unhappily.

"I hate this kind of thing," Simmons grouched. "All I need is another dead body I can't identify. The Sheriff is still pissed over that fellow we found dead on the express road last fall. Someone cut the poor fellow's throat, stripped him naked and left the body layin' in the middle of the road. We never did figure that one out…." For a long while, Simmons was quiet. "I could tell you to stay out of this," he said finally.

"Wouldn't do any good," Mitchell replied.

"Didn't think it would," Simmons admitted. "You might as well talk to the fellow who worked for Barrett, if you insist on digging into this mess. His name is Taggart... Brandon Taggart. I haven't had any luck finding him. Maybe you'll do better."

For a long while, Mitchell sat and watched as Simmons walked his horse up the Goshute Canyon road towards the turnoff to the Emma mine. Simmons seemed a decent sort—a man who liked his job, yet showed a distinct distaste for the kind of crime he was now forced to investigate. And Mitchell wondered just how much cooperation the deputy would get from Jack Ramsay or anyone else at the mine.

To Mitchell, it seemed that at the Emma mine there was only one concern... *dig*... and keep the ore coming out of the ground. Death meant nothing, and men were nothing more than tools in the process—tools to be used, worn out, and cast aside when they were no longer capable of performing the task they were hired for. It was a sad commentary on the ethics of the men who operated the Emma mine, but Mitchell knew the situation was not uncommon. There were few employers who saw their workers as a valuable repository of skills, and it was a condition that would probably never change as long as there were men who valued profit more than they valued the men who made that profit for them. Those gloomy thoughts persisted as he turned the dun back down the road toward town, resolving to look at his own behavior and take better care of anyone he might employ.

He had talked with nearly a dozen people before going up to the Emma mine and had gained little from any of those conversations... no one knew anything of Barrett's business... they knew nothing of his disappearance, and only one or two had ever had any dealings with the man. Barrett had kept to himself and had simply gone about his business with as little bother to anyone as possible.

Nathan Hawkins had sold Barrett a mule and repaired a damaged harness. Charles Allingham sold him dry goods for the boarding house and had once sold him ten pounds of blasting powder, when Barrett had run out and his shipment of mining supplies had been late coming from Tooele. Neither Hawkins nor Allingham had known anything of Barrett's other associations, and neither had any idea of what had happened to the mine owner. As far as they were concerned, the man had simply disappeared, and that was the end of it.

Mitchell let his eyes rove the weathered buildings lining the dusty track through the middle of town. It was a dismal picture. The buildings were faded and gray, and the rut-gouged track ragged and unkempt. The track might one day become a street, if the town survived long enough. But more likely than not, the town would eventually shrivel up and die if the mines in the hills above ever played out.

That thought brought him back to the body Ellen Wells claimed was her brother. If it was true, then Barrett was never coming back, and the person who had killed him might still be hanging around.

It could be anyone....

And his mind ran through the possibilities—a list that could not possibly include everyone who could have killed the man... *Ramsay, Deagan, Williams, Henry Forestall, Frank Gromley, Ellen Wells, or even Miranda Barrett....* Any of them could have done it....

Chapter 5

Utah Territory
Deep Creek Mountains—June 1869

Sarah Mitchell stood in the open doorway of the boarding house and gazed eastward toward the Onaqai Mountains. Collin had dressed and left their rooms well before daylight, while the early desert morning was still chilled enough that every breath hung in the air like thin tattered wraiths that drifted away and vanished as suddenly as they appeared.

Sarah shivered and felt the hair rise on the back of her neck. The thought of wraiths drifting about the desert skies under a waning gibbous moon brought back memories of Heber Valley and the shades of long dead conquistadors riding silently through deep forests of pine and aspen.

"Moody sort of place; ain't it…"

Sarah turned at the sound of the old man's voice.

"Mort! I thought you had gone off to meet some old friends."

The old man frowned. "Old friends? Once maybe…a long time ago. Eternal enemies now, you might say."

"That's dreadful," Sarah replied softly. "You can't patch things up?"

"No hope of that," the old man responded. "I'm just keepin' an eye on them… kind of temporary like."

"I've heard of such things," Sarah admitted, "but I've never had a friend turn on me with that kind of hatred."

The old man shrugged. "Takes a certain type," he replied. "And there are plenty more just like 'em."

Sarah shivered at the thought. "I hope I never meet any of them," she confessed.

The old man shifted uneasily. "They're all around us," he said gravely. "The trick is not to let them prod you into doing things you will end up regretting."

"I'll avoid them if I can," Sarah assured the old man.

Mort smiled. "You do that, ma'am. They're a hateful lot, and most folks would do better if they would steer clear."

Sarah brushed a wisp of strawberry blond hair from her face, and gazed back toward the orange-red fire of the sunrise. "Are you going to be around for awhile?" She asked the old man.

The old man raised an eyebrow. "A while," he answered cryptically. "There's a couple of folks I'm keepin' my eye on."

Sarah eyed the old man suspiciously. "I suppose you were planning to ride up the mountain today and take a look at Barrett's *Lost Crow Mine*?"

"As a matter of fact, that's exactly what I had planned!" The old man exclaimed. "You have a keenness of intellect lacking in most folks," he observed.

Sarah smiled. "Even more amazing is the fact that Susan and I were going to ride up there with Miranda Barrett."

"That is amazing," the old man agreed. "Say! We could ride up together, if you was to lend me that pigeon-toed critter of yours."

"Mort, that horse is yours as far as I'm concerned."

"I appreciate that, darlin', but I got no place to keep a critter like that. I'd rather just borrow him now and again, if you don't mind. He's a good one, and I've been showin' him some strange sights, but he ain't ready for the kind of life I'd be giving him. Besides, he'll be travelin' with another feller soon."

Sarah grinned. "He's still yours, Mort, but you leave him with us whenever you want."

"Howdy, Mort."

The Pratt kid's greeting held a tenseness that was typical of nearly every conversation he held with the old man. "You here to collect someone?"

The old man cracked a smile. "Nope. I'm just doin' a little participant observation."

"A little what?" The kid asked from the doorway behind Sarah.

The old man sighed. "I'm just along for the ride," he replied patiently. "I got some folks I'm keepin' my eye on."

"You ridin' up the mountain with us," the kid asked casually.

The old man shrugged. "Appears so," he responded.

The Pratt kid studied the mountains rising above the town. "I don't like it," he muttered absently.

"I got an invite," the old man objected.

"What?"

"I said: I got an invite. So it don't matter a whole lot whether you like it or not."

"Not you!" The kid blustered. "The ride up to that mine… I don't like it."

Sarah had retreated into the house, but the Pratt kid looked furtively over his shoulder as though expecting a sudden reprisal.

"They planned it this way," he told the old man. "The four of 'em.... His lordship says *no* and quick as a wink, they got me saddlin' horses and getting' stuff ready for a *picnic* ride up the mountain. I think it's a bad idea. We should at least wait until they can convince Brother Mitchell to come along."

"Collin will be busy all day."

The Pratt kid flinched at the sound of Sarah's voice directly behind him.

"Susan and I want to see this claim the two of you have bought into. Besides, Mort will be coming along now."

The Pratt kid eyed the skinny old man. He still had his doubts about the old man's sanity, and while Susan and Sarah seemed to accept the strange old goat readily enough, the Pratt kid still had his doubts.

"Not a nice place," the old man observed.

"Too dry," the kid replied.

"Too evil," the old man responded. "When the watchers fell, they settled out this way for a while."

"Watchers?"

"Apostates...two hundred of 'em. Broke their covenants and went bad to the core."

"Apostate Mormons?"

"Long before the Mormons ever came here, boy... long before the flood wiped men from the face of the earth."

The Pratt kid felt the hair rise on the back of his neck.

The old man gestured toward the western mountains. "West of them mountains... seems like... built up their secret society, secret murders... stuff like that. They was mighty bad folks, 'til Mouriel came for 'em. That finished 'em."

* * *

An hour later, Sarah eased her mount to a halt and studied the foothills of the Deep Creek range. Contrary to her first assumptions of a barren desert of windblown sand, this western desert was teeming with life and the mountains were covered with vegetation.

At its lower elevation, cheek grass and sagebrush battled for domination of the broken, shale like soil—a soil packed so hard the shoes of her mare hardly disturbed its surface. Often, the tall gray-green patches of sagebrush ended abruptly against the forbidding walls of stunted oak-brush covering the lower foothills, and wherever oak and sage failed to sink roots into the famished soil, the drab, slate-gray earth lay exposed like the twisted paths of a maze locked in the embrace of juniper and pinion pine.

"You're sure you know the way to your father's claim?" Sarah called to the raven haired girl leading the party.

Miranda Barrett turned in the saddle. "My father brought me here several times. He wanted me to know how to find his claims if something should happen to him," she called out. "I can find the one he called the *Lost Crow* easily enough. The other claims may be more difficult."

"Daniel's map may help," Susan suggested from her position in the line of six riders now pushing their way through a thick growth of oak brush.

The dark haired Miranda glanced back toward the Pratt kid who rode just a few feet behind her roan mare. "Are you good at reading maps, Mister Pratt?" She asked, letting a note of more than casual interest infuse her voice.

The Pratt kid shrugged. "Good enough I suppose."

"Excellent!" The girl exclaimed. "I was concerned that I might have trouble finding my way...." The girl slowed her mount until she was riding close beside the Pratt kid. "Now, I'm sure we can find our way, if we work together."

Sarah frowned at the girl's blatant display of interest in the Pratt kid and glanced quickly at the Campbell girl, who rode just a few feet ahead. The Campbell girl said nothing, but Sarah could sense the sudden tension in the girl and knew instinctively that Lynne was intensely angry.

Sarah glanced back, wondering if Susan had noticed the sudden change of humor. As though reading her concern, Susan nudged her mount and moved forward until they rode stirrup to stirrup.

"That's an encouraging sign," she confided casually.

"How so?" Sarah wondered.

Susan smiled disarmingly. "I thought you were familiar with all aspects of the Campbell and Pratt feud."

"Not so much as you might think," Sarah replied.

Susan laughed. "It seems Brother Pratt has continued his *pig farming* deception," she explained, remembering the boy's plan to allow the Campbell girl to believe he was lazy and shiftless, wanting nothing more than a small shack to live in and a few pigs to raise.

Fueled by the girl's belief that the Pratt kid was indolent and apathetic, the boy's initial plan had been to change, or appear to change, under the girl's guidance until she found herself in love with the object of her initial displeasure. The plan, of course, had been flawed from the beginning, and Susan had watched as the plan had been modified with each new revelation of the Pratt kid's expanding partnership in the business dealings of one Collin Mitchell—dealings that now included a ranch stocked with several hundred cattle and sheep, a small gold mine and more than one mine producing good quantities of silver ore.

The Pratt kid's share in all these dealings had already earned the boy enough to pay back a goodly portion of his debt to the Mitchells as well as deposit a tidy sum into a brand-new bank account. The Pratt kid might not be wealthy, but he was no pauper, and the Campbell girl was only beginning to suspect the Pratt kid's duplicity.

Susan looked at her older sister. "Lynne is beginning to question her original assumptions about Brother Pratt."

"Certainly took her long enough," Sarah responded. "Has Dȧniel finally decided to drop that silly business about pig farming?"

Susan grinned. "Lynne says he told her that he had decided there were better things to do with his life than raise pigs. Now she is suspicious that he never intended to be a pig farmer at all."

"That should have been abundantly clear to her from the start," Sarah said crossly. "The whole fabrication was as transparent as that night dress you bought last month."

Susan laughed, raising her eyebrows in mock surprise.

"Jealous of that one, are you?"

"Not in the least."

"Too bad… there was another... quite similar. They are made of a very fine Chinese silk."

Sarah's face flushed as she gathered her composure. For a moment, she studied the chocolate brown strands of her horse's mane.

"I did think it was beautifully made," she admitted, "but a little revealing."

"Much too revealing," Susan conceded as she leaned back, absorbing the fresh, raw scent of sage crushed beneath the heavy tread of steel shod hooves. "You'd like one though, wouldn't you?"

Sarah blushed, but nodded her head.

Susan grinned. "Good! Because I bought one for your birthday next week."

"You didn't!"

"I did."

"Real Chinese silk?"

"Every inch of it."

For a moment, Sarah let herself remember the feel of the silk when Susan had opened the package. The garment had been a thing of exquisite beauty.

"You gals ought to catch up with them kids, before them two kittens come to clawin' each other to pieces."

At the sound of Mort's voice, Sarah looked up to see the two young women and the Pratt kid nearly a hundred yards ahead. Deliberately, she nudged the mare into a trot and closed the distance.

She had gone less than fifty yards when she noticed several oddly dressed riders to the south—men riding parallel to her own path and keeping pace as she rode toward the Pratt kid and the two younger women.

Inadvertently, she slowed the mare to a walk. Mirror-like, the others slowed their mounts, matching her pace. Intrigued, she watched as one of the men leaped to the ground, scooped up a rock and hurled it in her direction. The rock sailed through the air, arching high then pounding into the ground where it skipped silently across the hard packed soil until it skidded to rest in a clump of dry brush and cheek grass.

Seeing the projectile fall short of his target, the rider stood for a long moment staring directly at Sarah. Then, deliberately, he spat in her direction before mounting and following his fellows who had turned away to the south.

"Reckon you ought to stay away from them fellers."

Sarah turned at the sound of Mort's voice to find the old man riding close beside her.

"He seemed rather hateful," she complained, "and I don't even know who they are."

"Ghosts," the old man responded. "Just shadows in a prison they chose for themselves... And they don't like you… Mostly 'cause they hate Mitchell. Guilt by association you might say."

"And I suppose you're not going to tell me why."

"No darlin', I ain't. But you stay clear of 'em. They're a bad lot, and they'll harm you just for spite."

Sarah turned and watched as the dust of the riders billowed upward and turned into a windblown haze. She felt a shiver of fear and knew instinctively that the old man was right, and the riders were malevolent creatures best avoided at all costs.

"I think I'll stay as far from them as possible," she responded gravely.

Chapter 6

Utah Territory
Deep Creek Mountains—June 1869

"*I* don't understand!"

Miranda Barrett stood in the center of a small clearing nestled deep in a tangle of juniper, and stared at the wreckage of her father's claim. The clearing was literally covered with scattered debris, as though the cabin and anything else related to the claim had been hit by a tornado.

"The cabin was standing beside those rocks," the girl murmured bleakly. "The head-frame and the hoist were just over there," she said, pointing toward an area where heavier timbers lay scattered about a dark hole in the ground.

Susan dismounted and hitched her mount to the limb of a stout juniper. For a moment she studied the wreckage.

"When were you last here?" She asked thoughtfully.

"A couple of months ago, Aunt Ellen and I came up with some folks from town. Mister Forestall was kind enough to remind me that some kind of assessment work would be necessary to maintain ownership of the claim."

Susan frowned. "Mister Forestall?"

"He's one of the owners of the Emma mine," the girl responded. "He offered, to help in any way he could."

"And you brought him here?"

"Several people came with us. They were all anxious to help us get things going again."

Susan sighed and stared intently at the head-frame now smashed and broken. There was no sign of a hoist—no block and tackle, nor rope or cable. Any equipment Barrett might have used was nowhere to be seen.

"What kind of equipment did your father have up here?" Susan asked. "He must have had something more than block and tackle to access the mine."

"What about help?" Sarah asked suddenly. "Didn't he have hired help… miners, teamsters, wagons, horses…"

The girl shrugged. "He had a fellow named Taggart helping him. He mentioned him all the time… but I never saw the man."

Susan scowled unhappily. "You never saw anyone else when you were here with your father… no one working the claim?"

"No. I never saw anyone," the girl replied defensively. "We came on Sundays. I always supposed my father had given the men the day off."

Susan walked to the wooden platform that surrounded the open mouth of the Lost Crow—a platform that had once served as a base for the head-frame and hoist. With the toe of her riding boot, she flipped a two foot length of broken beam into the opening, listening as it thumped and banged its way deep into the earth.

"It's certainly deep enough," she observed. "Your father must have found something worth all that work."

The Barrett girl edged cautiously toward the open shaft. For a moment, she peered into the blackness as though hoping for some explanation for the cause of her father's disappearance and the destruction of his claim and equipment.

"He was getting silver from the mine," the girl insisted. "He had enough to pay for everything we needed at mister Allingham's store. We had no debts at all until he disappeared and Aunt Ellen and I had to ask for credit at the store."

Susan frowned and turned to the Pratt kid. "Look around, Daniel. There should be a tailings pile nearby... a substantial one, judging by the depth of this shaft."

The Pratt kid nodded and began a meandering search of the surrounding trees. Moments later, his call drifted back into the clearing.

"Narrow gage track," he observed when the group joined him at the edge of the trees. He pointed to the narrow, steel rails disappearing into the trees on the lower edge of the clearing.

"Looks like someone pulled up about a hundred feet of track and ties, but what's left runs another hundred feet or so to the top of a small cliff. Barrett was dumping the tailings over the edge. There's a pretty big pile of the stuff at the bottom."

Sarah studied the ground where the tracks had been uprooted. "So, he *was* mining here," she concluded. "But it wasn't recently."

"He's been gone for six months," Miranda protested defensively.

Sarah nodded. "But you can hardly tell that there were ever any rails here," she pointed out. "Six months growth would hardly do that... a year perhaps... but not a few months."

"Barrett had three claims," the Pratt kid interjected. "He said one assayed at five-hundred dollars a ton, and with proper equipment he could increase production to two tons a day. He told us that was a conservative estimate. He never said which claim was producing. That was last September."

"Nine months ago," Susan observed as she examined the wooden ore cart still occupying the rails near the end of the track where a fifty foot drop led to the tailings pile at the base of the cliff.

"Mister Barrett must have worked this claim for some time," she concluded.

A hot breeze gusted upward from the ravine below, tossing her long, brunette hair. "Perhaps this claim played out," she suggested. "Or perhaps one of the other claims suddenly looked more promising?"

"That would explain the missing rails," the Campbell girl offered. "Mister Barrett could have moved them to one of the other claims."

Susan glanced back toward the abandoned ore cart. "You may be right," she conceded. "It doesn't explain why he left that ore cart, but it does make sense that Miranda's father would move the rails if they were needed elsewhere."

"Have you seen the other claims?" Sarah asked the Barrett girl.

"I never saw any of the others," Miranda replied.

"You don't know where they are?" Susan demanded.

"Only vaguely; Daniel's map seems accurate, but I've never been to either of the other claims. My only hope of finding them was to get a record from the claims office or have mister Taggart show me where they are located."

"And you haven't been able to find mister Taggart?" Susan suggested.

"No. He comes and goes around camp, but he seems to be avoiding me."

For a moment, Susan studied the clearing, noting the widespread destruction.

When? She thought suddenly. *When did all this happen*?

Once again, she inserted the toe of her riding boot beneath a shattered piece of debris and lifted it carefully. The piece was small, but beneath its weight lay the outline of its shape impressed into the yellowed grass. Suddenly interested, she flipped the sun bleached fragment away from its resting place.

"Interesting," she said quietly.

"What have you found?" Sarah asked.

"I'm not sure, yet," Susan responded.

"Cheek grass," she confirmed, carefully lifting several strands of the yellowed grass. The strands came up easily, still moist and clinging tenaciously to life

"They look dead," Sarah suggested.

"Not quite," Susan responded. "Notice anything else?" She asked holding the strands upright.

"They're limp?"

"Of course they're limp," Susan agreed, "but that's not what I'm talking about. Look at the length."

Sarah pinched one eye closed and squinted at the items in question. "Ten inches," she estimated.

Susan rolled her eyes in frustration. "Good heavens!" She squawked. "They are nearly the same length as all the other cheek grass in the clearing!"

"They are," Sarah agreed.

"So what does all this suggest?" Susan demanded.

Sarah frowned, concentrating and hating the feeling that Susan was just one step ahead in an analysis of what had occurred here.

"Recent," she blurted suddenly. "The yellow grass isn't quite dead, and it's nearly the same length. Whatever destroyed the cabin happened recently...within the last week or two."

"Exactly," Susan confirmed. The rails were taken out months ago and now this."

"Block and tackle up here!"

The Pratt kid stood at the southern edge of the sloping bowl that held the clearing and its odd assortment of debris. Not far from the Pratt kid a thin dribble of water welled up out of the thickness of the junipers and trickled down through the clearing and into the ravine below the cliff.

The Pratt kid stooped, grabbing the rope handle on one end of a large wooden crate and began dragging the crate toward the open mouth of the shaft.

The Campbell girl watched for a moment then frowned. "What are you up to?" She demanded crossly.

The Pratt kid dragged the crate onto the wooden platform and dropped it near the open shaft. "Sooner or later someone will have to go down that hole and see what made your father abandon it.... Might as well do it now."

"You don't know anything about mines," the Campbell girl protested. "We should wait until we can get someone who knows what they are doing to go down there. You can't possibly learn anything useful when you don't know what you're looking for."

The Pratt kid peered downward into the darkness of the shaft. "I'll admit I ain't all that excited about goin' down there."

"Lynne is right," Susan concurred. "There's no need for anyone to go down right now.

We can come back with help and send someone down there who can make a proper assessment of the mine and the feasibility of reopening it."

The Pratt kid shrugged and stepped back from the hole. "Reckon I wouldn't know a silver mine from a hole in the ground." For a moment, the kid stared at the black opening in the ground.

"Well... maybe I could figure that part, but I still wouldn't know what I was lookin' for down there,"

Susan looked at the Barrett girl, puzzled by the girl's lack of knowledge concerning the other claims. "At the moment, I'm more interested in the other claims," she told the Pratt kid. "Does your map show any locations for the other claims?"

"Nothing detailed… a couple of marks a little farther up the hill… two canyons west and a little higher up the mountain."

"Can you lead us to them?" The Barrett girl asked excitedly.

The Pratt kid shrugged and slipped the map out of a pocket. "I think so," he acknowledged. "We might end up huntin' around a bit… but if your dad did any work on them, we should find them easily enough."

Sarah took up the reins of her horse and climbed into the saddle. "I'll be very surprised if we don't find some extensive work at one of the claims," she predicted. "Those rails didn't wander off on their own, and I can think of no other reason Mister Barrett would remove them, unless he needed them somewhere else."

The Barrett girl crossed the clearing and grabbed the reins of her own mount. "I'm sure that's what dad must have done," she said defensively. "The bills were always paid, and Mister Taggart was always paid on time."

Sarah held her tongue, refusing to voice the sudden thought that the claims might never have produced profitable amounts of silver or any other mineral. Barrett could have simply sold Collin and Daniel a bill of goods and used the equipment money to keep his whole operation from going broke. Still, such a scenario seemed unlikely. Both Collin and Daniel had seen evidence that made them certain a partnership with Barrett had excellent potential for success.

Sarah waited as the others gathered their horses and prepared to leave the clearing. There was little they could do here until they could return with someone experienced enough to enter the mine and ascertain its condition, and she was anxious to move on to the other claims and see just what Barrett had been up to.

"Some fellers on the ridge across the way," Mort warned suddenly. "They ain't friendly," he added.

The words were hardly spoken when something buzzed past Sarah's head with a sound like the angry drone of a hornet. A second later, the sullen boom of a heavy rifle thundered across the canyon, pounding the clearing with an explosion of noise.

"That ain't good!" The old man bellowed. "Get into the trees!"

Sarah kicked her mount, and the animal leaped forward, into the juniper and away from the deadly hail of lead that cut through the clearing. For a moment, the others were close behind, but her terrified mount soon outdistanced the group until she found herself alone and careening through the trees.

After a hundred yards, Sarah felt as though she had been thoroughly thrashed by the unforgiving trees. The branches of the junipers felt as though they were axe handles pounding against her legs and arms. Deliberately, she sat back in the saddle, dragging hard on the reins. But the mare had the bit in her teeth, and the terrified animal plunged through the juniper at a wild gallop.

Sarah grabbed at the animal's mane in a near panic, struggling to keep her seat as the animal crashed between stiff, dry branches that threatened to tear her from the saddle. Eventually, the animal grew tired and with the impetus for its mad run left far behind, the absolute silence of the mountain soon calmed the animal into submission to Sarah's insistent pull on the reins.

Within moments, the animal slowed to a stop, its sides heaving and wet with frothy sweat.

"Wore yourself out, didn't you?"

Sarah dismounted and stood quietly, listening for the sound of pursuit. But the mountain was silent, and she was out of view, hidden deep in a forest of juniper beyond the crown of the ridge, west of the Barrett claim. Yet, now that the gunfire had ceased, her initial fear had dissolved into uneasiness over the welfare of the others.

In the moments before the mare's mad gallop into the trees, Sarah had seen them all mounted and urging their frightened animals out of the clearing and into the surrounding trees. There had been no coordination of direction, only a frantic scattering in any direction offering immediate hope of escape. Somehow, Sarah knew that the others were nowhere near, and her best option was to simply ride down the ridge until she reached the trail leading back to town. From there, she could turn east and reach town in less than an hour.

Couldn't be more than six miles….

The thought came randomly, but with it came half-a-dozen more. She knew that Susan would immediately begin searching for anyone separated from their party. But the mountain was no longer a safe place for any of them, and Sarah was convinced that the men who had fired those shots were even now crossing the canyon to finish what they had started. For a moment, Sarah wished she had listened to Daniel's warnings. They might all have been safer with Collin nearby—at least *she* would have felt safer, but that choice was already made, and her options were considerably fewer than they had been just an hour earlier.

Quietly, Sarah took up the mare's reins and walked the animal deeper into the concealing shelter of the junipers covering the ridge. The mare, now tractable and lulled by the tranquility of the mountainside, walked obediently into the trees and began grazing on the sparse cheek grass that lay in the cooler shadows beneath the protective covering of the junipers.

Sarah turned slowly, listening carefully in each direction for the telltale sounds that would announce the presence of pursuers on her ridge. For several long moments, she heard nothing…until the silence was broken by the barely discernable clatter of a stone dislodged and tumbling somewhere in the ravine below.

"Time to put some distance between them and us," she told the mare as she climbed into the saddle and eased the animal into a walk.

West… she thought… *then down the mountain and back into town…*

But riding west was impossible. According to Mort, the west face of the ridge was nothing but cliffs and impassable on foot or by horse. That route was out of the question.

Suddenly, she resolved to ride north to the head of the ridge. If she rode quickly and quietly enough, she might reach the head of the canyon and cross to the opposite ridge before the men on her trail knew where she had gone. Barrett's abandoned mine was less than a mile away, and she had hopes that the men now working their way up the mountain would first investigate the claim site before they started searching the mountainside for their escaped prey. If she could reach the head of the canyon quickly enough, she would be well on her way back to town before her pursuers realized what she had done.

* * *

Two hours later, she had crossed the canyon and worked the mare through the pinions and brush to a point nearly halfway down the ridge. There, she had stopped in a thick tangle of brush, searching for a way out - a trail of any kind. But there was nothing, only an impenetrable wall of leaves and branches on every side. Even the trail she had made forcing her way into the arboreal cage had closed behind her, leaving her no choice but to continue forcing her way through the unyielding growth.

"It appears we have no choice but to push on," she told the mare.

The mare stood quietly, feigning placid ignorance.

"You don't seem concerned," Sarah reproved. "We could end up fighting our way through miles of this stuff."

Finally, dreading the beating they were about to take, she thumped the mare with her heels, and they plunged into the brush. The dry branches of the scrub oak twisted and snapped in a rapid clatter, unable to withstand the force of the animal's passage, while Sarah, bent low and clinging to the animal's neck, suffered the snags, scrapes, and whipping of an unforgiving tangle of branches and leaves woven together in a chaotic mass. She could not defend herself against the whipping. She could do nothing more than cling to the mare and pray for a swift escape from the punishment.

Chapter 7

Utah Territory
Deep Creek Mountains—June 1869

The world was quiet. An hour earlier, the sound of gunfire had echoed from high on the mountains down into the foothills. But now, the only sounds were the steady thump of the dun's hooves, the whisper of a breeze, and the occasional clatter of wings as one of the ironclads plaguing the basin leapt from cover and fled the proximity of the invading equine.

Simmons was gone, and Collin Mitchell eased the dun gelding from the dusty path leading from the Emma mine back into town and waited in silence, listening to the sound of the wind. The breeze whispered through the tall cheek grass, hissing through the yellow-green stems like a voice whispering in his ear. He could almost hear the words, like the names of the dead rising up from the ground—names he could almost remember, faces he could almost see—drifting through his mind like wraiths from a long forgotten past.

Gravelly soil crunched beneath the dun's hooves as the animal shifted uneasily. The breeze petered out as though the world had suddenly gasped out its last breath. Mitchell felt his own breath catch as the sky grew dark and angry. In the distance, nearly invisible in the strange dimness that flowed out of the mountains to veil the valley floor, a large group of riders galloped eastward through a valley lush with tall green grass. Their horses plowed through the grass, leaving multiple wakes like ships on a forest green sea.

As the riders topped a distant hill and began to disappear, one of them stopped and looked back. For a moment, he seemed to look intently in Mitchell's direction. Then, as though compelled by an irresistible force, the rider turned his mount and followed his companions out of sight. Mitchell felt the hair bristle on the back of his neck.

"Them fellows don't seem too happy to see you."

Mitchell started at the sound of the old man's voice. "Dangit, you old fart! You gotta quit sneakin' up on a fellow like that!"

"Lucky it was me and not one of them fellows that rode off. They ain't all that friendly."

"Sure didn't stick around to welcome me to the neighborhood," Mitchell grumbled.

"Don't expect you're welcome here," the old man responded. "You was a bit *harsh* the last time you had dealings with the likes of them."

"Couldn't say," Mitchell responded. "Too far off to see any of 'em clearly."

"Don't matter none. They remember *you*."

"What are you doin' here, Mort?"

"Wanderin'... Question is, what are you doin' here? This place ain't on no map this side of hell."

"We came out to check on a missing friend," Mitchell replied.

The old man shook his head. "You're a bit off course for that. Steer back towards them mountains a bit more. This part of the valley ain't nothin' but a bad memory."

"What are you up to, Mort?"

"Watchin'... participant observation you might say."

"And just what are you watchin'?"

"You, mostly.... But them women folk of yours are interesting too. For a loner, you're gatherin' quite a formidable pack." The old man inclined his head toward the foothills. "You headed up on the mountain?"

"I was headed back to town," Mitchell confessed, "but I had the feeling I should ride up toward those cliffs."

The old man nodded. "Reckon that's a good plan," he admitted. "Sarah's up that way somewhere."

Mitchell frowned unhappily. "What's Sarah doin' up there?" he demanded. "I left her at the boarding house early this morning."

The old man shrugged. "Reckon she had her own ideas about how to spend her day," he suggested. "We all rode up there with her, but there was some shootin' and everyone scattered. We all met up on the way back to town... 'cept Sarah. She got cut off from us and rode higher up the mountain."

"You didn't go after her?" Mitchell demanded.

"I sure was of a mind to do just that," the old man growled.

"But you didn't."

"Voice says I was to stay out of your way," the old man grumbled. "Them gals have been the best friends a fellow ever had, an' them fellows are after her. If I had my way I'd drag them fellers down to hell in the blink of an eye, but the voice whispers, an' I keep my promises."

"To train me..." Mitchell responded, remembering that the old man was obsessed with the idea that he was the *angel of death* come to train Mitchell as his replacement.

"Sorta...."

Mitchell frowned. "I ain't certain I want any training."

"I ain't certain you need any," the old man muttered.

"You coming with me?" Mitchell demanded as he nudged the dun into a trot towards the mountains.

"Reckon so...."

They were into the foothills before either of them spoke again, and Mitchell was growing more anxious with every moment that passed. The dun couldn't run fast enough, and Mitchell struggled for patience as the miles slowly vanished in the wake of the dun's inexorable drive up the steep incline of the ridge.

"How far?"

"Not far," the old man answered. "The shootin' started just beyond them trees. There's a clearing, and Barrett's claim is smack in the middle of it."

Mitchell eased the lever action repeater from its sheath and examined the trees ahead.

"But Sarah ain't there," he acknowledged.

On the trail, twenty feet behind the old man shook his head. "Nope... I suspect she's a bit higher up the mountain."

Mitchell let his eye rove the peaks rising in the distance beyond the tree tops. "Rough looking country," he concluded.

"Pretty bad," the old man admitted. "West face of this ridge ain't nothin' but cliffs. That's why I'm sure your gal went up high. Weren't no other way to avoid them fellers that was shootin' at us."

By the time they rode into the clearing, Mitchell's nerves were on edge. He was filled with an inner conflict, knowing that he might be forced into a violent confrontation, yet hoping to avoid it if possible. The tracks of horses churning the ground of the clearing and heading into the trees on a route leading to the peaks above made it clear that there would be little chance of avoiding a fight.

"Quite a mess," he concluded.

"Pretty much the way we found it," Mort replied.

"The kid was goin' to take a look down that shaft over there, but that Campbell girl put up a fuss, and the kid never went down. Otherwise, we'd be tryin' to fish him outa there right now."

Mitchell scowled at the open mouth of the abandoned shaft. "Open hole like that ain't safe," he muttered. "Someone will fall in there and get themselves killed."

"Reckon so," the old man responded. "You don't look so good," he added.

"I don't feel so good," Mitchell admitted. "This place doesn't feel right... like something old and bad has been through here."

"How do you mean?"

"Makes the hair stand up on the back of my neck," Mitchell explained. "Like something dark and mean is watching every move we make."

The old man scanned the clearing and the trees surrounding it. "Something evil?" He suggested grimly.

"Malevolent," Mitchell agreed.

The old man frowned. "Reckon that pretty much describes things," he admitted darkly. "Some of them watcher fellers are real nasty, and they're pressin' the boundaries."

"You're talkin' ghosts again," Mitchell accused, "folks that have been dead for three-thousand years."

The old man frowned. "Dead... all depends on your point of view, I suppose...."

Cautiously, Mitchell swung down from the saddle and studied the ground. "Tracks go west," he observed, deliberately changing the subject.

Mort grunted tersely. "Figured as much when none of 'em followed the rest of us."

"Looks like they wanted to run you off."

"They done that all right," the old man admitted.

Mitchell let his eyes probe the clearing and the surrounding trees. The mountainside was still. No breeze touched the dry grass of the clearing. The junipers stood stiff and unmoved, watching silently.

"Quiet… Ain't it?'

Mitchell shrugged and fished a bit of jerky from his shirt pocket. Without warning, he flicked the bit of meat toward the brush tangled base of a nearby juniper. Like a rattler striking, the motley colored Lady-dog lunged from the brush, snapping the offering from the air.

"I think she's losing some of her sneakiness," Mitchell complained.

"Don't know about that," Mort confessed, "but that little bit of meat sure made that crow sit up and take notice."

Mitchell glanced upward, to where a gaunt-looking crow perched on a pinion limb quietly watching.

"Looks half starved," he observed.

The old man glared at the bird. "Carrion eater," he muttered in disgust. "They eat almost anything."

Mitchell fished another bit of jerky from his pocket and flicked it toward the grinning dog. The crow crouched as though ready to spring, but stopped as the motley colored dog snapped up the treat. The bird cocked its head and stared at Mitchell with one black calculating eye.

"I wouldn't do that," the old man protested as a third piece of jerky sailed toward the crow.

With a squawk, the bird leaped from the branch, beat its ebony wings against the sky and intercepted the offering as it reached its highest point and began to fall toward the dog now waiting below. With a growl, the dog settled down on her belly and waited.

The old man shook his head. "Them crows are smart," he grumbled. "That one thinks you'll feed 'im now, an' it won't be long before he tells all his relatives. You'll soon have a murder of crows followin' you—all of 'em expectin' to be fed."

"They can expect all they want," Mitchell responded lightly. "A little plug of jerky ain't gonna go far if he brings his relatives to dinner."

Suddenly, the old man shivered violently. Mitchell felt himself shudder at the sudden touch of bitter cold. In the blink of an eye the frozen breath was gone and the furnace like blaze of the summer sun bore down upon them like a mantle of fire.

"What in the hell was that?" Mitchell squawked in surprise.

The old man shrugged. "Natives hereabouts might call that a *ghost wind,*" he concluded unhappily.

"Ghost wind?"

"A breath of wind from a bleak, unhappy place. Enough to give an old man a heart failure."

"And the voices?" Mitchell asked cautiously.

"Voices?"

"On the wind," Mitchell admitted cautiously.

The old man turned and looked southeast, toward a valley hidden by the pinions that surrounded them.

"Watchers," he muttered.

"Watchers?"

"Them fellers you saw ridin' through the valley earlier."

"What have they got to do with this ghost wind, and voices?" Mitchell grumbled.

"Long story," the old man answered, "let's just say they don't like you.... We should be findin' that gal of yours instead of standin' here shootin' the breeze."

Mitchell let his eyes rove the edges of the clearing where wind tugged fitfully at the dry, unyielding branches and swept the tops of the pinions with the murmur of mournful voices—voices that whispered of pain and an ancient hatred.

"We should go," the old man warned. "Them fellers is supposed to stay put. No gallivanting around. But they know we're here now, and they'll make trouble if they can."

It was obvious that the old man had strong feelings about the riders he called *watchers*, and Mitchell had no desire to make their acquaintance if the old man found them so distasteful. The old man might have the most peculiar ideas at times, but Mitchell had never found him to be a poor judge of character.

Mort was an enigma. Mitchell estimated his age to be no more than sixty, but the old man seemed to change with each encounter and had always been just a little too knowledgeable for a down-at-the-heel old trapper who owned nothing more than a pistol and a filthy old buffalo coat. Mitchell however, found that he genuinely liked Mort, despite the old man's strange perception of reality.

Mitchell tugged on the dun's reins, drawing the animal toward the upper edge of the clearing and into the trees.

The old man followed, but let out a squawk. "Dangit!"

Mitchell stopped and looked back to where the old man stood scraping the sole of one boot against the sharp edge of a large rock.

"Horse piss an' mud," the old man growled. "Regular river of it runnin' down into that hole."

"You should watch where you step," Mitchell pointed out.

"It was your horse what done it," the old man retorted irritably. "Sarah will never let me near the house with this stuff all over my boots!"

Mitchell climbed into the saddle. "Reckon you'll be eatin' dinner out on the porch with the dog tonight."

They were hardly into the trees when Sarah's trail became obvious. The tracks of her sorrel colored mare had gouged deeply into the soft ground between the trees as she followed a narrow game trail along the top of the ridge. Mitchell plowed the dun through the tangle of branches, following the remnants of snapped and shattered limbs and the occasional explosion of fallen needles.

The old man followed closely behind, his passage warping the branches and snapping the driest of them in a constant racket that combined oddly with a rhythmic thump of hooves that soon set Mitchell's nerves at ease. There would be no surprises from behind; the old man would see to that, leaving Mitchell free to concentrate on the trail ahead.

It was not long before the trail suddenly changed. Mitchell reined in the dun and studied the torn ground. "Four riders following her," he concluded, as the old man came up beside him. "I think she had a good lead. Her horse seems to be letting up a bit, but the others are still digging in hard. It looks like her horse was a little spooked from the shooting and tried to bolt with her. She knew it would take those fellows a while to find a way out of that canyon. She was probably a mile or two higher up before they even got to this point."

The old man nodded. "She's a smart one," he replied. "They'll never catch her as long as that animal can stand up to this mountain."

Mitchell frowned, remembering the way Sarah's horse had been tiring more easily than normal.

"We'll push on a little faster," he said suddenly. "That animal ain't been up to snuff lately."

They moved on, picking up the pace, and for a moment, Mitchell's thoughts wandered. He listened for the wind and the whisper of voices, but the wind had died, and the voices were gone, leaving him with an uncomfortable concern for his sanity. He had never been prone to such phenomenon, and though Mort seemed perfectly at home with such things, the experience left Mitchell unsettled and wondering if his imagination had suddenly run wild. It was bad enough that the old man heard voices.

Behind him, the loud *crack* of a breaking branch sounded through the trees as the old man's pigeon toed horse forced its way past a dry, unyielding branch. The animal stopped suddenly, easing to one side, away from the jagged point of the threatening stub. The old man loosed a boot from a stirrup and kicked hard at the stub, snapping it off at the trunk.

Mitchell waited as the old man nudged his mount into a walk and brought the animal up beside the dun.

"This stuff is enough to make a fellow run screaming off the top of a cliff," the old man complained.

Mitchell nodded agreement and studied the ground ahead. "Looks like things are beginning to thin out a bit," he observed.

"That would be a relief," Mort grumbled.

* * *

An hour later, Mitchell eased the dun onto a rocky flat and dismounted. At the head of the ridge, they had turned south and crossed over a narrow draw and followed the next ridge down toward the valley below. They had followed Sarah's trail until they were nearly even with Barrett's Lost Crow claim on the opposite ridge.

"Feels like we're being watched," he grumbled, arching his spine backward, and feeling the relief of vertebrae popping back into place.

The old man swung down from the saddle and walked several paces toward the edge of the flat where the rocky ground sheered away in a sharp drop to the bottom of the canyon.

"Them old bones of yours are crackin' and a groanin' like you was a hundred years old," he cackled happily.

Mitchell pushed the dun's muzzle away from his shoulder and swiped horse spit from his sleeve.

The old man shook his head in disbelief, "Cuddly little fellow, ain't he."

Mitchell grunted humorlessly and shook the saliva from his hand.

"He's as bad as that dang dog for playin' games," he grumbled.

"Speakin' of which ... your mutt seems to have found something that interests her."

The Lady-dog sniffed at the ground, sneezed as though something had crawled up her snout, then shot down the trail and out of sight. Mitchell turned the dun toward the edge of the flat.

"Reckon I'll head back to town," the old man called out as Mitchell guided the dun onto the narrow trail leading down onto the northern face of the ridge.

"Reckon that mutt has found your gal, so I'll see you back at the boarding house."

The old man heeled the pigeon-toed Milo, and the animal lunged into the brush before Mitchell could respond.

With the old man gone, Mitchell turned his attention to the hard packed trail as it dropped off the edge of the flat and angled down the steep side of the mountain.

The trail appeared to be hard packed and well used, but there were no tracks to be seen, only the occasional scuff where something had passed, dislodging rocky shards from the surface of the trail into small scatters of loose detritus.

Although he was certain this was the path Sarah had taken, there was no real evidence that she had passed this way—no evidence save the dog's mad dash down the trail and the old man's word that the dog had indeed found the woman it was devoted to. Something ahead had captured the dog's interest, and though the motley colored canine followed Mitchell's every move, it was Sarah the animal seemed to adore.

Mitchell urged the dun forward until the trail rounded a bulge in the hillside and led down to a small, rough looking stone structure nestled like a cliff-house beneath the overhanging rock above.

In the heat of the afternoon sun, the silence was complete. The dog had disappeared. Nothing moved save the wind and the dark shape of a single crow against the blue of the sky. The groan of strained leather broke the silence as Mitchell swung down from the saddle and eyed the open doorway of the cabin.

"That dog ain't keepin' out of sight very well," he said firmly. "She's givin' you away."

Mitchell was only slightly surprised when Sarah stepped out from the corner of the building nearly fifteen feet from the shadowy doorway. She eased the Smith & Wesson's hammer down on a live chamber.

"I knew you would come," she murmured as Mitchell took her in his arms, "but I knew you would expect me to be careful."

Mitchell took a deep breath, relishing the scent of her hair and the feminine feel of her in his arms.

"Couldn't help myself," he admitted. "Might not have found you at all if that dog of yours hadn't high-tailed it down this way."

After a moment, Sarah released Mitchell and called the dog to her side. Fondly, she stooped down to ruffle the Lady-dog's ears. "Such a good doggie," she crooned.

Mitchell watched the animal scoot closer, basking in Sarah's attentions. "Never thought I'd be envious of a dog," he grumbled.

Sarah looked up and smiled. "You just want me to rub your ears and tell you what a smart, pretty boy you are."

Mitchell shrugged. "Don't know about pretty."

"Just trying to build your self esteem."

"It's working," he admitted. "But what's all this?" He asked, cocking his head toward the rock walls of the cabin.

Sarah stood and took Mitchell's hand.

"I'm not sure," she admitted, "but you should take a better look. It may be one of Mr. Barrett's claims. There seems to be a mine of some sort between this shelter and the cliff," she explained as she led him to the back of the cabin and into the forty foot gap separating the man made wall from the curving face of the cliff and the overhanging cornice above.

Sarah pointed toward a dark opening in the cliff face. "I found a lamp and went inside.... Only a little," she added as Mitchell gave her a disapproving look.

"Don't scowl," she reproved sweetly. "You'll scare the little doggie, and she won't follow you and eat all your jerky.... I only went in a little ways. It stops about fifty feet inside, and there's some kind of hoist going straight down as far as I could see. I didn't go any farther. I'm not all that fond of places like that."

Chapter 8

Utah Territory Deep Creek Mountains —June 1869

Susan Mitchell sat quietly in the parlor of Ellen Wells' boarding house. It was early morning, and superficially her attention was on the pamphlet she held in her hands, but Dr. Samuel Thompson's description of the properties and usefulness of lobelia for the treatment of maladies such as congestion of the nasal passages was of little interest at the moment. Her true focus of attention was split between worry for Sarah and a more subtle interest in the man now seated across the room in deep conversation with Ellen Wells.

Henry Forestall was a tall, unhappy looking man. The corners of his mouth turned down in a habitual frown that made anyone meeting him for the first time wonder how a man so wealthy could appear so unhappy. There was, however, more to Henry Forestall than met the eye. He was a man who kept his own council and had learned the hard way to keep his mouth shut and his most personal thoughts to himself. At present, he was gaunt and emaciated and had the appearance of a man deep in the throes of some illness that would soon drag him into the next life.

Immediately, Susan felt instincts prompting her to help the man. His conversation with Ellen Wells had already revealed that he was relatively new to the Territory.

"I was on my way to California," he told Ellen Wells. "I inherited a little money when my parents died. It was enough for a new start. I had been thinking of going to California for several years, then suddenly I had some money, and I wasn't getting any younger… I got as far as Salt Lake City when I overheard one of General Connor's men talking about a silver strike in the Deep Creek Mountains. I began to think it might be worth taking a shot at things here instead of going on.

"California's boom was twenty years ago, and I became convinced that I had a better chance of a good strike here… so I bought a claim from a fellow… I think his name was Perkins… We had no luck for quite awhile… just traces of silver and a lot of galena."

"Galena?"

"Lead-sulfide," Forestall answered. "It's a lead-sulfide compound," he explained. "Often, silver will attach to it as well. So it's a good thing, just not as profitable as I had hoped. Processing the ore takes a heavy toll on our profits. Our number two tunnel has been doing well. At least that's what my partner Frank Gromley has been reporting… a couple of tons of ore per day, I think. And that's the reason for my visit."

Now we come to it. The thought was sudden and Susan clapped a hand to her mouth, fighting an irresistible urge to vocalize her sudden doubts concerning Forestall's motivation.

Forestall shifted in his chair and leaned forward in a conspiratorial manner. "Frank and I have talked this over, and we want to make an offer on your brother's mining claims."

Ellen Wells hesitated. For an instant, her eyes flickered in Susan's direction then back to Henry Forestall. "I don't believe I'm the one you should be talking to," she responded.

Forestall glanced in Susan's direction. "Perhaps we should discuss things privately," he suggested.

Ellen Wells shook her head and waved a hand dismissively. "No need," she replied. "Susan is quite discrete. But you seem under the wrong impression. My brother left no will that I know of, and Miranda is his only child. You should discuss any Barrett claims with her."

Forestall nodded. "We took that into consideration," he admitted, "but we were unsure of her ability to act in certain legal aspects because of her age. We thought you might be acting as her guardian."

Ellen Wells paused a moment before responding. "Miranda is twenty," she said quietly. "I suppose that until her birthday in August, I would be her guardian. She has no other relatives in the Territory. Her mother's family is somewhere in Pennsylvania, I think."

Forestall smiled. "I think a court would certainly recognize that there is no one better suited, nor with a better claim to guardianship," he concluded. "Frank and I would certainly consider any agreement that you and Miss Barrett approved to be binding and we could easily renew any agreement on the same terms when Miss Barrett reaches her majority in August."

"Just what is it you wish to propose Mr. Forestall?"

Forestall slid forward until he perched precariously on the edge of the chair. "Frank and I would like to offer five-thousand dollars for seventy-five percent ownership."

Ellen Wells knitted her eyebrows in thought. "Seventy-five percent of which claim?" She asked carefully.

Forestall shifted backward in his seat, his face registering his surprise at the question. "Why… all of them," he responded defensively. "Of course, we would assume development of mining activities. Miranda would receive twenty-fire percent of the profits on a quarterly basis."

Susan sat quietly, giving no indication that she had paid any attention.

"I assure you it's a good offer," Forestall counseled. "Five thousand dollars is a goodly amount for undeveloped claims. Frank and I are taking a big risk. You know how a claim can look good one day and fizzle out the next. That five thousand could be your nest-egg, just in case things go poorly. Miranda would have no financial obligation. She would be a voting partner of course. But I suspect that there would be little need for any direct involvement with the administration or operation of any mines we might develop on the claims."

Ellen Wells sighed and shook her head. "I'm sorry, Mr. Forestall," she said. "Your offer seems reasonable enough, but Miranda could not possibly accept."

A look of irritation flashed across Forestall's face. "Why not?" he asked, the smile quickly returning and covering his true feelings. "If it's the cash… we might be able to offer a bit more."

Ellen Wells shook her head, clasping her hands in her lap, seemingly in distress. "It's not the money or the offer, Mr. Forestall."

"Then there is no problem."

"Mr. Forestall. My brother had partners… Miranda owns only a one third interest in the claims, and she cannot sell any portion of that interest without giving her partners the first option to purchase."

"Partners?"

"Yes, Partners."

Forestall frowned. "I knew nothing of any partners."

"My brother made a deal with them nearly a year ago. He needed money for better equipment."

Forestall shook his head in disbelief. "This certainly changes everything," he grumbled unhappily. "You're sure of this partnership?"

Ellen Wells shrugged. "James told me what he planned. He showed me the papers and explained the terms of the partnership. He showed me receipts for equipment he had ordered along with a thousand dollars that he had held back to pay his crew. He said he only owed part of it as wages, but he would need funds to pay his crew while they set up the equipment and the mine wasn't producing."

Forestall glanced toward the door, as though he had made up his mind to leave. "That leaves me in a rather awkward position," he acknowledged unhappily. "You see... Frank wants to cross-file on the claims. He believes that your brother did no assessment work this past year, making his claim to the sites invalid. Legally, they would be considered abandoned.

"Frank only consented to make an offer because I argued that it would be extremely unfair considering the circumstances. Frank can be rather bullheaded at times. Still, he agreed to make an offer. But I'm sure he will go to Tooele and file immediately, as soon as he learns there are outsiders involved."

"That's perfectly horrid!" Ellen Wells exclaimed. "I had no idea there was any such requirement for assessment work."

"I'm afraid there is," Forestall counseled. "At least that's what Frank has been telling me."

Forestall retrieved his hat from the table beside his chair and stood. "I'm sorry about all of this," he said awkwardly. "Let me talk with Frank again. Maybe we can find a way to work things out."

When Forestall had gone, Susan went to the window and watched his departure down the dirt path leading to the road into town. His movements were slow and measured, carefully paced as though walking was a chore. "I wonder that he walked all that way from town," she mused absently. "He seems too ill for a long walk."

Ellen Wells moved to the window and followed the movements of the departing mine owner.

"I've heard that he's been ill for quite some time," she confided. "Rumor has it that he nearly died from mercury poisoning several months ago and hasn't really recovered from it."

"I noticed his hands tremble a bit," Susan replied. "I've never heard of anyone poisoned by mercury. How on earth could that happen?"

Ellen Wells shrugged and went back to her chair. "Among miners, it's more common than you might think. Many of them use mercury to test their fines when they pan the streams for gold."

"Fines?"

"The heavy sands and minerals left in the pan when the lighter materials are washed away."

"And mercury?"

"The mercury can pick up even the finest particles of gold and form an amalgam. The miners then have to cook the amalgam to retrieve the gold. The mercury turns to a gas when cooked, leaving the gold behind."

"Sounds complicated," Susan confessed.

"Actually, it's a simple process," the older woman explained, "but it can be dangerous. The fumes from the evaporating mercury are poisonous and can be deadly. Too many of these fools hollow out a potato and put the amalgam inside. Then, they just throw the thing on the fire or in a stove and cook it. Few of them pay any attention to ventilating a room. They might walk away from the cabin, but as often as not, the fumes are collected and waiting when they come inside to retrieve the gold. It doesn't kill them all, but I've seen several fellows who showed signs of having poisoned themselves."

"And Mr. Forestall has been ill for some time?"

"At least six months," the older woman responded, "but no one seems to know how it might have happened. Mr. Forestall employs a number of fellows who would know how to use mercury safely. He would never need to handle it himself."

Susan turned from the window and looked at the older woman. "Surely, Mr. Forestall would be aware of the effects of mercury and know how to work with it safely," she concluded.

"One would certainly think so," Mrs. Wells agreed.

"Six months…" Susan repeated thoughtfully. "That's about the time your brother went missing. Isn't it?"

"Possibly… James has been missing since November."

"It seems rather coincidental, don't you think?"

"You think my brother's disappearance is somehow connected," Mrs. Wells asked disbelievingly.

Susan shrugged. "I'm not saying there is a connection," she hedged, "but it seems odd that one mine owner disappears suddenly, and less than a month later another is mysteriously poisoned and nearly dies.

For a moment, the older woman seemed shocked by the thought. "Somehow, I had never considered the possibility that the two could be connected. But to what purpose?"

"I have no idea," Susan responded. "But if there is a connection, it would surely have something to do with the mines. Mr. Forestall's interest in your brother's claims seems rather sudden; yet I wonder if their offer might have been made to your brother months ago?"

A look of doubt seemed to cross the older woman's face as she pondered the new possibilities.

"I'm sure James would have said something, if there had been an offer. He generally kept me informed of his plans and what was happening with the claims. He wanted me to know what was going on, in case something happened to him. He knew his work could be dangerous, so I knew most of the day to day problems he faced. But he never spoke of any offer from Mr. Forestall or Mr. Gromley."

Susan knitted her eyebrows in thought. "It didn't sound as though Mr. Gromley was interested in making an offer. His intentions seem more like those of a coyote waiting to pounce on its unsuspecting prey."

Ellen Wells sighed deeply. "I've heard nothing good of Mr. Gromley," she confided bleakly. "I've had no dealings with him myself, but folks around town say he's brisk to the point of rudeness and has little respect for any point of view other than his own."

Susan turned back to the window. Forestall's visit and the last few minute's discussion with Ellen Wells had served as a temporary distraction, but now her thoughts were drawn back to Sarah.

Where could she be?

The thought plagued her, along with the feeling that they should all have waited for Sarah to make her way back to their group. But Mort insisted that Sarah had ridden up the mountain, and that he would find Collin and go after her. That had been hours ago and Susan was growing more concerned by the minute. Quietly, she fought the urge to climb on a horse and go searching the mountain. She knew it would be a fruitless undertaking, but the urge was there nonetheless.

Her thoughts were still on Sarah's safety when the world exploded in a clap of thunder, and she felt herself slammed into darkness.

Chapter 9

Utah Territory
Deep Creek Mountains—June 1869

The house was a wreck. Every window in the place was shattered and scattered about the building like a glittering skirt. Curtains hung half-in, half-out of empty window frames. The front door gaped open and dangled precariously from one twisted hinge.

"That doesn't look good," Sarah groaned bleakly as Mitchell swung down from the saddle and tied the two horses to a hitching rail set near the southeast corner of the building. A moment later, she slid from the mare's back and into Mitchell's arms.

"You must be the Mitchell's."

The voice that came from the ruined doorway was friendly, calm and deep. And the man who followed the voice into the glass *carpeted* yard was short, heavy, and balding on top. What hair he had left was thin and gray and circled his head like a wide but well-oiled fringe of perfectly combed strands of fine thread. His dark suit had seen better days but had been recently cleaned and pressed, lending the impression that this was a man of wealth now down on his luck

"Everyone said you were up on the mountain, looking for Barrett's claims."

Abruptly, the fellow stuck out his hand. "I'm Frank Gromley," he confessed awkwardly.

For a moment, Mitchell considered the soft uncalloused hand. "You own the Emma mine," he said finally, shaking the offered hand.

"Part of it anyway," Gromley conceded. "Forestall owns the controlling shares—which is probably a good thing, since I know little about the mining business. Add to that an inexplicable terror of dark and cramped underground places, and I am incredibly useless and of no practical value to the company.

"Henry, however, seems disposed to forgive my lack of useful mining talents, and allows me to help out wherever I'm able. Mostly, I keep the ore shipments to the Tooele stamping mills on a regular schedule."

Mitchell thrust his head toward the ruined building.

"What happened here?" He asked.

"An explosion of some kind," Gromley responded. "No one was hurt though," he added quickly as Sarah pulled her hand free of Mitchell's grasp and started toward the canted door.

"Your sister is unharmed," Gromley assured. "I talked with her just moments ago. She has a bump on the head but insists that she's fine."

"I'll check on her all the same," Sarah answered firmly.

"I think that's a good idea, Mitchell agreed.

Sarah went into the house quickly, leaving Mitchell alone with the frowning Gromley.

"She seems quite anxious," Gromley muttered.

"She's had a long ride and a hard day," Mitchell responded.

"Bad one here too," Gromley admitted. "Strange kind of accident."

Mitchell stepped through the ruined doorway and examined the wreckage.

"No accident," he concluded. "The smell of burnt powder is still thick in here."

"Powder?"

Mitchell scowled. "Black powder," he explained. "Can't you smell the sulfur?"

Gromley shrugged. "I smelled it," he admitted, "but I never connected it with black powder."

Mitchell shook his head, wondering how anyone in the mining business could be unfamiliar with the smell of burnt powder; everyone he knew would recognize the smell. He strode across the room and surveyed the destroyed kitchen.

"From the look of that stove, I'd say someone tossed about a pound of powder inside and ran like hell."

"Not much left of the stove," Gromley agreed. "I would never have thought black powder could do so much damage."

Mitchell frowned. "You haven't done much mining, have you?"

"Not a bit. I made my money in shipping… back east."

"Shipping?"

"Cotton mostly."

"How did you end up in mining?"

Gromley shrugged. "Greed, I suppose... I heard all the talk about the big gold and silver strikes out here.... Kind of worked myself up until I just had to come out and see what it was all about…. Rode the trains all the way to Ogden.

"By then I was a little road weary, so I stayed there a week or so. That's when I heard that Henry was looking for someone to invest in the Emma. I thought the deal looked good, so I paid ten-thousand dollars for a forty-nine percent partnership.

"Everyone said the Emma was following a good vein of silver, but Henry had overextended on equipment and hadn't made payroll for three weeks."

"Ever meet Jim Barrett?" asked Mitchell.

"We talked a few times," Gromley admitted. "Last fall, I heard he was looking for financing to get the equipment he needed for his claim. By the time I caught up with him, he had already gone to Salt Lake and got the money he needed."

Mitchell caught a glimpse of Sarah wandering the back yard, beyond the rupture that left most of the kitchen open to the elements. She seemed preoccupied, and scrutinized the ground as though searching for something. Mitchell looked back at Gromley.

"I'd like to continue our conversation later," he said. "Right now, I need to look after my family."

"I understand," Gromley replied, turning away.

"There *is* something you could do for me," Mitchell proposed to Gromley's retreating back.

Gromley paused and looked back.

"What might that be?"

"I'd like to take a look at the place in the Emma where you found that body."

Gromley frowned. "Is there some reason? I mean... It just seems odd that you should be interested."

Mitchell scowled. "Jim Barrett was my partner. He came to me last fall and we struck a deal on a partnership."

"Partnership...."

"That's right. Barrett sold one third to me and one third to another fellow to raise the money for the equipment he needed."

"And now you want me to let you into the Emma? I'm not sure it's wise to let the owner of a competing operation into our mine."

Mitchell's face hardened into a scowl that Sarah sometimes referred to as his killer face. "I'm not interested in your operation," he growled. "I just want to see the pocket where the body was found. Ellen Wells is sure the dead man was her brother. Besides, you have to admit it's pretty strange to find someone encased in solid rock six-hundred feet down."

Gromley shrugged. "It's pretty obvious that no such thing happened. Those two fellows working the face were responsible for the whole thing. Deputy Simmons just didn't have the skill to discover how they did it."

"I'd still like to look around. Even if it wasn't Jim Barrett, the man had been shot between the eyes, and Simmons says there was no weapon with the body. Now, that's not proof that he was murdered, but it sure makes you wonder."

For a moment, Gromley stood frowning.

"Fine," he conceded. "Come out to the gate in a couple of hours... about three... I'll take you down myself."

When Gromley was gone, Mitchell hurried up the staircase to their rooms. Sarah was just entering the hallway, carefully closing the door to Susan's room behind her.

"She's asleep," she reported quietly. "You ought to stay out of there and let her rest."

"Is she hurt?"

"She's well enough," Sarah replied. She took a pretty good knock on the head, but she's fine, nothing broken…"

"Did she say what happened?" Mitchell demanded coldly.

"She was nearly asleep… Ellen gave her a bit of laudanum, so she wasn't able to explain much of anything… she says they were in the parlor when the kitchen just exploded. She thought the explosion must have thrown her across the room and against a wall. She hit her head on something, and that's all she remembered."

Mitchell scowled and marched back down the stairway. "I saw the stove in the kitchen," he explained as Sarah caught up with him. "And I smelled burnt powder when we came in."

"There must have been a lot of powder," Sarah concluded as they entered the kitchen. "There's still a cloud hanging over everything."

Mitchell surveyed the room in amazement. The door between the kitchen and the parlor was simply gone, and the room itself was still shrouded in a gray-white cloud that smelled of rotten eggs. At the back wall a stove-sized hole opened the room to the glare of the sun and a view of a yard cluttered with shattered bits of lath and plaster. Ten feet away lay the twisted object that had once served as the boarding house stove.

"It's a wonder the house didn't come apart at the seams," he grumbled. "Blew the doors off and shot the thing through the wall like a rocket."

"Where are the doors?" Sarah asked thoughtfully.

Mitchell glanced around the destroyed room. It took a moment, but they soon discovered the missing doors. One of the heavy steel plates had been flung diagonally across the room, where it had cut edge-on through the face of a cupboard, burying itself in the wall beyond. The other had shot upward through the ceiling and into the room above, and only a blackened edge now protruded downward into ruins of Ellen Wells' kitchen.

"I hope no one was in that room," Sarah said appraisingly.

"Lucky no one was in the kitchen," Mitchell replied. "Of course, if someone *had* been in the kitchen, no one could have sneaked in and loaded the stove with black powder."

"Who would do such a thing?" Sarah murmured unhappily.

"I had a fire going in that stove all morning." Ellen Wells said as she stood in the open frame of the parlor doorway surveying the damage. "I've been in and out of here all morning. No one could have come in here without my knowing it except when Henry Forestall was in the parlor visiting with us. Any other time and I would have caught them in the act."

Mitchell frowned and went to the back door. In the yard, the ground was littered with debris, and the door itself lay thirty feet away in several shattered pieces. Two-hundred yards beyond, the earth surged upward in a steep hillside nearly barren of vegetation. Thoughtfully, Mitchell stepped down into the yard and studied the littered ground.

The soil was hard, yet the surface was covered with a thin layer of wind-blown dust and a myriad of footprints… most of them the hard-soled prints of boots like those worn by most of the miners in the area. It was plain to see that the back door of the boardinghouse had been designated as the proper avenue of entry and departure for the men who lived here and worked in the mines.

The boot tracks led in every direction. Some wandered off and disappeared in the surrounding desert. Some wandered the yard aimlessly. But most led only a few paces from the sun-bleached porch and stopped near a wooden trough filled with water. Here, the ground was littered with the burnt-out remains of cigars, butts of hand rolled cigarettes, and the dried-up leavings of chewed tobacco.

In all the yard, only four sets of tracks stood out, each set slightly different, but all of them belonging to women. These Mitchell followed carefully until he was satisfied that he had learned all he could of their movements. After an hour, he returned to the house.

"You were out there an awfully long time," Sarah pointed out when he returned to the damaged parlor.

The place had been swept clean and much of the furniture returned to its proper place. Broken things had been removed, and save for missing windows and a canted door, the room seemed almost as it had been. Quietly, he found a chair and settled his weight carefully onto its seat.

"There are a lot of tracks out there," he replied after a moment.

"And did you discover anything useful?"

"It seems the back door is the preferred route in and out of the house."

Sarah glanced quickly at Ellen Wells. "That's a rule of the house, isn't it Ellen?"

Mrs. Wells glanced quickly at Mitchell. "It is," she admitted. "The men are absolutely filthy when they come out of those mines. If I didn't make them clean up before they come into the house, I'd have a pig sty in here every day. I wouldn't be able to keep up with the cleaning."

"I thought that might be the situation," Mitchell observed. "They smoke outside also?"

"Yes they do... I can't abide the smell."

"And the women?"

"There's only Miranda and myself."

"I found footprints of another," Mitchell advised. "Have you had any women come calling at the back door recently?"

"None that I know of."

"No one visiting one of your boarders or your niece?"

"I suppose they could have... Are you suggesting a woman blew up my kitchen?"

Mitchell scowled and shifted uncomfortably in the chair. He had no idea who might have done the deed, but deep down, he had a feeling a woman had done it, and the feeling was hard to ignore.

"I don't know," he answered finally. "The boot tracks are everywhere... coming and going constantly. Your tracks and Miranda's come and go multiple times. Only this other woman... she came and left again the one time, and that was today, I think.... Not one of her tracks were disturbed or walked over by any of the miner's boots. I think she was here today, but I can't be sure what she was doing here. We can talk with your boarders and see if anyone was expecting a visitor, but I doubt we'll have any luck on that. I'm almost certain she's responsible, whomever she is."

"But why blow up my house?"

"I can't be sure," Mitchell answered, "but someone may be trying to scare us off."

* * *

It was the cool of the evening. The red-orange disc of the sun brushed the tips of the Deep Creek Range and sank beyond, turning the mountains into shades of fire and shadow. Mitchell sat in a sturdy chair of tightly woven willow branches and tipped back against the west wall of the boarding house. The last heat of the evening sun swept up the wall, racing ahead of the ragged shadow-line that had sped from the foothills to Mitchell's feet in a matter of minutes.

Behind him, muffled by the clapboard of the sun-bleached wall, the chatting of women and the bump and clatter of their cleaning efforts came through the wall as the soul easing sounds of home. It was a background murmur that filled Mitchell with an inner contentment that was too often ignored in the rush of daily events.

Quietly, he took a deep breath. He let it out slowly, relishing the knowledge that Sarah and Susan were both safe inside, and feeling the pent up stress of the day drain away. Too often, both women had been in the thick of events better left to men more inured to the buffetings of the world—events that often required a more calloused attitude than either woman had yet acquired or ever would.

Both women had gumption. That much was certain. But deep down, Mitchell had a niggling fear that too close an association with the meanness of life might somehow darken the brightness and joy both women seemed to exude like the warmth of the sun. That fear sometimes prompted him to overprotective behavior, but either woman soon put him in his proper place when that happened. Neither woman rejected his right as a husband to be their provider and protector, but there were limits. And Sarah had once made it very clear that she would not be kept as a "caged bird." She had even quoted verses from Elizabeth Browning's *Feminine Education of Aurora Leigh.* Just to put him in the proper perspective.

In any case, there were limits. But Mitchell had his own ideas about just how far he would let those limits bind him to inaction. He would not cage them. But as Susan had once said, "they might be she-wolves capable of taking care of themselves, but *he* was the dire-wolf, and no one in their right senses would trouble his pack."

Mitchell, however, did not see himself as a dire-wolf, although popular opinion seemed to agree with Susan's assessment. When he took the time for introspection and self-examination, he saw himself as a simple soul who loved his God and his family. He was an impossible distance from the Christ-like man he wanted to be, and knew it well. But the goal was there, however distant and unreachable it might seem.

"You're very quiet."

Mitchell opened his eyes at the sound of Susan's gentle observation.

"Just thinking," he admitted.

"Ah… Deep thoughts or just the frivolous things that knock about in one's head from time to time?"

"Just thinking how comforting the sounds of a good woman puttering about the house are."

"Thinking and writing," Susan observed, pointing to the journal that lay atop a large stone next to Mitchell's chair.

Mitchell tipped the chair forward and stood. For a moment, he considered the volume resting on the stone. Then quietly, he led Susan to the chair.

"Read as much as you like," he offered. "Let Sarah have it when you're finished. It ain't all good, but it ain't all bad either. Still, I think there are some things easier to get a handle on if you read about it first."

"You can't just tell me?"

For a moment, Mitchell studied the rocky slopes and canyons of the mountains so close at hand to the west.

"Probably," he admitted. "But it might lose something in the telling. The written word is a lot like a photograph. If you get the focus just right… capture the details, things that were obscure become clear… Anyway, I've got a couple of horses to feed and water. When I'm finished, we can talk about anything in there that troubles you. Most of it's from memory, and there ain't much in there, 'cause I've only been working on it for a couple of months. But

I'd like you to read it, 'cause there are a few things I've been meaning to tell you about for a long time. They didn't seem important at first, but I never intended to keep them to myself like some dark secret."

Susan set the journal in her lap and looked up. She smiled mischievously. "Like the fact that you studied at Harvard for nearly four years?"

Mitchell scowled and shook his head in disbelief. "Now just *how* did you discover that bit of information," he groaned.

Susan smiled and raised both eyebrows as though surprised "So it's true! I've suspected something of the sort for a long time. Every now and then you slip out of that down-home Mormon dialect you've adopted and say something completely out of character for a fellow as uneducated as you pretend to be.

"But rumors started last fall, I believe, when Deputy Turner told his wife. She told Sister Murphy at the dry goods store in Heber City. Sister Murphy told her husband. Brother Murphy mentioned it to the blacksmith, who told brother and Sister Campbell, who told Lynne, who told me, and I told Sarah. I may have left someone out of the gossip chain, but most of Heber City knew about it before we ever left town.

"Sarah and I learned of it just last month when Lynne commented on how odd it seemed that a fellow so highly educated would want to live out in the middle of nowhere and raise cattle and sheep."

Mitchell groaned unhappily. "I intended to tell you long before this."

Susan stood and wrapped her arms around his neck. "Don't worry," she murmured against his chest. "We're not angry. But we *will* read your journal... just to make sure you haven't forgotten to tell us anything else so revealing about the mysterious gunman we've married."

"Not so mysterious and no gunman," Mitchell replied quietly.

Chapter 10

Utah Territory
Deep Creek Mountains —June 1869

Heat waves shimmered in the distance; dogs lay panting in any patch of shade they could find, and the morning wash hung dry as a bone by the time Sarah stepped onto the sagging planks of the boardwalk in front of Charles Allingham's dry goods store.

Sarah leaned close and peered into a dingy window. It was a drab little store, hardly more than a slat-walled room, perhaps twenty feet on a side. Like every other building in town, the store had never seen a drop of paint, and the combination of weather and the brain roasting heat of the sun had turned every stick of wood from its natural color to a bleached-out gray that was miserable to the eye.

Sarah hesitated for a moment. She could see nothing through the dust covered window. She had little hope of finding the material Ellen Wells had asked her to find, and fully expected the undertaking to be a complete waste of time. The shop was so small that she could hardly expect to find anything more than the most meager of necessities. The things needed at the boarding house would have to be ordered and shipped from Salt Lake City; and that could take weeks.

Still, the effort was necessary. Most of the boarding house's furnishings had been ruined in the explosion. The kitchen had been totally destroyed. The parlor had survived, but every bit of glassware had been shattered.

The windows were gone, and the curtains in tatters. It was a miracle no one had been killed in the blast.

Quietly, she stepped back from the window and turned her attentions to the stillness of the town. There were few people to be seen—less than one might expect—even for such a small place. The cause, she suspected, lay in the hours worked by the men at the Emma mine, which seemed to be the principal employer for the majority of the men in the area. Most of those men appeared to be single and worked long, hard hours, leaving them exhausted by the end of their shift and with hardly enough time to eat and sleep before they found themselves back in the abysmal depths of the Emma's bowels.

Only the miners laboring in drift number two of the Emma worked a twelve hour shift—an oddity that Sarah had noted only by accident—a bit of information that Henry Forestall had barely mentioned during his visit to the boarding house.

"You seem preoccupied."

The voice came from the doorway of the shop and startled Sarah from her reverie. She turned to see the fellow standing in the doorway. Apron tied about his waist, broom in hand, he was a tall man, thin of body and face. His once dark hair, now missing on top and gone gray at the temples, lay matted and damp from the sultry heat inside his shop.

"I was noticing how few people are out and about today," she replied.

"Too hot," he grumbled. "Most of the night crews are trying to get some sleep before their next shift. Other folks come and go as they please.... Mostly, they have their own chores to take care of, unless they've got a need for something.... Is that why you're out and about, Ma'am? Can I help you with anything?"

Sarah shrugged. "Not for me. Ellen Wells asked me to come into town and look for some curtain material."

The man nodded his head sagely.

"Heard the explosion. Rattled everything in the store. Knocked a couple of quarts of jam off the shelves and broke them. Made a sticky mess. Took me half an hour to clean it up."

Sarah smiled. "Made a mess of the boarding house too. But I think it will take a little longer to clean things up over there."

"I can imagine."

"Do you have any curtain material?" she asked.

"I've got some material," he replied. "I don't know if it would be any good for curtains though."

"May I look at what you have?"

The man stepped away from the door. "Sorry, ma'am. I didn't realize I was blocking the door."

Sarah smiled again, sensing a change in the man's attitude. It was as though the prospect of a sale had changed his whole day. "No need to apologize," she responded as she stepped through the doorway and into the dim interior of the shop. "You must be Mr. Allingham," she suggested.

"Guilty," he confessed.

"Have you been here long?" Sarah asked casually.

"About two years," Allingham responded. "Wasn't much of a town then, but it looked like things could grow a bit... especially if the mines in the district did well."

Sarah let her eyes rove the shop, looking for the material, but all the while assessing the success of Allingham's business.

"And have you done well?" she asked.

Allingham frowned and looked around the shop.

"Not as well as I hoped," he admitted. "As you can probably tell...."

Sarah wandered. After a moment of fruitless searching, Allingham pointed her toward the back of the shop. Near the back wall, she found a small table stacked high with a dozen or more bolts of cloth stacked in its center.

"That's the lot of it," Allingham confessed.

"There might be something here," Sarah suggested hopefully. "Some of these colors are quite dark though. They would turn a room into a dungeon. I'm thinking something lighter would brighten up a room—especially the parlor. Everything in there was quite dark... Although there is little left of the parlor now."

"What about this one?"

Allingham dragged a bolt from the bottom of the pile and unrolled a section the length of his arm. He took the bolt to the window and held it where the sunlight passed through the window in a wide angular beam. The cloth lit up like a glowing lamp shade as the light turned it the soft tawny color of a hawk's feather.

"That's quite nice," Sarah admitted.

"I brought it in for shirt material," Allingham admitted. "No one bought any. I think I have two bolts."

Sarah nodded approvingly. "Yes.... I think that might just do the job."

Allingham held the cloth to his chest. "You could always use it for shirt material," he suggested dryly.

Sarah grinned. "I might just do that," she concluded happily. "Collin has one old shirt that I just detest. But he won't get rid of the thing. It's been mended a dozen times. If I make a new one, I might convince him to give up the old one. If I can get it away from him, I'll cut it up for quilt material. That's if there is any part of it worth using."

She was still holding a length of cloth draped over one arm when the door of the shop squealed open on dry hinges and a shabby looking fellow stepped into the dim interior of the shop. Surprised, Sarah paused to consider the picture he made, standing framed in the open doorway like a full-sized portrait of a man gone to seed and in need of a good scrubbing.

From head to foot, he was unkempt, wrinkled, and stained. His hat rested at an angle upon his head like a crumpled wad of cloth that had lost any shape or resemblance to any hat she had ever seen. It hung limply down the back of his neck until it brushed the threadbare collar of a coat that fell nearly to his knees.

His shirt was no better. Lacking any visible button, it lay open from throat to navel, and he stood, hands shoved into pockets, shadow veiled eyes staring into the dimness.

Finally, when his eyes found Sarah, he stepped forward cautiously, as though his advance might startle her and send her bolting from the shop like a frightened deer.

"Hold on now!" Allingham challenged sharply. "What are you after?"

The ragged fellow stopped and hooked a thumb in Sarah's direction. "I came to talk to the lady," he protested.

Allingham glared at the man. "What business do you have with her? You work up at the Emma mine, don't you?"

"I did," came the response, "until this morning... Ramsay let a couple of us go.... That's why I came to talk with you," he said, looking towards Sarah. "I heard you folks own half of the Barrett claims."

Sarah laid the bolt of cloth on the table and focused her attention on the unemployed miner, wondering if he was about to ask her for a job.

"If I understand things correctly, my husband is a partner in the Barrett claims."

"Could we talk for a minute?" the man asked quietly.

"I have a few minutes," Sarah admitted, "but you really ought to speak with my husband, if you're looking for work."

"I could use a job, but that ain't why I came to see you."

The miner glanced quickly at Allingham. "Art told me not to talk with anyone else," he said quietly.

Sarah looked quickly around the shop. One corner, near the front was clear of tables and merchandise.

"We could talk over there," she offered.

The miner frowned, as though the suggestion offered less privacy than he wanted. Finally, he nodded. "That'll be fine."

Sarah stepped quickly past the man to a spot near the window.

"My name's Deagan," he said quietly when he stood beside her. "Mike Deagan.... Art Williams and me worked up at the Emma mine until this morning. Art's out at his shack, but we both thought we should talk with your husband as soon as we could."

"Something about the Barrett claims," Sarah asked casually.

"Something about the Emma...."

"The Emma?"

"We was the ones that found that body," Deagan explained. "Art said we'd get fired over that business.... Turns out he was right."

"And you want to talk with Collin about the body you found?"

"Some.... We heard that Mrs. Wells went over to the post office to look at the body after Deputy Simmons brought it up out of the mine. We heard she thought it was her brother. Art thinks the whole business is queer, but we can't make heads or tails of it. Art thinks he might be on to something. He thinks something fishy is going on."

Sarah raised an eyebrow. "Do *you* think something fishy is going on?"

The miner frowned, and Susan realized suddenly that this was no old 'veteran' of the mines. He was a young man, still insecure in his own knowledge of his trade.

"But Mr. Williams is sure something fishy is going on..." She prompted.

"So he says. Small things mostly, but they're things that just don't add up."

Sarah glanced toward the back of the shop where Allingham stood rearranging the bolts of cloth. He placed the two she wanted on top.

"These small things must add up to something," Sarah replied.

"I guess they do," Deagan admitted. "But Art wouldn't tell me what it is. He just tells me it's better I don't know, and if I wasn't so green I'd have figured it out by now."

"Mr. Deagan..."

"Call me Mike."

Sarah smiled. "Mike... As soon as I see my husband, I'll tell him that you and Mr. Williams would like to speak with him as soon as possible."

"I appreciate that, ma'am." Deagan turned away, and under Allingham's critical eye, the miner left the shop.

Sarah watched though the window until the miner had disappeared from view. When he was no longer visible, she crossed the store to Allingham and his bolts of cloth.

"I'll take those two," she declared.

A good choice," Allingham confirmed.

Quietly, Sarah followed Allingham back to his counter. "You seemed uncomfortable with Mr. Deagan," she suggested casually. "Is he a trouble maker?"

Allingham shrugged. "Don't know," he responded. "Never dealt with him before, but I know the type. They come into the store and things disappear.

"You have to keep an eye on them every second or they would pick the store clean… Thieves… the lot of them!"

Sarah frowned. Deagan had not seemed like the sort who would steal from anyone, let alone Allingham.

"I would have thought the mines paid enough for a fellow to live on," she surmised.

"They do!" Allingham exclaimed. "But these fellows will drink and gamble away a month's pay in a few days. They're always broke. They can't stay away from the card game that's going twenty-four hours a day over in the back room at the freight office. Most of them are wearing rags like the fellow that just left, and I doubt if any of them have had a decent meal since that game set up six months ago."

"And these men have been stealing from you."

"I couldn't prove anything," Allingham admitted, "but things *have* gone missing."

Sarah frowned, shaking her head in disbelief. She paid for the cloth, and Allingham dropped a ten-dollar gold piece and some change into her hand. Pretty coin," she observed absently, wondering how she would manage packing two bolts of cloth back to the boarding house.

"You can leave the cloth here," Allingham offered. "I'll see that it gets over to the boarding house."

"Thank you," Sarah responded, dropping the change into her handbag. "I should have planned better. I suppose I wasn't really expecting to find anything suitable today."

"No problem," Allingham said reassuringly. "Happens all the time."

Moments later Sarah was out the door and back into the furnace of late morning. She looked south towards the stables where Mitchell had gone earlier in the morning. For a moment, she thought of walking down to find him and tell him that Deagan and Williams wanted to talk, but the scorching heat from the torch overhead engulfed her like the blistering breath from the depths of hell. In a matter of minutes, she was sweltering and hunting for shade, but the west side of Main Street was awash with the heat, and the only refuge lay on the east in the narrow strip of shade hugging tightly to the buildings and growing thinner with every passing moment.

She crossed to the other side. In the shade, she pressed against the front wall of the Post Office, and the temperature dropped fifteen degrees. The change brought instant relief. Ninety-five was almost bearable.

"You folks should go back where you came from."

Sarah stiffened. The voice came from behind her, through the open window of the Post Office. She started to turn, intent on confrontation.

"Don't turn around. This is a friendly warning, but I don't want them to know I warned you."

"Who are you warning me about?" Sarah asked quietly.

"I don't know who they are," came the answer. "I was in the back room just a few minutes ago. I heard a man and a woman talking… couldn't make out much of what they said, but they are up to no good. So watch your back."

Chapter 11

Utah Territory
Deep Creek Mountains—June 1869

The morning sun was a red-orange disk balanced on the tips of the ragged peaks of the Onaqui Mountains. A dusty wind had kicked up only moments before, and Collin Mitchell grabbed at his hat as the wind snatched it from his head and tumbled it through the open doorway into Ned Hawkins' stable. The hat came to rest leaning against the gate post of one stall, perilously close to a freshly shoveled pile of wet manure. The stable boy was after the hat before it had touched the ground and had it in hand before the wind could take hold again to send it skimming across the muck spotted ground.

"That was close," the boy observed as he returned the battered headpiece to its owner.

Mitchell brushed at the hat, removing loose bits of hay, searching for more offensive material.

"Pretty beat up anyway," he replied, "but I don't think I want to be wearin' any of *that* stuff."

"Reckon not," the boy replied.

"What's your name son?"

"Tom... Tom Hawkins...."

Tom Hawkins

The name whispered across Mitchell's consciousness like a shaft of brilliant sunlight.

"Tom," he whispered, holding out his hand. "Pleased to meet you, Tom Hawkins. My name is Mitchell."

Hesitantly, the child's small hand came out to be buried in Mitchell's calloused grip.

"You make a big light. Folks around here are all cloudy. Do you know the angels?"

Mitchell smiled and released the small hand. Amused, he looked down at his homespun trousers and beat-up riding boots. "I might," he replied. "Do they make really good bread?"

"Don't know. I seen 'em walkin' down by the boarding house though… Pop said it's my *'magination.* That's like make believe, ain't it?"

"I suppose it is," Mitchell agreed cautiously. "But some folks just can't see as good as a young fellow like you. I'll bet you can climb a tree better than your Pa, can't you?"

The boy was quiet for a moment, thinking. "I think so…. I never seen Pop climb a tree…"

"You like your Pop, don't you?"

"Yup… He takes me places, an' he don't beat me none. 'Lizbeth's pop beats her when she's bad."

Mitchell glanced around the stable. "How old are you, Tom Hawkins?"

"Seven."

"You keep a clean stable for a fellow just seven years old."

"Pop says I'm strong. He told my mom I'm a good fellow, but I ain't smart…. They was talkin' real quiet. I wasn't supposed to hear. Mom says they'll have to take care of me 'till they die….

"I got a baby cat. The other kids don't like me 'cause I got a baby cat. Mom gave it to me for my birthday. She lets me feed it some milk. You want to see it?"

Mitchell smiled and wandered over to a rough-sawn bench that had been pushed up against a nearby wall and sat down. "You go ahead and bring that cat," he laughed. "I'd like to have a look at her."

"You'll wait here?"

"I'll wait here."

Mitchell watched as the boy launched like a startled jackrabbit and was out the back door on the run. He was back before the slamming door had stopped vibrating.

"I got a bed for her in the shade out back. My Pop says she'll take care of the mice for us when she gets big.... I thought mice had moms and pops like boys do... I guess cats like to help so the mice moms and pops can get some rest."

Mitchell took the proffered animal and held the little black and white ball in his lap. Gently, he rubbed a thumb across the tiny forehead.

"She got a name?" He asked.

For a moment, the boy looked puzzled. "Cat," he concluded finally.

"Good name," Mitchell approved. "You like working in the stable?" He asked as *Cat* started to purr.

The boy shrugged. "Pop says I got to learn. He says I got to work or I can't buy food. Mom cries when they talk about me."

"Tommy!"

Mitchell glanced toward the back door of the stable. "Sounds like your mom is looking for you."

"She just wants me to come in for breakfast."

"You probably ought to go then. You wouldn't want to worry her."

The boy turned as the back door swung open and a middle-aged woman stepped into the shadowy interior of the stable. For a moment she stood quietly, waiting for her eyes to adjust to the dimness.

"Tommy, I've been calling you."

The boy looked down at his feet.

"Who's your friend?" She asked softly.

"I forget." The boy murmured, looking at his feet.

The woman marched to the boy's side and took him by the hand, half shielding him from Mitchell's sight.

"Don't mumble," she instructed. "It's okay that you forget."

The boy looked up at the woman and gripped her fingers more tightly. "I seen some angels today."

The woman pulled the boy close and wrapped one arm around his shoulders. "We'll talk about your angels later tonight," she instructed.

The boy's eyes darted toward Mitchell, then back to his mother. "They made a light like him... not so big though... Hey! He's got a cat, mom. Can I hold your cat, mister?"

Mitchell plucked the purring animal from his lap and handed it into the boy's outstretched hands.

"I'll bet your mom would let you have this one, Tommy," Mitchell suggested gently. "But you'll have to take good care of her."

The boy hesitated, glancing from the kitten to his mother.

"It's okay, Tommy."

Mitchell shifted his attention back to the woman. "I'm looking for a miner named Art Williams," he explained. "I was told someone at the stables could tell me how to find him. Tommy saved my hat from certain destruction when the wind tried to tumble it into a pile of manure. Tommy and I just hit it off after that."

The woman sighed and shook her head. "I'm not sure I know anyone by that name," she confessed. "My husband may know something about him though. Most of the men working the mines have little to do with us. Few of them own a horse, but my husband does a little business with some of them. He charges two-bits a head to take them out to the Emma and the Lost Treasure and back again when their shift is done. The fellow you're looking for might be one of them... I just don't know.

Mitchell noted the wagon backed into a shadowy corner of the stable. "I'd really like to talk with your husband ma'am."

For a long moment, the woman hesitated. "I'll get him," she said finally.

* * *

They found Art Williams entirely by accident. After an hour of riding in circles, Mitchell had finally spotted a boot track in the softer soil on the bank of a small dried-up stream. They had followed the track into a thick cluster of juniper and tall buck-brush. There, they found Williams' place tucked tightly and invisibly within the trees.

"Not much of a place," the Pratt kid muttered as he eyed the rough built structure. "Looks like someone dragged in every stick of dead wood they could find and made a big pile to live under."

"Looks a bit like a hogan," Mitchell concluded. "Guess a fellow by himself don't need much more."

"Hello the house!" The Pratt kid bellowed. "You home Williams?"

There was no answer. The Pratt kid waited a few seconds. "Williams!"

Mitchell studied the hogan and the surrounding trees. All was quiet. The hint of a dry, hot breeze played with the leaves of the buck-brush, and the sun beat down hard upon the dry earth, hunting for the moisture it had long since baked out of the rocky soil. Mitchell took off his hat and wiped the sweat from his forehead with the big blue bandanna Sarah had made for him that winter. It was her small effort, she claimed, to keep him from using a perfectly good shirt sleeve for the wrong purpose. More often than not, he forgot the bandanna and used the shirt sleeve anyway.

"I suppose we ought to take a look inside," he suggested.

"I don't think I like that idea," the Pratt kid grumbled. "That fellow could be sittin' back somewhere just waitin' to shoot us for trespassin'."

"Could be," Mitchell answered. "But I don't think so. There's just a little bit of smoke coming out of that pipe he's got for a chimney, and I got a feeling he ain't in any condition to shoot anyone."

"You think he's dead. Don't you?"

"Almost like I can smell it."

"Crap! You're startin' to sound like Mort."

Mitchell scowled and pointed at the shelter. "Just see if he's inside," he demanded.

"Fine!"

Reluctantly, the Pratt kid dismounted and pushed open the door. The woven branches swung stiffly inward on wire hinges, and the kid poked his head inside.

"Well, he looks dead all right."

Unhappily, Mitchell dismounted and went inside the shelter.

The tiny dwelling was sparsely furnished. A cot, a chair, a table and a stand for a small, portable cook stove were the only furnishings. A rough plank attached to the outer wall held a nearly empty sack of flour and a quart bottle filled with dry beans. There was no other food to be seen, except the few cooked greens on the tin plate Williams had eaten from. Aside from the plate, a small pot, a bent fork and a hunting knife were the only utensils to be found. It was an impoverished little hut and Williams lay dead in the only clothing he owned.

"Doesn't look like he's been dead very long," he observed.

"Guess not," the Pratt kid replied from where he stood near the door. "That ain't much of a cook stove he's got, and that little bit of a fire wasn't nothin' but a few twigs and some little branches. The coals are still hot. I don't expect it would take more than an hour or two for the lot of 'em to burn down to nothin'."

Mitchell looked away from the handmade cot and the remains of the man who had built it.

"Anything here seem odd to you?" he asked quietly.

"The whole world seems odd to me lately," the kid complained.

"Look at that table," Mitchell insisted.

"Okay," squawked the kid. "I see food."

"Half eaten," Mitchell prompted.

"Couldn't stomach his own cooking," the kid replied.

"Maybe... But look at the whole picture."

"Okay," the kid grumbled. "He didn't eat his vegetables, and he left the potato on the coals."

"That potato is strange though. Isn't it?"

The Pratt kid moved closer to the small home-made cook stove. With one finger, he nudged the burnt stub of wood sticking up from the skin of the potato.

"Why toothpicks?"

Mitchell dropped into the dead man's chair and pushed the half-finished plate to the opposite side of the small table.

"Pull that spud out and set it here," he instructed.

"Still warm," the kid observed, dropping the object on the table in front of Mitchell.

Mitchell held the object down and plucked out the wooden sticks. "It's an old method for separating gold from mercury," he answered. "Fellows on placer claims can pan out gold dust that's too fine to see or separate easily from the black sand and other fine materials they find in a stream. They end up with a mix of gold, magnetite, iron… all kinds of stuff.

"That stuff is still worth some money, but you have to get the gold and silver separated. So they take a little mercury and roll it around in the fines. The mercury sucks up the gold—silver too, I think. Anyway, the mercury and gold become an amalgam. The next step is to recover the gold. That's where the potato comes in."

"I'm lost," the kid muttered.

"You cut the potato in half, hollow out a pocket, drop the amalgam in the pocket, pin the two halves back together and bake the danged thing. The mercury gasses off from the heat and leaves the gold in the pocket."

"You're sayin' there's gold inside that potato."

Mitchell pulled the two halves apart, exposing a small golden spherule. "I'm saying there's gold in that potato," he answered.

The kid glanced toward the cot. "Kind of a raw deal," he complained. "A fellow finds a little gold, then up and dies before he can use it."

"That's what seems odd," Mitchell reasoned. "Everything here makes it look like Williams died from mercury poisoning."

The kid shook his head. "I wouldn't know about that stuff," he replied.

"When you bake that potato, the mercury turns to a toxic gas. It's bad stuff. Heavy exposure can cause chest pains, hearing trouble, lung trouble, delirium, lots of bad stuff…"

"So the fumes killed him," the kid concluded.

"No," Mitchell argued. "I don't think they did."

He dropped the halves of the potato on the table and studied the walls of the hut.

"This place ain't tight enough to keep the wind out. About all it's good for is a little shade. Any real weather would blow through here without hesitation. There's been a little bit of a breeze all morning. So I can't see how cooking out that little drop of mercury could have saturated this place with enough fumes to kill the man. Make him sicker than a dog maybe.... But even that seems unlikely."

"What's this," the kid asked, pushing at a small piece of paper that lay under the plate.

Lifting the plate, Mitchell retrieved the paper and examined the angled lines that crossed the sheet in several directions. "Strange... seems a waste for a fellow that has so little..." Carefully, he folded the sheet and placed it in his pocket.

Mitchell turned in the chair and took a closer look at the body of the miner. The man's clothing was worn and dirty, as though it had been weeks since he had last cleaned them. The woolen blanket on which he lay was in no better condition, and his battered hat hung atop an equally worn coat on a hook near the door.

All in all, Williams had the appearance of a dirty, sun burnt character that had been living a hand-to-mouth existence.

"If the mercury didn't kill him, what did?" The kid asked bleakly

"I'm not sure."

Mitchell stood and leaned over the body.

Something odd...

"His nose is broken," he said finally. "There's a little blood on his face."

"Maybe he fell," the kid offered.

"Maybe... It's on his shirt too."

"Blood on this shirt too," the kid added, dragging the wadded article from behind a small stack of firewood.

For a moment, Mitchell stared at the shirt. It was clean, white, and it was something Williams had never worn.

"I guess we ought to get the county sheriff out here," he concluded grimly. "That's a woman's blouse, and whoever owns it may have killed this fellow."

* * *

"That deputy thinks *we* done it," the Pratt kid complained as they rode away from Williams' hut for the second time. "He'd arrest us right now if he thought he could prove anything."

Mitchell jerked forward in the saddle as the dun took a jolting lunge onto the flat bottom of a creek bed and turned east, away from the Deep Creek Range.

"He knows we didn't do it," he called back. "He's just the type that grabs up the first idea that comes into his head and can't let up on it no matter what. He won't believe anything we tell him, even if his nose is rubbed in the proof."

"Well, I don't like it," the kid objected.

"I don't like it either," Mitchell agreed, "but there ain't a whole lot we can do about it, and I still want to talk with that Deagan fellow."

The Pratt kid jumped his horse out of the gully and onto the dry, brush covered flats between the foothills and the southern edge of town.

"I heard that deputy say Deagan was rentin' a bed at the Emma bunkhouses."

"Probably those buildings across the road from the cemetery," Mitchell responded. "We'll head that way and see if Deagan is there."

The ride to the bunkhouses was quickly over, and when they found Deagan, the man was nervous and ready to bolt.

"Art's dead?" He repeated. "We was supposed to go out to the Yellow Boy Mine first thing this morning and see if we could get hired on. Art never showed up."

Deagan sat down hard on the bunkhouse steps. The thin slats of the porch bowed under his weight, squawking noisily in protest.

Mitchell leaned up against the bunkhouse wall and watched as the wind rocked the branches of the sagebrush and kicked up a fine, dry dust that filled the air with the scent of sage and the salty taste of old lake-bed soil.

"I think someone killed your friend," he advised

"Why?" Deagan responded incredulously. "He didn't have nothin'. He lived out in that little shack he built and lived on flat-bread an' beans. He sent just about every dime he made to his family back in Kansas. You wouldn't think it, but he was only thirty-two."

"Was he doing any placer work," Mitchell asked.

"I don't think so. When would he have time? We worked twelve hour shifts, sometimes eighteen, if someone on the night crew didn't show up."

"Was he taking any ore from the Emma?"

"What do you mean?"

"You know what I mean."

For a moment, Deagan looked scared." Well…"

"He was. Wasn't he?"

"Only a couple of times," Deagan objected. "He thought there was somthin' fishy goin' on at the mine. So we took some small samples."

"What did you do with the samples?"

"Art took 'em over to the assay office and had 'em tested."

"Seems to me the assayer would have wondered where your samples came from."

"He did, but Art told him we was prospectin' down south of Dry Creek. The assayer never said nothin' after that. 'Specially when the samples was no good."

"No good?"

"No minerals of any real value. A little galena… that was all. Cost us two bucks for the assay, but Art wasn't upset or nothin'. I was with him outside the assay office when the results came back. He just slapped his hat against his leg and says 'I knew it.'"

"He knew it?"

"That's what I wondered. I asked him why we wasted two bucks if he already knew the samples was no good. He just says 'we're driftin' kid, and I know where.' When I left, he was still mutterin' about the whole deal. I couldn't figure nothin' from that, so I just shut up and forgot about that dollar I wasted."

"Drifting?"

"Yeah. I figured maybe he found us a better outfit to work for. We heard some of the mines up on the Comstock was doin' real good."

"Did Williams ever cook gold or silver out of a mercury amalgam?"

"Probably, but I never seen him do it. Most of the fellows I work with have done it one time or another. Old Jake Tompkins probably done it more than most, and I think it's just about killed him. He's got the shakes so bad he can't hardly hold a coffee cup. No one will work a face with Jake anymore, 'cause he can't remember if he's rammed a charge already or not. He ain't safe. They say he was out of his head one time an' tried to kill himself.

He shoved the drill down a charged hole and gave it a whack with a single jack before his partner could throw him down and holler for help. The whole crew was still down below. Could have been bad for 'em all 'cept Jake couldn't remember which hole was charged an' shoved the drill down the wrong one."

"So you don't think Williams would have been cooking any amalgam this morning?"

"I doubt it. Where would he get it? You gotta have black sand to make it worth usin' merc. The merc don't come for free, and Art ain't had a spare dime for weeks. We both put in a buck for that assay work 'cause Art didn't have enough cash to pay it on his own. He damn near talked my ear off before I finally let loose of that dollar. But Art figured he could get us a stake, and we'd light out for the Comstock and maybe stake our own claim out that way. He just never told me no details of what he was up to."

Mitchell looked south to where the deputy and two other riders jumped their horses out of a dry wash and headed toward town.

"Tell me what happened when you found that body down in the Emma."

"Not much to tell. We blasted the face, an' there he was."

"Give me details," Mitchell demanded. "Everything you saw—everything you did. Were you and Williams alone?"

"Not at first. When we come on shift, there was maybe a dozen muckers sortin' ore an' loadin' the carts. While they was busy with that, Art an' me was drillin' the load face. "We drilled the pyramid shots first. That's three holes set like a triangle on the load face. We drill 'em about thirty inches deep, but they're drilled on angles so they come to a point back inside the face... like a little pyramid stuck top first into a wall. We were using single jacks, so things went pretty fast. Art's a little faster than me with a four-pounder. So he was workin' on that last hole when I started drillin' one of the edger holes... see, you got to drill seven holes... three for the triangle, one on each side for edgers, one on top—that's the reliever, and then the lifter on the bottom.

"They don't go off all at once, y'see. The triangle shots go first; they break up a pretty good pocket, then the reliever and the edgers go off and make the pocket even bigger. Finally the lifter shot goes and picks up all that loose rock an' throws it out on the floor of the drift.

"So that's what we was doin'... drillin' those seven shots. That took a while. Then we had to load the shots. We ain't got a blaster to load the charges, 'cause Ramsay fired him a couple of weeks ago. So me and Art was doin' the whole business. We rammed the charges, cut and set the rat-tails, then we hollered for everyone to clear out. We gave 'em five minutes to get back to the hoist and up the shaft; then Art put the spitter to the rat-tails, and we hauled our butts a couple of hundred feet back to this little spot we got shored up real good and waited for the shots to go off. After that, we waited five or ten minutes for the dust to settle before we went back down to the load face."

Mitchell frowned. "It's a wonder the blast didn't disintegrate the body," he muttered.

Deagan shook his head. "The shots are all drilled towards a single point back in the face," he explained. "All the force of each shot pushes the rock back out into the tunnel, not back into the rock. Some of the force went back inside though... couldn't help it I guess, what with that pocket so close to our charges. Normally, there's nowhere else for it to go but the tunnel, but I guess that rock between the shots and the pocket was just thin enough for the blast to pop out a hole just big enough for a little kid to walk through. We had to open up the rest with a pick and shovel."

Deagan looked south to where the deputy and his companions drew steadily closer.

"You think that deputy is gonna cause me trouble?"

Mitchell shrugged. "Who knows? That fellow was jumping at any idea that popped into his head when I talked to him earlier."

"Must not be that Simmons fellow that came out to the mine. He seemed like a decent sort."

Mitchell moved over to the porch and sat down beside Deagan.

"So, when you and Art got back to the load face, you found the blast had opened up a pocket?"

"Yea… I didn't think nothin' of it at first. You see lots of strange things down there. One time I left my coat hangin' on a nail stuck in one of the support beams. We shot the face, and when we come back, there was my coat hangin' there pretty as you please. But that nail was drove six inches into the beam, and there was this two foot long spear of rock stuck through the collar of my coat holdin' it right where I left it.

"So that pocket in the face weren't all that strange. I seen 'em before. But Art went up close enough to see that fellow all jammed in there like a pea in a pod. He made me come take a look, an' I can tell you right now, I never seen the like of it in my life."

Mitchell pulled out the blue bandanna and wiped the sweat from the back of his neck. "Did you see anyone or pass anyone in the drift on your way back to the load face?" He asked thoughtfully.

"Nope. That deputy asked the same thing about a dozen different ways. I told him no every time. There just ain't any room for anyone to hide. Once the ore carts come down the track, there's hardly enough room to unhitch the mules and bring 'em back past the carts so we can hitch 'em up on the other side.

"When Art an' me walked back down the drift, we was side by side, checkin' the beams for damage an' lookin' for places that might need some extra timbers to shore things up. There just wasn't any place for someone to hide or slip past us."

Mitchell glanced sidewise at Deagan and cracked a smile. "I'll bet the deputy wasn't happy with that story."

"Not one bit!"

"So, how do you think that body came to be there?"

"I don't know. And I just quit thinkin' about it. But Art wouldn't let it go. Every time we went past that spot, he'd look all around the drift an' start grumblin' to himself, askin' '*How the hell did that fellow get in there like that?*'"

"Did he come up with an answer?"

"If he did, he never said nothin' to me."

"What do you know about the Barrett claims?"

Deagan looked down at the dirt between his shoes. "Not much. I heard Barrett had a couple of claims somewhere near the Emma mine. Rumor had it that they had a small strike of gold."

"Any truth to the rumor?"

"I don't know. You should talk to Taggart about that. He was workin' for Barrett. All I know is there was talk that Barrett thought he had hit a good vein and had found partners in Salt Lake to put up the money for the equipment he needed."

"You and Williams never went out there?"

"Nope. I heard Gromley and Forestall made Barrett an offer, an' he turned 'em down. But I don't think Barrett told anyone much about his operation... least wise not fellows like me an' Art."

"Where can I find Taggart?" Mitchell asked.

"He ain't been around for a while. I think he used to do some prospectin' out around Granite Peak... about thirty miles northeast of here... over toward Skull Valley. Maybe he went back there. That's where I'd look if I was you."

Mitchell took a deep breath and sighed quietly. The world smelled hot and dry, but the odor of sage drifted on the air like a spicy flavor that had become the taste of home.

"Smells good," he told the younger man sitting beside him. "It used to bother me... when we first came to the valley. Even the colors seemed bleached out and dull back then. The whole valley stank when the wind blew across the lake and stirred up a stench like something was dead out there. And we all wondered why God would drive us two thousand miles from any decent place and make us settle in a grasshopper infested hell.

"Something changed though. One day I woke up and a thunder storm was blowing in from across the lake. I could smell the sage and the lake, and then the rain came, and it was like the world changed in an instant. The heat was gone. The air was wet and clean. And there was something else... No one was trying to drive us out."

Mitchell stood and dusted off the seat of his pants.

"You should go home," he advised the miner sitting glumly on the porch.

"Too much trouble back there," Deagan muttered unhappily.

Mitchell studied the young man's face for a moment, listening to the whisper of the wind through nearby trees.

"That trouble is over and done with," he said finally, "and your pa wants you back to take over the farm."

"You don't know nothin' about it!" Deagan challenged.

Mitchell's eyes narrowed to an angry squint. "Go home," he growled harshly. "That fellow ain't dead, and there's no warrant out for you. Your family needs you. But if you go to the Comstock, you'll be dead by the end of the year."

Mitchell turned away and strode to the hitching rail where the Pratt kid stood silent and unhappy beside their horses. "You look a little nervy," He observed as he gathered up the dun's reins and mounted.

"You scared the bejeebers out of that fellow," the kid observed gravely.

Mitchell shrugged and climbed into the saddle. "Enough to stay away from the Comstock, I hope."

For a long while, Mitchell studied the road and the long stretch of hard, dry ground that lay between the bunkhouses and town. Suddenly, he felt a prickling of uneasiness—a sense of something gone wrong. Abruptly, he turned the dun toward town and kicked the animal into a lope.

Chapter 12

Utah Territory
Deep Creek Mountains—June 1869

Susan peered through the front window of Kate Pendleton's restaurant, watching intently for her sister. Sarah was late; and Sarah was never late. There was no sign of her on the street, and there were few people out and about at the moment. A few minutes earlier, there had been a man and a woman down near the stage office. They had been too far away to see their faces, but they had argued hotly for a moment then gone their separate ways.

Two dogs shot across the dusty street, nipping playfully at one another, but they were soon out of sight, disappearing down an alley and into the shade between the buildings.

Susan turned her attention back to her companions and the table they shared. They had yet to order. They had been waiting for Sarah.

Kate Pendleton had refused to let them sit chatting idly, and had brought a fresh loaf of bread with butter and honey to keep them occupied while they waited. But the loaf was half gone, and Sarah was now ten minutes late in a town that could be walked end to end in less than five.

"She probably went back to my place," Ellen Wells suggested. "It's like an oven out there. She may have decided on something lighter to wear. I know that dress she wore this morning looked much too heavy for this kind of heat."

Susan smiled, but the suggestion did not set well. Part of her wanted to accept the idea that all was well, but another, more pessimistic part—fired by some intuitive sense or instinct—refused to be pacified.

Five minutes....

The thought came suddenly with the force of a decision that could only be changed by Sarah's appearance. Five minutes more and she would go after Sarah.

Miranda Barrett craned her neck. "Isn't that Mr. Forestall?"

"I believe it is," her aunt replied. "He seems rather frail today," she added.

"He looks as though he doesn't eat enough," Miranda observed. "His wife should feed him better."

"I didn't know he was married," Susan confessed thoughtfully.

"You wouldn't guess it just seeing him around town," Ellen Wells replied. "I don't think I've ever seen them together, and you hardly ever see her at all. She keeps to herself. Mostly up at the house they have about a quarter mile west of the Emma bunkhouses."

Susan took a bite from her slice of bread, but kept her eye fixed on the small watch she had taken from her handbag and laid beside her plate. "Is she ill too?"

"Not that I've heard of," the older woman replied. "Just not the sociable type, I suspect. Some folks are that way you know."

Susan knew exactly what Ellen Wells meant. Her own personality was often unsociable, and Sarah was much the same, although their activities of choice were often quite different.

Sarah liked to make her bobbin lace and weave and read. And though Sarah loved the outdoors, her passion was for things of the home. Susan, on the other hand, had always been more of a tomboy, and though fancywork and sewing were just not that appealing to her, she loved reading, growing herbs, riding her horse, and shooting targets with the Smith & Wesson pistol Collin had given her only a week ago.

So, in many ways, she could relate to a woman who kept to herself and enjoyed her privacy. Yet somehow, it seemed odd that a woman who was married to a man so prominent in such a small community would be so reclusive.

"Have you seen her often?" she asked.

Ellen Wells paused for a moment. "Actually, I'm not sure I've ever seen Mrs. Forestall."

"I don't understand."

The older woman shrugged. "I've heard her mentioned from time to time, but I've never met her. I'm not sure I've even seen her. I thought I saw her once about three months ago, but I could have been mistaken.

"Winter was still hanging on, and it was bitterly cold for a few weeks. Several of the miners living out at the bunkhouses were ill. Miranda and I suddenly realized that those men had no one to take care of them. None of them have families out here, and ill as they were, they were not going to be helping one another, and when they got well they went back to working their shifts with the other men who were healthy.

"Anyway, Miranda and I made a big pot of soup one morning and took it out to the bunkhouses. There are five buildings out there, and we found seven men who were too ill to take care of themselves. So, Miranda and I made up a pot of soup each day and went round to each of those fellows for two weeks. By then, they were all well enough they didn't need us.

"Anyway, one day when we were crossing from one building to another, the wind was blowing from the north, and it was freezing cold. We had our backs to the wind and were in a hurry to get out of the cold. But I dropped one of my gloves. When I stopped to pick it up, I happened to glance towards the Forestall place.

"That's when I saw a buggy pull up at the front of the house. It's quite far off, but I saw a man and a woman get down from the buggy and go inside. The man was Mr. Forestall. I just assumed the woman was his wife."

Susan glanced out the window again and sighed in relief. Sarah had just crossed the street and now stood at the front of the post office, back against the wall, fanning herself.

Miranda Barrett leaned forward. "I heard she came into town just this morning," she reported in a conspiratorial whisper. "She went to Allingham's and then got back in her buggy and went straight home. Janet O'Neil told me she hardly even spoke to Mr. Allingham… just paid and left."

"Seems like a lonely kind of life," Susan responded quietly. "Mr. Forestall is probably at the mine every day. She must have little or no companionship."

Ellen Wells laughed. "That might be a blessing in disguise," she confessed. "I had a friend once who could talk your ear off. She had something to say about everything, and once she got going, it was a description in detail. And no one could get a word in edge-wise."

Susan smiled. "I've met a few like that. I suspect Mrs. Forestall is not one of those."

"I'm not sure anyone has had a chance to find out," the older woman answered.

Susan drew her eyes away from the window. Her gaze panned about the room—two women at a table a few feet away-Kate Pendleton setting plates of food in front of them—a man at a table near the back wall... her eyes stopped.

The man was a large man. Not tall and muscular like Collin—similar in height certainly, yet thinner, older and more angular, and quite recognizable though hidden behind his newspaper. Susan turned back to her friends, but watched the man as he sat limply in his chair, rattling and clattering his newspaper and periodically making the oddest assortment of sounds. His face was hidden behind the newspaper, but from beyond that thin wall came a contorted serenade of grunts, sighs, and unrecognizable bits of sing-song-like humming.

Amused, Susan brought one hand up to mask her smile. The old man peeked over the top of the paper and gave her a wink. Susan waited a moment, then excused herself from the table and crossed the room to the old man's table.

"What are you up to, Mort?"

The old man's face cracked into the faintest of smiles. "Readin'... and keepin' an eye on you."

"Do I need an eye kept on me?"

"Not really. I should be over to the post office, but then I'd be tempted to interfere."

"Interfere with what?"

"Pretty much anything," he confessed cryptically. "I tend to be a little nosey," he admitted.

Susan raised an eyebrow. "I thought you were out wandering the hills with Collin."

The old man looked thoughtfully at the ceiling where a large fan turned slowly, stirring the air.

"I might be... I forget..."

Susan laughed. "You're sitting here with me, and you know it... You silly old coot."

"Mort, where is your family? Don't you have any kin you could settle down with?"

The old man frowned. "You tryin' to get rid of me?" he asked bleakly.

"Certainly not!" Susan protested fervently. "You're part of our family no matter what!"

"That's pretty nice of you," the old man confessed "Ain't sure that gunman you're married to feels the same."

"Collin has already agreed that you can stay with us as long as you like," Susan answered.

"He did, did he? Well, I do have some family," the old man admitted.

"Where are they?" Susan asked excitedly. "Are they back east?"

"Naw, they're somewhere hereabouts."

"And you haven't gone to see them!"

"I check on 'em from time to time."

"Someday you should go visit... just so they know you're alive and well."

The old man shrugged. "I suspect they know I'm doin' okay," he reasoned.

"You should still visit them," Susan repeated stubbornly. "Siblings or other family?" She asked suddenly.

"Both," the old man admitted.

"An older brother... two young cousins."

"Even more reason to visit them," Susan pointed out. "Maybe I should write them a letter, and let them know how you're doing? What are their names?"

"Well... there's Mouriel. He's my brother. Then there's Araliel and Analiel."

"I should write them."

"I'd rather you didn't."

"But, Mort...."

"No buts... they're doin' okay, and so am I."

"Stubborn old goat."

"Nosey little pest."

Susan squawked indignantly then grinned happily. "I should get back to our lunch," she confessed. "They'll think me rude for just walking away like that."

"I reckon so... I was just reading' this here newspaper... Absolutely ridiculous the stuff they put in here... can't believe even half of it. 'Cept this thing about some new way to generate electricity... calls it a dynamo.... This feller *von* Siemens built one in 'sixty-six'. Another other feller named Wilde built this thing he calls an alliance generator the same year... runs a light house with it. Pretty fantastic stuff if you ask me. "

"I'll talk with you later, Mort."

"Might be a day or two before I get back."

Susan raised an eyebrow. "You're going somewhere?"

The old man laid his paper back on the table. "Willow Springs, I think... then out to some mountains northeast of here. Won't be gone long—just a day or two."

Susan looked back toward her table. Sarah had not come in.

"What is she up to?" She grumbled crossly.

"She, who?"

"Sarah. She was supposed to be here for lunch fifteen minutes ago. I saw her across the street a few minutes ago, but she still hasn't come in."

For a long while, the old man was silent, watching the door. "Maybe you ought to check on her."

For a moment, Susan stared at the door. "This is silly," she concluded impatiently. "She should have been here by now. I'm going after her."

Suddenly anxious, she turned back to the old man. "Come with me, Mort. I have a feeling something is wrong."

The old man sighed, and shoved his chair away from the table. "Reckon so," he responded grimly.

Without another word, Susan crossed the room and drove herself out into the heat. Anxiously, she scanned the walkways on both sides of the street. Sarah was gone.

"She was over in front of the post office just a minute ago," she complained.

"Couldn't have gone far," the old man said reassuringly. "Maybe we should start by lookin' over to the post office. You could even ask that mean lookin' fellow comin' up the street to give us a hand."

Susan did not hesitate, but stepped down from the boardwalk and crossed the street, angling directly toward the point where she had last seen Sarah.

Mitchell crossed on a tangent that would intercept her at the post office. "Thought you was having lunch at the restaurant?"

Susan looked up at the sun-burnt face of the man she loved. "I was, but Sarah was late, and I began to worry. I saw her standing right here just a few minutes ago, but now she's wandered off. You know she's never late."

Mitchell leaned back against the clapboard wall of the post office and let his eyes rove up and down both sides of the street. Sunlight scorched the boardwalks; a fitful breath of hot air lifted puffs of dust from the street, and the flag in front of the post office fluttered limply from its mast, but Sarah was nowhere to be seen.

"She could have gone into one of the shops," he suggested. Susan frowned and shook her head. "Why?" she asked. "She knew we would be waiting for her. Something has happened," she insisted. "I can feel it."

Susan studied the buildings on both sides of the street. "Five minutes," she declared suddenly. "That's all the time Mort and I spent talking. Where could she go in five minutes?"

Mitchell frowned. His own feelings were growing darker by the minute.

"Ten minutes now," he pointed out, "and addin' up every second. All we can do is start looking. We'll split up. You and Mort check every building on this side of the street. I'll check the alleys and the areas behind everything. When you find her, give a holler. If we need to, we'll go to the other side of the street and do the same."

Susan left quickly and was soon opening doors, poking her head inside and scanning the interior of each shop along the street. Mitchell, on the other hand, slowed to nearly a complete stop as soon as he stepped into the alley between the stone walls of the bank and the clapboard walls of the post office.

Here, the ground was soft—ground shaded from the scorching heat of the sun, a place where rain had softened the soil and given weeds a chance to take root near the walls of the two structures. Here, on the slightly harder ground of a path pointed directly towards the Wells' boarding house, the prints of a woman's shoes darted down a narrow track towards the back of the buildings.

The woman hurried, and Mitchell was instantly certain that the tracks were Sarah's. Suddenly worried, he raced down the alley—and found nothing. The back lots were empty.

Frustrated, Mitchell searched the ground. He found the tracks again and followed. Suddenly, there were other tracks—boot tracks and a scuffle. Sarah's handbag hung cradled in the center of a solitary, gray sagebrush, its contents strewn upon the ground.

Behind him a twig snapped on the ground.

Like a rattler, Mitchell turned. The butt of the Smith & Wesson was in his hand in an instant, and the muzzle centered on the old man's chest in the blink of an eye.

"Pretty quick," the old man conceded.

Mitchell scowled and holstered the pistol.

"You're gonna get yourself shot sneakin' around like that."

"I might, if you was the kind that *liked* pullin' the trigger. Reckon I'm safe enough."

"Thought you was helpin' Susan."

"I was. She found Sarah comin' out of the butcher shop."

With a sigh of relief, Mitchell dropped down on one knee and began gathering the scattered contents of the handbag. By the time he had finished, Susan and Sarah had arrived.

Mitchell brushed the dust from the bag and stood quietly considering the object. "Pistol's gone," he reported. "I'm not sure about anything else... How do you pack this thing? It must weight twenty pounds."

"I, at least, carry my own things," Sarah retorted primly. "I don't throw a month's supplies into two huge bags and make my horse carry them around."

Mitchell grinned and returned the bag. "What happened?" He asked, changing the subject.

Sarah sighed and shook her head. "I was standing in front of the post office, trying to escape the heat. I was trying to decide if I had enough time to go back to the boarding house and change into something lighter. The heat was just too much.

"I was standing near an open window. Someone inside started whispering to me, telling me to be careful, that someone was after us. About then a man came out of Allingham's store and started walking directly towards me. The person inside the post office suddenly got excited and started shouting 'that's one of them! Run!'

"So I hurried down the alley, thinking I would cut across the back lots and up another alley and across to Pendleton's. But someone was waiting and grabbed me as I came out of the alley. I fought and finally got away. But I lost my handbag. When I looked back, both men were going through my things. After a minute, they got on their horses and rode south, out of town."

Mitchell frowned unhappily.

"Did you recognize either of them?"

"The one who grabbed me had his face covered. I never got close enough to the other one to really see his face."

Mitchell looked at both women and sighed

"I guess I'll be riding south," he observed grimly.

* * *

Kathryn Pendleton was oddly quiet when she came from the Kitchen and placed Sarah's lunch on the table near the window. Sarah took notice of the silence, remembering the woman's friendliness just moments before.

"You seem quiet," Sarah observed cautiously.

The tall woman paused. Slowly, she drew one of the chairs away from the table.

"Do you mind?" she asked quietly.

Sarah shook her head and motioned for the woman to sit. "Please do. I've been hoping to talk with you."

Sarah watched as the tall red-head seated herself then scooted her chair forward until she could rest her folded arms on the table. She glanced quickly around the room, then leaned forward and spoke in a conspiratorial whisper.

"They say your husband is a notorious gunman… Is it true?"

Sarah paused, her eyes half-lifted from the table. For a moment, she struggled for an answer to the woman's question. "Not really," she said finally. "He's very good with a gun, but he's certainly not what the dime novels depict as a gunman. In fact, he's quite a gentle man. What makes you ask such a thing, Mrs. Pendleton?"

"Miss.… Call me Kate; I'm not married."

Carefully, Sarah set the cup back in its original position on the table. She did it slowly and deliberately, waiting for the explanation she felt was due after such a question.

Kate Pendleton shifted uneasily under Sarah's cold glare.

"I'm sorry. I'm prying into your personal life and that's rude. It's just that after hearing all the rumors that are flying about… I just wondered if your husband came here looking for anyone in particular."

Sarah sat quietly for a moment, considering her answer.

"As far as I know, he came here looking for his partner, James Barrett," she said finally. "Is there someone else he should be looking for?"

The woman shook her head, and Sarah settled back in her chair with the uneasy feeling that she would now have to *pry* into Kate Pendleton's life for any information, no matter how important.

Kate Pendleton glanced around the room as if looking for someone. There were few people in the dining room, and when she had looked quickly at each of them, she turned back to Sarah.

"I just wondered, because there are a number of strangers in town," she offered, forestalling the need for Sarah to begin her own *prying* questions.

"Mostly men," the red-head continued. "They seem to have money, but no purpose... wandering and poking about, but doing nothing for days on end. Some of them may work for Desert Range Mining, but if they do, they aren't doing much for their pay... And some of them are very rough characters."

"And why would this have anything to do with my husband?"

Kate Pendleton hesitated a moment before answering. Her green eyes darted around the room again.

"One of them has been coming around quite often," she said finally.

"Coming here for dinner," Sarah suggested.

"Coming around to visit," Kate replied dismally.

"And these visits are not welcome," Sarah concluded.

"Not welcome at all. The man scares me."

"He's threatened you?"

"No... not at all. But there is something about him... It's unsettling... When he first came around, I was flattered that he would pay any attention to me. We don't get many new fellows in town. Those who do come here are mostly fellows looking for work at the mines, and they either find work or move on. The few who stay soon find that they have little time for a social life."

Sarah glanced quickly around the dining room, there were few people in the room; none of them men. "How do you stay in business if the miners don't eat here?"

Kate Pendleton smiled. "Oh, they eat here… at least enough of them to keep the place open. They come in at odd times though, depending on which shift they work. Sometimes, the place is packed."

"And this fellow you're afraid of?"

"He comes around quite often… I feel a little foolish, now that I've brought it up. Grady has never done anything… It's just these silly feelings…"

Sarah waited, but the woman was silent and finally slid her chair away from the table and stood.

"Be careful," she said quietly. "There are people here who don't like Mormons, and they need very little excuse to cause trouble."

Kate Pendleton turned away and hurried back into her kitchen, leaving Sarah to ponder everything she had just been told. And in the end, it added up to very little… nothing more than a few strangers in town and a scared young woman.

Sarah left the restaurant and wandered south along the boardwalk until she came to Allingham's store. A small woman in a faded dress stood on the boardwalk with a broom in her hand. She looked up as Sarah came near and stepped to one side of the doorway, making way for Sarah to enter the store.

"Morning," she said quietly.

"Good morning," Sarah replied.

"You're one of the Mormons come to see Ellen Wells," the woman's statement was flat, bold, and matter-of-fact.

"Yes I am," Sarah replied in the same matter-of-fact tone. "We've come to find out who killed James Barrett and get his claims up and producing, if we can."

"I'll not fault you for that," the woman replied. "James Barrett was a good man. And his family could use some help getting things straightened out. They could use the money, and they got no other way to earn anything until those claims are producing. That boardinghouse barely keeps them in food."

Sarah stepped through the open doorway and into the cooler interior of the shop.

"We've been wondering who might profit by Mr. Barrett's death, or if he was a man with enemies."

Janet Allingham stepped inside the shop and placed her broom behind the front door. "I only heard of one person who had trouble with James.... Jack Ramsay had an argument with him last fall. I have no idea what it was about, but it could have been something to do with Miranda. She turned twenty last summer, and she was a little too friendly with some of the boys... nothing bad, you understand... she's a good girl, but she seemed taken with Jack Ramsay, and James was very upset.... He thought Mr. Ramsay was too old for her, and the two of them argued about the girl. Nothing serious enough for a killing though. No, nothing like that."

Sarah was silent for a moment, considering what Collin had told her of his meeting with Ramsay. According to Collin, Ramsay was a mean spirited kind of man, the kind no one wanted to associate with—an arrogant, hard-nosed type who pushed people aside and made little effort at being sociable. He had been employed at the Emma long enough to know the situation there, and Collin had the feeling that Ramsay was not the kind to sit idly while his livelihood disintegrated. In fact, it was rumored that Ramsay had a claim of his own in the mountains south of Goshute Canyon. But no one knew where the claim might be, nor had anyone heard of Ramsay bringing in any ore, if such a claim existed.

"My husband says he seems like an ornery cuss," Sarah suggested.

Janet Allingham glanced towards the front of the store and shook her head. "No more than a lot of folks in this place," she answered. "There are rumors that the Emma mine isn't doing very well, and that has a lot of people worried and on edge. The Emma pretty much keeps this place alive. Something goes bad at the Emma, we all suffer."

"Do you think the rumors could be true?" Sarah asked.

"I don't know. Mr. Forestall says things are fine, and that's what I'd like to believe. But we have a family, and everything we have depends on this store doing well. If the Emma shuts down, we can't survive here.

Chapter 13

Utah Territory
Granite Peak—June 1869

The earth was the color of sand. Sometimes it was a tan, granular mix that shifted beneath Milo's hooves; sometimes it was the washed out gray, plate-like layers that had been compressed beneath a thousand feet of water for a million years. When the water had disappeared, the sands had baked under a blazing desert sun until the ground lay seamed and cracked like a gigantic jigsaw puzzle. Here and there, clumps of salt grass and stunted sagebrush dotted the flat expanse of the lake bed. Otherwise, nothing grew in the salt-killed sands.

For a moment, Mitchell pondered the possibility that God's creation of the Earth had spanned many millions of years rather than the shorter times demanded by so many biblical scholars. Personally, he found no difficulty in accepting the idea, though in the daily crush of life, it made little difference what pace God set for himself in creating the universe and the tiny globe Collin Mitchell stood upon. It made little difference, yet the mental exercise broke the monotony of the sands and the constant blast of the sun overhead.

Quietly, Mitchell reached down, stroking Milo's shoulder reassuringly. The big quarter horse was hot, but his shoulder was hard as iron, and he was breathing easy, as though the last fifteen miles had been but an afternoon walk.

Mitchell had been surprised when Mort had walked the pigeon-toed Milo to the front of the boarding house, saddled and ready to go.

"The dun's gone lame," he explained. "Milo here is a good old boy. You take him. He'll do you right."

Now, twenty miles east of Silver Creek, Mitchell was impressed. He'd owned the animal for nearly two years, but had never ridden him. Mitchell knew little of the animal's breeding, but it was obviously good.

The American Quarter Horse had been bred for a number of traits, and Milo seemed to have them all. At twelve-hundred pounds and fifteen hands at the shoulder, Milo was fast, smart, and he had stamina.

In the last twenty miles, Mitchell had put the animal through hell. Milo had knocked out a quarter mile run in twenty-one seconds. That was as fast as any racer Mitchell had heard of, and Milo had done it packing nearly three-hundred pounds of rider and gear. Even now, after spending most of the day in an unrelenting furnace, the animal was lathered in sweat, but breathing easy and fighting the bit as he caught the scent of water and fresh grass.

For hours, Mitchell had been following the old Pony Express trail, crossing the northern edge of Snake Valley and skirting the northern tip of the Fish Springs Range. Now, less than a mile away, the trail turned south, running between the marshy flats of Fish Springs and the foothills of the mountains to the west.

Milo tossed his head. The big roan smelled water and wanted to run. Mitchell felt the tenseness in the animal and leaned forward, giving him a touch of the spurs. Milo took off at a jump, running flat out past the turn in the trail and into the salt covered flats, following the trail of Sarah's assailant.

There were other tracks now—a wagon and a team, and two more horses joining the one Mitchell followed. He felt certain the wagon belonged to Taggart, but the others....

Suddenly, he felt the hair rise on the back of his neck. They were up to no good... he knew it without a doubt, as though a still small voice had whispered it, telling him to be wary.

Milo slowed, his excess energy burned off for the moment, and Mitchell eased the animal to a walk. To the north, the salt flats stretched into the distance, blending into waves of heat. To the south, Fish Springs dotted the land with small ponds that fed the long grass surrounding the waters.

It was mid-afternoon when they came up on a small pond on the northern edge of the springs. Mitchell swung down from the saddle and led the roan to the water's edge. For a moment, he let the animal drink.

"Not too much now," he advised, tugging at the reins.

Reluctantly, the roan turned away from the cold waters of the spring, letting Mitchell lead the way to a thick patch of grass. Quickly, Mitchell stripped the gear from the horse, and rubbed the animal down with a dry rag. When the animal was grazing, Mitchell turned to his own needs.

There was shade here... though only a little and of the spotty, almost useless variety, but shade nonetheless. It was low to the ground and jammed tight against the base of a small clump of Russian Olives that had taken hold in the moist soil near the water. There was barely enough shade for Mitchell, and certainly no room for the quarter horse, but Milo seemed content with the grass and the cooler air drifting across the springs.

Thoughtfully, Mitchell studied the terrain ahead. They were on the northernmost edge of Snake Valley—a somewhat lush valley twenty-five miles wide and stretching nearly one-hundred miles to the south.

Fifteen miles to the north-east, lay Granite Peak, and beyond that lay Skull Valley—all of it arid, hot, uninviting land. Yet some folks were drawn to that stark beauty as though the sheer emptiness of it brought them quietude and peace.

Mitchell however, was not so fond of the blazing heat of the western desert. Yet there were few places in the Territory that offered anything much better, and a place that was cooler in the summer was generally colder in the winter.

Deliberately, Mitchell forced his thoughts away from the desert and back into the moment. He made a quick survey of his camp site, rousted a sleeping rattler from the shady hollow of a large rock, and sent it off to parts unknown. When the rattler was well on its way, Mitchell eased himself to the ground and leaned back against his saddle. He was asleep within minutes.

Light flashed across the valley like lightning shot from the ground, pounding the hillside with a staccato thunder of explosions that turned the night bright as daylight. Stark in the glare of a man-made hell, the old man dumped the empty cases from his pistol and reloaded….

"You got any pastries in that stuff Sarah packed for you?"

Mitchell came awake with a start. Mort stood nearby, rummaging through Mitchell's saddle bags.

"Sneaky old fart!" Mitchell hissed.

"Sneaky! You was sleeping like the dead. You got the sleepin' sickness or something?"

"Just restin' my eyes."

"An' dreamin' I'll bet."

"Nightmare," Mitchell confessed unhappily. "Like a war with hundreds of Gatling guns and razor wire everywhere...dead men tangled in the wire...."

The old man frowned. "Trenches?"

"No trenches," Mitchell responded. "Desert...like this...a wide valley...rockets like fireworks all over the sky."

The old man shook his head. "Bad place that one...glad I got no part in it."

"You know it?"

"I know where it'll be...."

"I've been having a lot of nightmares lately," Mitchell muttered. "Thought you were staying back in town?" he challenged.

The old man shrugged. "Reckon I was...'til I found me a horse. Then them gals of yours sent me along with enough food and the like to last a month. I had to bring that mule along to carry it all."

Frustrated, the old man dropped the flap on the saddle bag. "There ain't no food in here."

"Other side," Mitchell instructed. "They threw in some biscuit-like things filled with apricot jam."

The old man turned the bag and fished around with one hand until he found the pastry. A moment later, half of it was gone in one bite. "That's mighty good," he sighed. "Mighty good."

Daylight was quickly disappearing when they found the tracks of two horses and a wagon turning eastward into the mouth of a steep, rocky canyon.

Mitchell removed his hat and wiped a sleeve across his forehead.

"Looks like we lost that other fellow," he confessed. "This outfit is probably Taggart's team and wagon."

"Reckon so," Mort agreed, "but that other fellow isn't out here for the scenery."

Mitchell glanced at the western sky.

"We've got another hour of daylight at most. Think we should go on up and see if we can find Taggart before dark?"

The old man shrugged. "See them crows?" he asked, pointing to a dozen birds circling over head. "Like them, I'm just taggin' along so you'll feed me."

Mitchell glanced upward at the crows and shrugged. "They came a long way for nothing," he replied.

"You better water that sneaky dog of yours too," the old man advised. "It's a wonder she ain't dried up an' blowed away like dust."

Mitchell stepped back from the wagon track and turned full around, searching for the dog. The animal was invisible.

"She's danged good at that hidin' game," he conceded as he took the canteen from his saddle and poured water into his hat. Carefully, he set the hat on the ground and whistled. He waited, but the dog did not appear.

Mitchell whistled again. "Come outa there, you mongrel!"

He watched the rocks, but the dog remained hidden. "You'd think she'd come to water," he complained.

The old man chuckled. "She did," he advised. "Sneaked right up out of them flats. Look behind you."

Mitchell tuned and found the motley colored dog sitting less than a foot away, panting and grinning.

"Go get your water," he growled.

Mitchell waited while the dog lapped the water from the hat.

"Them crows are actin' mighty strange," the old man reported, pointing to where the birds now flew in a series of crazy dives and steep climbs over the rocky foothills three-hundred yards to the south.

For a moment, Mitchell watched the birds, but an uneasy feeling soon crept over him. Abruptly, he climbed into the saddle.

"Those crows are makin' me nervous," he told the old man. "We're like a couple of prairie dogs out here in the open."

Mitchell kicked the roan into a fast lope, and with the old man hard on his heels, they followed the tracks of the wagon for nearly a mile.

The wide mouth of the canyon narrowed quickly, until the bottom ranged two-hundred feet on either side of the rocky path the wagon followed. Mitchell slowed the roan to a walk, picking their way along the narrow track left by the wheels of the wagon. A mile-and-a-half in, the trail forked in three directions.

Mitchell gave Milo a loose rein, trusting the animal to find the best footing through the narrowing canyon. Instinctively, Milo followed the path of the wagon up the middle fork until they reached a point where the trail became impassable. Yet there was no wagon.

The old man turned his horse in a small circle, searching the surrounding hillside.

"That's pretty tricky," he acknowledged thoughtfully. "Disappearin' a wagon and a team like that."

Mitchell shook his head and studied the slopes on both sides. The canyon had curved to the right and now ascended steeply to the south, with steep, rugged slopes rising on either side. Strewn with broken rock and shattered cliffs, the terrain was extreme and offered no route for a wagon. Only one direction seemed reasonable—back down the canyon.

Mitchell scowled and swung down from the saddle.

"He must have taken the wagon back down," he suggested.

"Reckon so," the old man agreed. "Think he's still up here?"

"Nothing but rock up here," Mitchell pointed out. "Maybe he unloaded here and took the wagon and the team down to a better location. That left hand fork seemed a little greener a hundred yards from the turnoff. Maybe he camps there and works a claim up this way?"

The crows danced overhead then dived into the gulley beyond the northern ridge.

They found the camp by following the crows. The wagon was burned to the ground and still smoldering with a wispy, gray smoke that dissipated almost as soon as it lifted into the air. Taggart's horses lay dead and rotting in the heat, and the crows stood atop one of the carcasses and watched as Mitchell made a quick search of the camp, hunting for Taggart.

"Someone shot them horses," the old man pointed out. "Don't reckon that Taggart fellow would kill his own stock."

Mitchell swung down from the saddle and looped the reins through the rim of a fire-blackened wheel. Heat still radiated from the ruins of the wagon, and thin smoky tendrils snaked upward from a dozen half-dead coals. The smell of smoke was in the air, but that smell was overwhelmed by the stench of rotting horse.

"Looks fairly recent," he concluded. "Maybe last night… maybe early this morning. Looks like a couple of coyotes have been at the horses."

The old man let his eyes rove the abandoned camp. "They shot up his water barrel," he complained, pointing to a barrel shot full of holes. "They wanted him dead.... If you can't kill a man outright, shoot his animals and leave him afoot with no water...."

"They must not know this country very well," Mitchell replied. "It's only fifteen miles to Fish Springs. A fellow could walk that far if he had to. There might even be a spring or two somewhere back in these canyons. So I don't think they could count on him dying of thirst.

"I'll bet they're out there right now prowlin' around, huntin' him. They were probably hoping for a quick kill. Otherwise, they would have kept that barrel of water for themselves. Come to think of it, Taggart could have shot up that barrel to keep them from getting it."

The old man frowned. "Quick kill, eh? That Taggart fellow is probably pretty dry by now, if he got away with no water. An' we ain't gonna be no help to him tonight. It's almost dark now."

Quietly, Mitchell walked the camp, searching for anything that might better explain what had happened to Taggart. It was obvious that Taggart had been attacked, but it seemed unlikely that the miner had been taken captive.

The ground was hard and dry, but there were tell-tale signs... horse tracks, the imprint of a boot heel, scuff marks where a man had stumbled, scraping a boot sole across rocky ground... blood....

"Blood here," he reported.

"Not surprisin'," the old man responded. Probably find him holed up in them rocks on that other ridge."

"Any findin' will have to be done when there's better light," Mitchell replied. "We can set up camp here, and I'll see if I can track him down in the morning."

The old man frowned and shook his head. "You go up in them rocks alone, and you'd best be watchin' your back. If that Taggart feller ain't dead, he's hurt bad. He'll likely shoot you full of holes an' not think twice about it. An' he ain't the only one. Them others are still somewhere about. We never seen hide nor hair of 'em when we come in here. Likely, they're still up in them rocks huntin' that feller."

Mitchell led the pigeon-toed Milo to a place in the lee of a huge boulder and began stripping the animal's gear. He was not happy with the prospect of hunting a wounded man through the rugged terrain above, but their options were limited. They could turn their backs and ride away from a man who might be bleeding his life away, or they could search him out and lend what aid they could.

Mitchell lugged his saddle and other gear to a clear spot of ground. Tomorrow, he would climb into the rocks and pray he didn't get shot for his trouble.

* * *

Daylight came slowly, first lighting up the tops of the Deep Creek Mountains thirty miles to the west, then pushing the shadows down the mountains and into the salt flats. For the moment, the air was cool, and morning dew still beaded the wispy blades of cheek grass that lay on the mountain like sparsely seeded hair on a bald man's head.

Mitchell was in the rocks searching for blood nearly two hours before the sun finally peeked over the top of Granite Peak and breathed down on the world like the fires of hell gone mad. Sweating and feeling like a pig at a barbeque, Mitchell took off his hat, wiped the sweat from his forehead, and looked down on the burned out camp.

"I don't like leaving the horses with no one to keep an eye on them," he confessed unhappily.

"Them horses will be just fine," the old man replied. "Besides, somebody's got to watch your back."

Mitchell scowled as the breeze picked up, whirling through the rocks, filling his mind with the faint whisper of a voice and dragging his heart down into misery.

"Tommy...." he whispered.

For a moment, the old man's face scrunched up in surprise. "Oh my...," he muttered unhappily. "That's gonna be a rough one."

For a long time, Mitchell stared at the trail and the rocky ground ahead. "I think some of your crazy is rubbing off on me," he complained.

"Hearin' things, are ya? Well... it ain't so bad most times...."

Mitchell looked ahead to the trail leading through the up-thrust rocks. It was a desolate place of broken stone, stunted grass, and oppressive heat. And when the breeze died down and transformed into waves of heat dancing on the white glare of the salt flats, Mitchell felt the sun boring down like a branding iron.

"I think we're close," he said finally. "There's more blood... and someone is following him."

"Don't surprise me none," the old man grumbled.

Mitchell pointed the barrel of the Winchester toward the rocks above. "Tracks are still hard to find, but the trail seems to be meandering towards those rocks near the ridge line."

Cautiously, he moved up the trail, watching for signs of Taggart or the man who followed him.

"Boot print in the blood," he reported.

"You gonna give me and inch by inch description of what I'm seein' with my own eyes?"

"I just figured you were getting feeble and having trouble with your eyesight..."

'I ain't feeble an' I see just fine."

"That why you're wearin' that apricot jam in your whiskers? Want me to wipe that off for you?"

"You just worry about finding that Taggart fellow, and let me worry about jam in my beard!"

"You can borrow my bandanna..."

"I seen you blowin' your nose in that thing!"

"Still got a clean spot."

The old man rubbed at his beard with one hand, smearing the sticky preserves deep into his whiskers.

"Dang it!"

Mitchell grinned and turned back to the trail, moving slowly toward the ridge above. At a bend in the path, he paused to lever a round into the chamber of the Winchester and listen quietly.

On a mountain silent but for the whisper of the breeze, there came a sound like the hammer of steel on steel. Mitchell rounded the bend ready to fire, but the trail was empty—a dead-end jumbled with broken sticks of lumber.

"Strange place for a pile of lumber," the old man observed.

The sound of hammering had stopped, but it came again suddenly from beyond the stack of broken wood. Mitchell eased past the lumber.

"Thought so," he announced, looking down into the open mouth of a mine shaft. "You down there, Taggart?"

For a moment, there was silence.

"Taggart!"

Finally, a tired voice called out of the pit. "Shoot and be damned! You won't get much out of this hole!"

Mitchell moved to the edge of the shaft and hunkered down. "We ain't here to jump your claim. We came to talk about Jim Barrett. My name's Mitchell."

Taggart was silent. "You that gunman he partnered up with?"

"That would be me... That your blood trail we followed up here?"

"Well, I'm shot all right. Some no good coyotes come up on my camp yesterday and shot up everything. Killed my horses and put a bullet in my leg before I could get away. Toss down a rope or something and get me out of here."

Mitchell leaned over the mouth of the shaft and peered down into the dimness. The shaft appeared to be twenty feet deep with sides smooth and free of obstructions. There was no ladder, and what had once been a head-frame with ropes and pulleys was now a tangled pile of broken lumber. Yet, in the dimness twelve feet below, Taggart sat uncomfortably perched on the steel shaft of a four foot long drill bit driven straight into the wall of the shaft.

"How did you end up down there?" Mitchell asked when Taggart was finally out of the shaft.

"They shot up my water," Taggart explained. "I knew I wouldn't last long without it, so I headed up here. I had a couple of jugs stashed down in the mine, so I went down to get it, thinkin' I could get back out and hide in the rocks. I was bettin' they had less water than I did. 'Course they caught up before I could get out.

"They fired a couple of shots down the shaft, but they didn't have the nerve to come down after me. So, they pulled up the ladder, busted up my head-frame and took off. They was laughin' the whole time. Thought there was no way out, and I'd starve down there. 'Course they didn't know nothin'.

"Once they was gone, I got the single-jack and them drill bits and started drillin' holes and workin' my way up the wall of that shaft. Took a while, but I'd drill one in a foot or so, then sit on the bit and drill the next... kind of like a ladder, only I had to keep reaching down to pull out the lowest bit. I only got the three of 'em, so I couldn't leave any behind. But I was getting' mighty close to getting' myself out of there when you came along.

"I tied them water jugs to the end of that rope. You oughta haul 'em out of there; we'll be needin' 'em."

By late afternoon, Taggart's camp was too hot for comfort, and Mitchell was beginning to feel jittery.

"We should head out of here," he said finally. "We're using water pretty fast."

"We could make it to Fish Springs in just a few hours," Taggart replied. "We could wait until sundown and travel when it's cooler."

"We could," Mitchell admitted, "but we aren't escaping the heat by waiting. We might as well be moving as sitting here using up water. We water those horses a couple of times, and we'll be crossing fifteen miles of salt flats dry. We might take only five or six hours getting to Fish Springs, but I'd rather have some water just in case.

"We've got plenty of food," he explained. "Mort brought the pack mule, and she's loaded up pretty good. But we're going to be shy on water, and I think we ought to go careful."

Taggart thought quietly for a moment. "I can go along with that," he conceded finally. "I just want to get out of here in one piece. They done a pretty mean job on my leg, and I'm feelin' a little rough."

Quietly, Mitchell went to the horses and began saddling the pack mule. He was feeling uneasy again. There had been no sign of the men who had shot Taggart. They had simply disappeared, and that was worrisome. They might have ridden away after stranding Taggart in the mine shaft, but Mitchell was doubtful. There were few places they could have gone without leaving some trace of their passing.

Mitchell slipped the lead rope through the halter, and felt the angry buzz of something ripping past his ear. The pack mule stiffened and collapsed, and the roar of a large bore rifle thundered up the canyon and into the rocks of Granite Peak.

Chapter 14

Utah Territory
Deep Creek Mountains—June 1869

Susan felt the ground buckle as the edge of her shoe cut through the hard, tabular fragments on the surface and bit into the softer soil beneath. Her foot slid downhill several inches before the rocky fragments compacted enough to support her weight. For a moment, the ground held. Then suddenly, as though anxious to be rid of her, the ground collapsed, sending her sliding down the hillside in an unladylike tangle of skirts and petticoats, until she came to rest at the bottom of the gully between Frank Gromley's small house and the much larger Forestall home.

Susan groaned and sat up. She knew she should have been more careful on the trail above. It had been much too narrow, and that alone should have been warning enough to go another way. But the tracks of the two children had drawn her step-by-step until there was no retreat. She had been lucky the trail hadn't led to a more dangerous place and a more serious fall. She felt battered from the uncontrolled descent over rocky ground, but nothing seemed broken, and after a moment she gathered up her handbag and got painfully to her feet.

Quietly, she surveyed her surroundings. The gully started as a deep cut, but it grew shallow quickly, running down to the southeast. There, she could see the road to the Emma mine cross a shallow wash and wander up the canyon until it disappeared around the curve of the mountain.

"Are you hurt?" called a voice.

Susan looked to the lip of the gully where Henry Forestall stood peering down at her, the edge of one hand to his forehead.

"Slightly battered, but not hurt," she called back. "It was my own fault. I should have been more careful."

"That slope is treacherous," Forestall advised. "It looks solid enough, but the soil is soft below that top layer. It's a wonder you didn't have half the hillside follow you down. You could have been buried in that stuff."

Susan looked up the gully to the fresh scarring on the hillside and the small alluvial fan of talus that had broken away and followed her into the gully.

"I don't think I'll walk across there again," she conceded. "I was searching for two lost children, and thought I found their footprints."

"Footprints!" Forestall exclaimed. "There must be two dozen children in town... They wander everywhere. I shouldn't wonder you found footprints. There are probably hundreds of them around here."

"A boy and a girl," Susan explained. "The footprints I followed seemed to be the right ones, although I could be wrong."

"That's Frank's place," Forestall protested. "Why would they be hanging around there?"

"Probably just wandering, like you said," Susan responded. "I'm more concerned with where they are now," she added.

"Could be anywhere," Forestall concluded. "These people don't seem overly concerned with keeping track of their offspring."

Susan ignored the statement and brushed at the dirt on her skirts.

"May I ask you a question?" Forestall said suddenly.

"I suppose..."

"Why are you here? I've heard rumors that your husband is a rather notorious gunman, but I fail to see what would bring you folks to a place like this, unless you are some relation of Ellen Wells...."

Susan watched as Forestall dug the tip of his cane into the ground and leaned more heavily on it for support.

"We're no relations of Mrs. Wells," she replied casually. "We're here simply to find James Barrett, if he's still alive."

Forestall shifted his weight as though the simple act of standing caused him pain. "I suspect Barrett is dead," he advised.

"Suspect?"

"I think the body was a failed attempt at some kind of sick humor, and someone took it into the Emma to cause trouble."

For a moment, Susan studied the man standing above her on the edge of the ravine, wondering if he truly believed it was all a badly played joke.

"I followed those tracks from behind Allingham's store clear up the side of the mountain," she said, changing the subject. "They wandered around a bit, but the ground was still damp from the last storm and their tracks were easy enough to follow. They led right up the ridge to a windmill of all things. . . not more than a quarter of a mile up the hill. It was all boarded up with a steel bar across the door and a very large lock on it."

Cautiously, Susan began picking her way down the draw stepping over rocks and weaving through a tangled maze of brush that blocked her path to the road. Forestall was waiting when she finally stepped out onto the road.

"What were those kids doing up at the mill?" he demanded.

"I have no idea," she replied. "Their tracks led to the door of the mill then turned down this way. They seemed to be running away from something."

Forestall shook his head. "I can't imagine why," he confessed. "We seldom use the mill anymore, and no one goes up there. We keep the door barred to keep the kids out, so they don't get hurt on the equipment."

"What kind of equipment?" Susan asked casually.

Forestall shifted his weight and leaned on his cane. Susan watched the tip of the cane sink into the softer ground at the edge of the road.

"We built the mill when I bought the claim," he explained. "We needed timbers for the Emma, and cutting our own seemed to be the best option. So we built the mill. There's hardly any water around here, so we had to come up with some way to power the mill. Wind seemed to be the best way. It's up on the ridge because there's a lot of wind right there."

"But you're not using it now?"

"Seldom any more. We found it was less expensive to buy precut timbers from a mill in Salt Lake. A few of the mine owners went in together on large orders to cut costs. It was more costly to pay a crew of twenty men to go out hunting lumber. By the time they found suitable trees, cut them, hauled them back, and ran them through the mill, the cost was nearly double what we pay on a consolidated contract with the other mines. So we locked up the mill and pay to have the lumber brought in. Since then it's been unused. I don't know why those kids would go up there. There's nothing of interest up there."

"Nothing of interest for an adult," Susan suggested. "But you know how children are… the things they're told to stay away from become the very things they're most interested in."

Forestall grunted incredulously. "An old building?"

"A windmill," Susan corrected excitedly, "with white canvas sails slowly revolving against a cerulean sky!"

"They're a tattered, dirty brown," Forestall protested, "and the gears are locked down so the thing doesn't turn."

Susan dismissed his response with a wave of her hand. "Doesn't matter," she concluded. "Children see what they want to see… it's like a game of *let's pretend*. The fact is… they went to your windmill and then ran down the ridge and into the foothills."

Forestall looked southeast into the barren slopes of the foothills. "They'll come back in time for dinner," he answered crossly. "If not, they'll miss their supper and not be so foolish the next time."

"You disapprove of children?" Susan asked quietly.

"I disapprove of their unsupervised nonsense," Forestall grumbled.

Susan turned toward town and started quickly away. "What about supervised nonsense?" she called over her shoulder.

"Even worse," Forestall complained. "Their parents should keep them under control!"

Susan kept her eyes on the ground as she strode the rocky path back to town. The ground was dry, but the road was littered with fist-sized stones, some loose on the surface, others half-buried in the hard, dry earth. And the stones, like cunning little demons, waited for her attention to waiver so they could dart beneath her feet and send her crashing to the ground.

"I've been looking for you."

The sound of the Campbell girl's voice brought Susan to a stop. She looked up from the road into the girl's red-rimmed eyes.

"Something's wrong," she observed tiredly.

"Yes...." the girl admitted unhappily.

Susan clenched her fists at her sides and waited for the girl's answer.

It must be the children, she thought bleakly.

"It's Daniel," the girl groaned.

Susan sucked in a ragged breath and let it out slowly. "Good heavens! Don't scare me like that! I thought you had bad news about those missing children!"

"It's Daniel," the girl groaned again.

"What about Daniel," Susan demanded crossly. "He's not hurt, is he?"

"He's flirting with that Barrett girl," Lynne wailed.

Susan raised an eyebrow. "And this bothers you?"

"Of course it does!"

"And does Brother Pratt know his attentions to Miss Barrett irritate you?"

"Of course not!"

"Yet you want him to stop?"

"He's making a fool of himself..."

Susan smiled and took the girl by the arm, steering her back towards town. "Collin says most men make fools of themselves over a woman sooner or later."

"Well, Daniel should behave himself. That girl will take advantage of him."

"In what way?"

"She thinks he has money, and when she finds out he's poor as a church mouse, she'll toss him aside."

"And you're concerned that Brother Pratt's heart will be broken."

"Of course...."

"And you walked all the way up here to tell me that the Barrett girl is trying to get her claws into your man?"

"Exactly... I mean...."

"I know exactly what you mean. But you can't expect Brother Pratt to spend the rest of his life trying to win you over. I don't think there are many men who have the patience for long drawn-out courtships, let alone the kind of games the two of you have been playing."

"But he has no ambition! First, he wanted a pig farm in Heber City. Then it was sheep... Now it's mining... at least that's what he's been telling that Barrett girl—that he's a partner with her father and Brother Mitchell."

"And you don't believe him."

"I don't know what to believe."

Susan sighed impatiently. "Do you really care that much about what Daniel does for a living? I would think that honest work and his best efforts to provide for you would be enough... if you really care for him."

"But pigs...."

"And what do you have against pigs? Do you think Daniel will build two pens—one for the pigs and the other for the two of you to live in? Be reasonable girl! Daniel is looking ahead. He believes that more and more people will come into the Salt Lake Valley, and many of them will live in town. He thinks the market for those pigs you dislike so much will grow year by year."

"I hadn't thought of that."

"Well, I suspect Daniel has changed his mind about the pigs anyway."

Susan stopped suddenly and looked back towards the steep ridge behind Frank Gromley's house.

"Have you seen Miss Barrett today?"

"Earlier," Lynne admitted. "She was at Allingham's store when Daniel and I stopped there half-an-hour ago. I left when Daniel started acting like a puppy who wanted his ears rubbed."

"Let's go find them," Susan urged thoughtfully. "I have a couple of questions I want to ask her, and while I'm doing that, you can rescue Daniel from her clutches."

The girl smiled and examined her fingernails as though checking a weapon for sharpness. "Daniel was going to the stable to check on our animals," she said darkly. "They should be there by now."

Ten minutes later, Susan threw back the tall, sun-bleached doors of the Hawkins' stables, flooding the dimly lit interior with bright afternoon sunlight. Far towards the back of the building, the Pratt kid forked loose hay into one of the stalls. The Barrett girl stood close by, watching the work and chatting happily at the silent worker.

Susan led the Campbell girl to the pair, and for a moment, they stood watching as the Pratt kid tossed the last of the hay into one corner of the stall.

"That oughta do it," he concluded as he set the hay fork to one side and turned to find himself surrounded by the three women. "I ain't in trouble, am I?"

Susan shook her head and took the Barrett girl by the arm. "You are not in trouble," she advised, "but I do need to ask Miss Barrett a few questions."

For a moment, the Barrett girl looked surprised. "Questions..." she repeated.

"Questions," Susan affirmed, steering the girl to the front of the building and into the fresh air beyond the doorway. "I want you to tell me about the windmill on the mountain above town," she explained.

From deep in the stable, Susan heard the Pratt kid's frantic whisper. "Where the hell did you go?" he moaned. "That gal damn near talked my ear off.... She sucked in one breath of air and never stopped talkin' 'til you come back... I never seen the like... Don't ever leave me like that again!"

"The windmill?" asked the Barrett girl, who stood too far outside to hear the exchange at the back of the stable.

"Yes, the one Henry Forestall built to cut timbers for the Emma mine," Susan explained.

"I don't know much about it," the Barrett girl confessed. "We hear it running now and then."

"Then you missed me?" Lynne asked quietly.

"Of course I missed you!" hissed the Pratt kid.

"You seemed quite focused on the low-cut dress that female is wearing," Lynne replied.

Susan frowned. "You can hear them cutting lumber?"

"Not exactly." the Barrett girl replied. "Sometimes there's a loud hammering noise. It's far enough up the mountain that no one pays much attention any more. For a while, it was really irritating. It would start clanging away early in the morning, wake everyone in town, and then stop after about an hour."

"It was an accident!" the kid squawked. "I forget you gals wear that kind of thing so fellows *won't* look at you!"

"When I wear that kind of thing, you may look all you want Brother Pratt—anyone else...you be mighty careful where your eyes are wandering."

"Mss. Pendleton finally went to Mr. Forestall and complained." Miranda continued. "They must have fixed whatever was wrong, because it's much quieter now, and they only run it at midday."

"I hadn't noticed it," Susan acknowledged.

"I don't think they've used it since you've been here," the girl admitted.

"Do they use it often?"

For a moment, the Barrett girl was silent, pondering her answer. "Maybe twice a week... for an hour or two."

Susan frowned and knitted her eyebrows in thought. The two conversations were driving her mad, but she wanted to hear both. "Yet Mr. Forestall just told me that they seldom use the mill any more. I wouldn't describe twice a week as *seldom*," she said.

"You mean that?" the Pratt kid asked quietly.

"Of course," Lynne replied.

"I don't know about that," the Barrett girl replied, "but you can ask anyone in town. I'm sure they've heard it too."

"So they're still hauling trees up there and cutting timber for the mine?"

The girl shrugged. "I haven't noticed any lumber coming or going."

"No wagons? No people?"

"Nothing. I heard someone say they've seen smoke up there occasionally, but that's all."

"There's something I've been meanin' to ask you," the Pratt kid said suddenly.

Susan glanced quickly toward the pair at the back of the stable then looked up the mountain toward the mill. The tall sails of the windmill were invisible, hidden below the rim of the ridge that ran northward between the windmill and the town. No smoke drifted on the wind; no hammering echoed down the long slopes between the scattered pinions. The day was silent, the sky clear and blue.

"*Something* is going on up there," she said quietly.

"Something is going on up where?"

The Pratt kid's question startled her, and Susan turned to find Daniel and Lynne standing in the open doorway of the stables.

"There's a lumber mill of sorts about a mile above town," Susan replied. "I followed the tracks of two children up there. The two of them wandered around the windmill, and then ran down the mountain like they were scared to death. Both of them fell once or twice, but they just got up and ran again.

I followed the tracks down to the road that leads up to the mines, but the tracks ran across the road as though they never even noticed it. That's where I stopped following and came back to get help."

The Pratt kid frowned and looked back to the stalls and their animals. "You want me to take my horse and go find them kids?"

"I want you to find Collin," Susan replied anxiously. "I have a bad feeling about this, and I'd feel a lot better if he was here."

The Pratt kid frowned. "He followed that fellow down towards Willow Springs... I can ride down that way, but that's awful big country. He could be anywhere by now."

Susan paused for a moment, realizing that the Pratt kid was right. "You're right," she said last. "Saddle our horses, and bring them over to the boarding house. I need to talk with Sarah. We can all look for those children, and then I want another look around that windmill."

Chapter 15

Utah Territory
Granite Peak—June 1869

Mitchell dropped to the ground behind the dead mule. A second shot boomed though the camp, and another bullet thumped into the body as Mitchell scrambled quickly into the rocks on the south edge of the canyon.

Taggart had gone into the rocks as well, but the old man and the two saddle horses had disappeared.

"Did you see where them shots came from?" Taggart called out.

"Above us somewhere…" Mitchell answered, "back in the rocks near the top."

"That old man took out of here like a jackrabbit," Taggart reported. "Took both them horses with him."

Mitchell jacked a round into the Yellow Boy, and quickly scanned the mountainside. The ridge-line was a jumble of jagged rock. Below the rocks, alluvium fanned out for twenty yards before the slopes became relatively smooth and covered with a scattering of rock and the sparse vegetation that seemed to cling to life wherever it could. The rocks at the bottom of the ravine were nothing more than the weathered and eroded chunks of rock that had broken loose and gathered enough momentum to reach the bottom.

"Why the hell are they shootin' at us?" Taggart bellowed. "I ain't found nothin' but a crappy little glory hole of silver. I dug down nearly twenty feet, and I ain't made more than fifty dollars!"

"I think they're shooting because they don't want you talking to me about Barrett's claims," Mitchell replied.

"Don't know why," Taggart objected. "That shaft on the ridge west of the Emma was a bust. Barrett and me even moved some of the equipment over to the Polecat claim at the cliffs, but I never got anywhere near the number three claim! I think he had another fellow helpin' there for a while... 'till the fellow quit and headed out for the Comstock."

Mitchell ducked down as a bullet *spanged* off the rocks and whined overhead. "Barrett pretty much told me the Lost Crow was a bust," he admitted.

Taggart shoved himself tightly into a seam between two large rocks. "We knew *that* when Barrett went to talk with you," he answered. "We had a head-frame up and we were followin' a skinny little vein. We were down two-hundred and fifty feet, that's when we broke through into some kind of crevasse and lost the vein altogether. Barrett thought we could find the vein again, but we had some good color at the cliffs, so we quit the Crow and moved over to the cliffs. But Barrett knew he couldn't run two mines without more money and equipment. We moved some track and such over to the cliffs, but we needed more equipment. That's why he went to you.

"I thought we was gonna get back to the Lost Crow and work on her some more. Then for a while, I thought Barrett was gonna sell the claim. Some fellow even come out and took a look at it... had a woman with him. They went down and looked around, but I never seen 'em after that.

"After Barrett come back from seein' you, we worked about a month at the cliffs, and then Barrett up and disappeared. I went up to the cliffs one morning and he wasn't there. So I went down to the Lost Crow. Most all the equipment was still there, so I went down the shaft, but there was no sign of Barrett, and the bottom of that crevasse was all choked off with debris... That was back in November. Since then, I've been out here diggin' my own holes."

"The man and woman who came out to look at the mine...who were they?"

"I got no idea... never seen 'em before."

Mitchell shifted to the east side of his rocky hideout. He was uneasy about being pinned down, though they were safe enough for the moment. The angle of fire from above gave no opportunity for their assailants to hit anything but the rocks at the base of the mountainside. Here, they were safe temporarily, but that would not last. The men on the ridge above would soon grow impatient, and they would look for ways to flank their quarry. Mitchell let his eyes probe the rocks, searching for a way out—a way protected from view. Taggart had no options. He crouched behind a pair of man-sized boulders with open ground on all sides. Any movement on his part would be begging for a bullet through some tender part of his anatomy.

"How are you fixed for ammunition?" Mitchell called out.

Taggart opened the pouch at his belt and shook his head unhappily. "Not much," he replied unhappily. "This old army Colt is loaded up, but I ain't got but three or four rounds after that."

Mitchell took the Yellow Boy by the barrel and estimated the distance separating them.

"I'm going to toss this rifle to you. Just let it come to you and don't go reachin' for it unless you want another chunk of lead in your gizzard."

Taggart pushed tighter against his rocky outpost. "I ain't movin'," he replied. "Don't need no extra holes."

Mitchell hefted the gun then tossed it butt first across twenty feet of flat, gravel packed ground. Taggart held tightly against the rocks, but snatched up the weapon as soon as it touched the ground.

"You know how to work that thing?" Mitchell asked dryly.

"Ain't never even seen one before," Taggart admitted.

"Hammer and trigger work the same as that Army Colt," Mitchell explained. "Load the cartridges through that little gate on the side; just ram 'em up into that tube under the barrel. It holds fourteen rounds. You can't load when the lever on the underside is open. Jack the lever open, and it'll throw out whatever you got in the chamber—the hammer cocks when you open the lever."

Taggart worked the lever twice, then picked up the ejected rounds, brushed them off, then pushed them through the gate and into the magazine.

"Handy little thing," he acknowledged. "How does she shoot?"

"You should be able to put some holes in those fellows on the ridge-top," Mitchell advised. "About a hundred yards," he suggested, "after that, she drops pretty fast."

Mitchell shifted a bit and drew one of the new Smith & Wessons.

"Lob a shot up there with that Colt every now and then," he told the miner. "Get their attention."

Taggart nodded, reached up with one hand, and without looking, popped a wild shot into the rocks above.

Mitchell moved quickly, not waiting for a reaction from above. He crawled thirty feet, hugging closely to rocks so small he was certain to be seen. The shots came suddenly, pounding the rocks and blasting chips like hail around him.

He squawked as a sharp-edged splinter sliced his cheek beneath one eye. "Damn!"

Taggart fired again, and Mitchell scrambled to a more protected spot. He moved again and again until suddenly, he found himself in the bottom of a shallow ravine. Barely ten feet across, jagged stone rose steeply on either side, creating a 'V' shaped defile that ran up-slope for more than three hundred feet before opening out on the ridge top.

Mitchell hurried up the narrow trace. For the moment, he was a sitting duck, and he wanted out of the ravine as quickly as possible. But speed was impossible. What started as a narrow trail leading upward along the floor of the ravine soon turned into a jumble of massive stones sheared from the vertical walls on either side.

Mitchell climbed and wormed his way through the rubble, moving as quickly as he could, but the rocky debris grew larger and more difficult to traverse until he was forced to leap from one large rock to the next. For a moment, he paused, listening as Taggart fired another round toward the ridge-top. The bullet ricocheted and whined off into the distance.

The world grew silent. No shots responded from the ridge above, and Mitchell grew nervous. Their enemies were on the move. Suddenly apprehensive, he crouched down, wedging himself in the space between two large boulders.

It was a bad decision. He knew it from the moment he pressed his back against the rocks. There was nowhere to go. In desperation, he might slip around the curve of one boulder and into another crevice, but that option afforded little hope of escape, and if the men above discovered him, they would cut him to ribbons.

He heard them long before they came into view—a man on either side of the ravine, walking the edge, searching the rocks below. Their boots crunched on the gravelly surface of the ground at the edge of the cliff-like face of the ravine. Mitchell tensed as the first man stepped into view.

The man stood on the lip of the ravine scanning the rocks below. Sweat darkened the front of his shirt, and the red dust of the desert coated the legs of his trousers. Quietly, Mitchell raised the muzzle of the Smith & Wesson.

"Don't see how anyone could come up through that mess of rocks," called a voice from behind Mitchell.

"Me neither," replied the man framed in the sights of the forty-four. "I don't like this...."

"What's eatin' you," the other called back.

"This whole business.... I got a bad feeling, Ross, and I think we should get out of this."

"What about our money?" Ross demanded.

"To hell with the money! This has already gone further than I expected. Bad enough we shot Taggart and chased him down that hole. Killin' 'im wasn't part of the deal... Now there's two more."

The man behind Mitchell was silent for a long while. Finally, a boot scraped the ground, thumped a rock and sent it clattering into the tangled stone where Mitchell lay hidden.

"I don't like givin' up that money," the man grumbled.

Mitchell waited. After all that had happened, he had no desire to shoot either of the men who stood above him. In fact, it seemed likely that shooting one might make Mitchell an easier target for the other. The prospect was unappealing. So Mitchell waited, hiding in the shadows between the rocks, watching the man across the iron sights of the forty-four, waiting for the life changing decision. When the decision came, it came quickly as the enemy spun on the sole of his boot and strode out of sight.

"I'm out of it," he called to his partner.

Mitchell heard the sound of boots crunching away towards the ridge-top.

"Damn!" Ross growled. "Wait up, Jenks! I'm with ya!"

Again, Mitchell waited, the pistol cocked and ready. He wanted both men well on their way before he climbed out of the ravine. Quietly, he holstered the pistol and took a piece of jerky from his shirt pocket. With a jackknife, he nipped off a piece.

Absently, he cut a second piece for the dog. But the dog had been missing for a while and was unlikely to be hiding anywhere near. Mitchell chewed the jerky, impatient to be out of the ravine and free of the growing feeling that he was boxed in. Something evil was nearby... watching. He could feel it, like a hot wind on the back of his neck. Still, he waited; and the feeling grew. Finally, he pushed out of the crevice and started the climb out of the ravine. He went quickly, climbing the sharp-edged stones that had scaled away from the eastern wall onto the gravelly mountainside. The evil was there.

The bullet droned like an angry bee, knifing across his back, and the sound of the shot boomed down the mountainside and fled across the salt flats. Mitchell spun, snatching the pistol from its holster. The muzzle jumped, and sixty feet away, the forty-four caliber slug plowed the bushwhacker to the ground. Mitchell thumbed the hammer back and took two quick steps toward the unmoving body. The man lay still, and Mitchell closed distance until he could reach down and pry the Yellow Boy from Taggart's unyielding grip.

"Damn! What the hell got into you?" Mitchell growled.

Taggart's eyes followed the muzzle of the pistol. "I figured you'd come after me sooner or later," he groaned.

"Hell, man! All I wanted was answers to some questions about Barrett's claims."

"Don't know nothin'," Taggart moaned. "I worked for him. That's all."

"Did you tell anyone where the claims were located?"

"Ramsay paid me some money to show them where Barrett was getting' his gold. I was broke, so I took the money and showed them where the little vein was hid."

"Who's *them*?" Mitchell demanded.

Taggart was silent.

"Who..."

Taggart lay still on the hard mountain soil. His jaw was slack, his lips unmoving.

"Damn fool!" Mitchell growled at the dead miner. "Now I got to bury you, and try to explain to that damn deputy."

Angrily, Mitchell bent down to retrieve the bag of rifle cartridges, but he stopped at the sight of Sarah's new pistol tucked in Taggart's belt.

"Now how did you come by that," he muttered unhappily as he yanked the Smith & Wesson from the dead man's belt and wiped the dust from it.

There was no doubt the weapon belong to Sarah. It was custom-made, nickel plated, and hand engraved. With a three inch barrel and ivory grips, there was only one other like it in the territory, and Susan's gun had ebony grips.

For a long while, Mitchell studied the surrounding mountains. He was confused. Had Taggart been in league with the men who had shot him? If Jenks had been telling the truth, they had been offered payment for something, and had ended up shooting Taggart and chasing him down into his mine.

The heat was oppressive. The air was dry, and Mitchell felt a sudden pang of thirst. But he had no water. In the heat of battle, he had gone to cover without taking any with him. If there was any nearby, it would have to be with the dead pack mule, and if not there, he was going to be mighty thirsty in a short while.

The old man had disappeared, taking the horses with him, and if Taggart's partners, if partners they were, had really given up and left the mountain, then he was thirty miles from the nearest settlement, without food or water, alone and on foot. The nearest water he knew of was at Fish Springs, fifteen miles to the south, and he had no desire to make that trip on foot. His prospects seemed grim until he saw the pack mule lying near the burned-out wagon and the packs still strapped to the animal's body.

Chapter 16

Utah Territory
Deep Creek Mountains—June 1869

Sarah looked down at the journal she held in her lap. She had read nothing as yet, but the prospect of looking into Collin's past was tempting beyond the endurable. He had given it to them and told them to read it, yet something inside her made her hesitate—a hesitation she drove aside as she opened the cover.

The journal was old, battered, and leather bound. Sarah was sure that Collin had kept the thing in his saddle bags for a long time, stuffed in among food, clothing, and ammunition, and it was not until the journal lay open that she realized Collin had been keeping this record for more than fifteen years. Quietly, she began the first entry.

10 January 1854
Trouble at home. Left school with $50.00 in my pocket.
Bought a horse and a used rig for $20.00—found a used Navy Colt for $10.00

26 May 1854
Nearly broke. Still a long way from home. Tried to find work. Got a day job for room and board. Stayed two weeks. Left with $5.00 pay.

19 June 1854
Ran into a couple of fellows who offered me a temporary job tending their horses. I'm to bring the horses down to the spring outside of town at daybreak day after tomorrow.

21Jun1854

I shot a man today. God forgive me; I may have killed another. That horse tending job was no job at all. Those fellows were getting set to rob the bank down in town. I overheard them planning last night, so I got on my horse and rode out of there as fast as I could. Ten miles away, I realized they were just going to rob that bank anyway.

Felt guilty just riding off. Rode back to town and found the sheriff. Told him everything. The sheriff rounded up some fellows, and before daybreak, he had us all set where he wanted us.

Bank opened about 9 am. Those fellows shoved the door open, yanked out their pistols and went right for the vault. The sheriff hollered for them to throw down their guns, but they started shooting, so we cut loose on them.

26 June 1854

Sheriff kept me around town for a few days. Gave me $25.00 – my share of the bounty on two of those fellows robbing the bank. Camp for the night, about 100 miles east of Springfield.

Sarah closed the journal. That skimpy glimpse into six months of Collin Mitchell's life had shown her how easily a person could become entangled in someone else's nightmare. Collin had been caught up in just such a nightmare, and its effects had followed him for the past fifteen years. It made her experience of the previous day seem almost trivial by comparison, yet there was something… something similar….

"Deep thinking?"

Sarah looked up to find Susan looking down at the journal.

"I was reading the first few entries," she replied.

"I found it very hard to be critical of what I've read so far," Susan confided.

Sarah tapped the journal with one finger. "It got me thinking," she said.

"Thinking of what?"

Sarah stood and walked to the empty frame of the parlor window. "Thinking of how *we* keep getting caught up in other people's nightmares. It's like we're somehow meant to be involved in things that are beyond the normal."

"Destiny?"

"Not destiny," Sarah objected. "You know I don't believe in fate. This makes me feel as though someone is watching over us and giving us a chance to prove ourselves."

"Ah… The refiner's fire," Susan concluded.

"The fire… yes," Sarah admitted. "For just a moment, I saw the way Collin moved step by step through a dozen choices and how each choice led to an event that tested what kind of man he was. It was a chain of choices and consequences that made him what he is today."

"So, you've had an epiphany?"

"I suppose so, but it made me think about yesterday. And I began to wonder what choices I had made that led me into that alley and ended with that man attacking me. Even then, he didn't really attack *me*. He just took my handbag and dumped everything on the ground."

"And took nothing," Susan added.

"Ten dollars," Sarah corrected. "I had about thirty dollars, but he took only one coin and my new Smith & Wesson."

"You're lucky that's as far as it went," Susan reproved.

"I managed well enough," Sarah retorted.

"Well enough," Susan admitted thoughtfully. "But I didn't come in to talk about yesterday... I thought I should let you know that the whole town is in a panic."

Sarah turned her back on the window and the hot, dry breeze that coursed through the empty frame, turning the parlor into a kiln that sucked the moisture from everything.

"Must be something dreadful to panic a place as rough as this," she responded grimly.

"Dreadful enough," Susan answered gravely. "Two children have gone missing. One of them is that little boy Collin talked with at the stable."

"Tommy Hawkins?"

Susan frowned unhappily. "And a little girl about the same age," she explained. "Her name is Debbie Allingham. Her father owns the dry goods store."

"I met him yesterday," Sarah replied. "How long have they been missing?"

Susan shook her head. "All night, at least. Mrs. Hawkins remembers Tommy hanging around the street near the front of the stable. He was showing his cat to Debbie just after dinner last night... about five. He didn't come in when she called for him half-an-hour later. They met with the Allingham's around six and spent the rest of the night searching."

"I suppose the whole town has been searched by now," Sarah concluded.

"More than once," Susan replied gravely.

"And no one has any idea where they might have gone?" Sarah asked.

Susan shook her head. Mrs. Hawkins says that Tommy stayed around the stable most of the time. He wanted to show his father he was a good helper. Once in a while he would play with the other children who live out here, but there are only half-a-dozen even close to his age. Those were some of the first places they checked."

Sarah felt her chest tighten at the thought of two young children wandering and perhaps lost in a landscape so totally unforgiving. There would be little chance of them finding water. The heat of the summer had already cleared the snow from the tops of the deep Creek Mountains, and the perennial streams had metamorphosed into bone-dry gullies that would only see moisture when the unpredictable storms of summer rumbled across the mountains and down into the valleys.

The pair might find shade, but the days were already reaching temperatures of more than a hundred degrees, and while shade might help for a short time, the blistering heat would soon suck the moisture from their small bodies and leave them sluggish, drained of energy, and eventually without life.

"They won't last long in this heat," she predicted unhappily. "I'll bet it's a hundred-and-five in the shade."

Susan shuddered at the thought of two small children dead from thirst and heat, their bodies lost and desiccated in some snake infested gully.

"There are a dozen men searching the mountains west of town, but only a few have gone down along the foothills. Two of them went north, but no one is searching southeast towards Willow Springs."

"You think they went down into the foothills?" Sarah asked.

"I do. That's where those tracks were headed, and I think someone ought to be looking there."

* * *

It was late afternoon when Sarah reined in the dun and let her eyes rove the depths of the gully running southeast and away into the northern end of Snake Valley. She was southeast of the stables. The hills to the west were nearly barren of vegetation and the ground beneath the dun's hooves threw back the sun's heat like the kiss of a branding iron. Her straw hat did little to stop the heat, and she felt like a sponge—soaked, then wrung out and left in an oven to dry.

The dun blew out a huge breath of air, shaking his head and stamping his feet impatiently.

"You're not lame at all, you lazy hammerhead," Sarah accused crossly. "I'll bet you wanted a shady stable and cold water and grain. I think Collin has been spoiling you since the grulla was killed last fall."

The dun settled down at the soothing music of Sarah's voice, but the animal laid back both ears when she leaned forward and stroked his neck just a little too close to a ragged and gnarled looking ear.

"Don't like that, do you?"

Sarah examined the lopped-off tip of the animal's ear where a bullet had literally exploded the sensitive flesh before smashing through Collin's gun-belt and plowing a half-inch furrow above his hip.

Sarah leaned back in the saddle, settling into the comfortable half-seat of the Hope-style rig. She felt the padded cantle snug up against the base of her spine and let herself relax as she nudged the dun into a walk and dropped down into the bottom of the gully.

Only then did she notice the small footprints disturbing the softer sands where the spring runoff had deposited loose soil and detritus in the bottom of the wash. The tracks were faint. The children were small and lightweight, and though the sands were softer than the hard-packed ground above, the shattered flakes and rubble of the runoff gave little beneath the feet of a small child.

Where are you going? Sarah wondered thoughtfully.

The tracks ran eastward—away from town—dodging between tall sagebrush—first running, then walking carefully and hiding among the larger clusters of brush. Finally, Sarah dismounted, leading the dun by the reins. Slowly, she followed the tracks, watching carefully for fear of losing the trial. Three miles east of town, the tracks disappeared like the promises of a politician after Election Day. Nothing remained. The tracks were simply gone.

Sarah stared at the bed of the gully. Here, the runoff from several perennial streams had converged and turned into a powerful surge that had risen nearly half-way up the banks of the channel, stripping the riverbed of lighter sands and detritus and scouring it down to bedrock.

Carefully, Sarah led the dun down the rocky channel. They moved slowly, the dun's steel shod hooves clattering and slipping on the smooth surfaces of the water-worn stone. A hundred paces and she began searching for a way out of the gully. Another fifty and the banks grew lower and less steep. Fifteen more, and she saw the blood—great spots spattered across the stony riverbed—and the little body crumpled and nearly cut in half by the blast of a large bore gun.

The dun tossed his head, pulling away from the smell of fresh blood. Sarah threw her weight on the reins, dragging the animal's head downward, speaking softly until the animal settled down and let her come closer to the child's body. Sarah shuddered at the sight of the torn little body and fought the urge to vomit.

"Shotgun," she muttered bleakly.

She felt sick at the prospect of informing the Allinghams that their only daughter had been brutally murdered. The family would be devastated, and she had no desire to be the bearer of such news. Dazed and unhappy, she led the dun around the body and down the dry watercourse. Twenty feet away, she hauled back on the reins and stopped the dun in his tracks. She couldn't leave.... She couldn't leave the little girl lying broken and uncared for in the middle of nowhere.

Suddenly, her heart felt as though it weighed a hundred pounds. The tears came as she slid from the saddle and untied the wool blanket. She turned back to the little body, laying the blanket just so....

The sobs came. She couldn't stop them—great racking sobs that shook her frame and left her gasping for air—weeping for the little girl, weeping for her parents who would never hold her again in this life, weeping for her own children who even now were more than a hundred miles away, yet safe with her own parents.

Even the dun felt her pain and pressed his nose to her shoulder as though trying to reassure her. But the sobs went on... until at last she was weak, wrung out, and silent. Methodically, she piled rocks on the blanket, knowing that the scavengers would come and that the blanket would afford little protection. She hated abandoning the remains of the little girl, but Tommy was still out there. She prayed he was safe, but someone had murdered Debbie Allingham, and if Tommy Hawkins had escaped the same treatment, he would need help and quickly. Unhappily she climbed into the saddle and heeled the dun. The startled animal leaped forward and lunged up the bank of the gully and onto the flats above.

Sarah flinched as a sullen *boom* rolled off the mountains behind her and *crackled* across the flats. The dark menace of a thunderstorm boiled eastward, flashing lightning and spattering the ground with a sudden downpour of rain.

Lightning flashed again, and before the deep rumbling of the thunder could reach her, she heard the sharp *crack* of two quick gun-shots. Sarah kicked the dun into a lope, dodging the animal around rocks and tall brush, jumping anything that got in the way of their mad rush in the direction of the gunshots. At a quarter-mile, the dun dodged a stunted juniper and struck the running boy a glancing blow, sending him tumbling across the hard-packed flats. The boy staggered to his feet, stumbling away.

Sarah hauled on the reins, dragging the dun back on its haunches in a sweeping turn that sent them charging back to the dazed little boy. Like a hawk seizing a wounded jackrabbit, she leaned down and snatched the boy by the collar, dragging him across the saddle. A hundred yards to the north, two riders plowed their horses through clumps of waist-high sagebrush, bearing down on the dun and firing wildly. Sarah turned the dun east, slapping its flank with the reins until the animal raced through the growing darkness of the evening.

Dark clouds poured over the top of the Deep Creek Range. Bald Mountain vanished in a roiling blanket of black and gray. Water poured from the sky in a torrent; dark chunks of mud tumbled through the air behind the dun's flying hooves, and in the growing darkness, the animal leaped some invisible obstacle and stumbled. Sarah fought to stay in the saddle. They were near the road when the riders fired again, and Sarah felt the dun flinch.

Shot in the rump, the animal stumbled and collapsed, dumping Sarah and the boy headlong onto the hard-packed surface of the old express trail.

Tommy struck the road, bounced, and vanished in the darkness. Sarah plowed through a water-filled depression and slid to a stop near the center of the road. Dazed, she struggled to her knees.

Lightning flashed overhead, and she saw the men less than ten yards away—two on her left, and a third to her right, standing in the center of the road, his clothing drenched, and a pistol in his fist. Sarah froze, unable to move as the men fired and red-orange flames stabbed through the heart of the gathering darkness.

* * *

Thunder boomed down Goshute Canyon, and a cold rain rattled like hard pellets on the brim of Mitchell's hat. Mitchell reined in the roan and worked his jacket out of the tightly bound roll lashed to the front of the saddle. Wind blasted out of the canyon, dragging at the jacket. The cloth popped open like a sail, nearly yanking him from the saddle. Mitchell fought his way into the jacket, but was soaked before he could get it buttoned.

Behind him, Sarah leaned forward, pressing herself against his back. She was already wrapped in a woolen blanket and an oversized slicker, and Mitchell was grateful for the warm barrier she made against the storm.

"Goshute Canyon," he called over the noise of the wind and rain. "We're only three or four miles from town."

"And the rain will quit just as we reach the boarding house," Sarah predicted.

"No doubt," Mitchell responded. "We should have gone over to Willow Springs and stayed the night."

"But we need to find Tommy!" Sarah protested.

"I know," Mitchell agreed, "but this weather ain't helpin' any. You can't see ten feet in this stuff."

"He can't be far," Sarah insisted, "and the storm seems to be passing. We can't leave him out all night. He'll be soaked from the rain, and he'll die from exposure."

We ain't leavin' him," Mitchell promised. "But we've been up and down this side of the road, and there ain't no sign of him. I think we should cross over the road and start looking where the dun fell. After everything that's happened, Tommy's probably scared to death. He may have gone back the way you came, trying to find home...."

Sarah rested her head against Mitchell's back, clinging tightly to the man who had come out of the night like a destroying angel.

"Ain't any...." She corrected softly.

Mitchell took the roan to the west of the road, and for a hundred yards, they moved slowly to the south, searching for any sign of the boy's passing.

The wind died. The rain changed from a torrent to a drizzle and finally stopped. The dark thunderhead rolled ponderously to the northeast, its trailing edge like a dark curtain, opening the sky to a waxing gibbous moon and a billion glittering stars that lit the desert with an eerie nocturnal glow.

Finally, in the cold light of the stars, they found the place where the dun had fallen. The animal was gone, but when Mitchell slid from the saddle and searched the ground, he found Tommy's small footprints leading the limping animal back toward town. Quietly, he reached up and took Sarah by the hand.

"We'll find him now," he promised.

An hour later, they found the boy. Tommy was soaked to the skin, bedraggled, and barely able to walk. The fall from the dun to the express road had left him bruised and battered, and Mitchell was surprised that the boy still had the strength to lead the dun through the darkness, fighting fatigue and the mud clinging to his shoes.

The boy was barely aware when Mitchell dropped to the ground beside him and scooped him up into his arms. Tommy looked into Mitchell's face. "They killed Debbie," he sobbed quietly. "I couldn't do nothin'.... The *shadow man* just shot her... and then she just laid there all torn up...."

Mitchell held the boy close to his chest and turned back to where the pigeon-toed Milo stood waiting. The roan pressed his muzzle against the boy as though sensing his distress. Carefully, Mitchell lifted the boy into Sarah's waiting arms where she wrapped him tightly in Mitchell's coat.

Silently, his heart filled with an anger that threatened to drag him into a killing rage, Mitchell gathered the two horses by the reins and started the long walk home.

Chapter 17

Utah Territory
Deep Creek Mountains—June 1869

Mitchell snugged the collar of his coat closer about his throat and leaned into the deeper shadows at the base of a weather beaten pinion. The last orange flare of the evening sun shot down the canyon from the west and fled into the flats below, leaving an unnatural chill in its wake.

On the ground, three dozen crows stalked among the fallen needles beneath the pines, walking with stiff little staccato steps, hopping two legged, beaks stabbing like daggers at the carpet of needles and the tiny appetizers hidden beneath it.

"Them birds make me nervous," the Pratt kid grumbled from where he lay concealed in the brush ten feet away. "Someone is gonna see them pecking around out here and wonder why. Then one of them guards is gonna cut loose with a scatter gun. 'Course he'll miss them crows, and I'll catch a load of buckshot right in the butt!"

Mitchell grunted unsympathetically. "Should have hid behind a tree," he advised. That brush ain't gonna stop any buckshot."

The Pratt kid grumbled unhappily as he scanned the hillside for a more protected spot.

"Better stay put," Mitchell advised. "Ten minutes and it'll be dark enough we can get down near the fence and maybe get inside."

The Pratt kid rolled over on his back and stared up into the evening sky where the brighter stars were already beginning to appear.

"Reckon we'll see anything useful?" the kid asked.

"I'm not sure," Mitchell answered, "but I'm curious about those wagons Susan told us about. I can't see any reason for loading them up at Gromley's place and shipping them out from there.

"What would they have at Gromley's place?"

The Pratt kid stared at the sky and picked at his teeth with a twig. "Maybe Gromley is skimming off some high-grade ore and shipping it out when he thinks it's safe."

Mitchell pondered the idea for a moment. "Maybe," he admitted finally. "But I don't see bringing the ore wagons down from the Emma warehouse… seems a little too obvious, if you're stealing high-grade. Why take a chance with partial loads stashed at your house when it would be easy enough to set some high-grade aside at the warehouse and make up a special load for parts unknown?"

"Beats me," the kid replied. "There must be some reason for all that extra work."

Mitchell sucked in a deep breath of air. The smell of pine was thick but mingled with the scent of sagebrush and the salty taste of red mountain dust.

"They're movin' another wagon," he told the kid.

"Maybe two," the Pratt kid suggested. "I can hear something coming down the road from up towards our claims."

"Now that don't make any sense," Mitchell replied. "There ain't any claims up that way but ours."

"Well, something's comin' down the road," the kid insisted.

"I don't like it," Mitchell growled unhappily.

Quietly, the Pratt kid got to his feet and made his way to Mitchell's tree.

"I'm going down to the road," he said quietly. "I can get to the wagon, sneak up from behind and check the load. If it's ore they're moving, then there's a good chance it came out of that Polecat claim we ain't seen yet."

A moment later, the Pratt kid was gone, leaving Mitchell listening to the sound of the ore wagon from the Emma warehouse growing closer and finally passing the gate and rolling down the road towards town.

Mitchell hesitated only a moment before he lunged from his hiding place and rushed down the hillside. He took the scrub covered slope at a break-neck pace, leaping shadowy rocks and dead-fall until he reached the side of the road only a few paces behind the wagon. The clopping hooves of sixteen mules covered the sound of his progress as he closed the distance and grabbed the tailgate of the wagon. Quietly, he heaved himself over the gate and onto the bed of the wagon. In the dimness, he wormed his way under the canvas covering the load.

"You see that?" The driver asked, turning towards his partner who sat slumped and half asleep.

"Just the road," the sleeper grumbled. "Keep your eyes on the road. I don't want to go off the cliff because you keep watchin' the back end of the wagon."

For a long while, Mitchell lay quietly on the rocky cargo. He felt the wagon jolt as it turned to the east, dropping into the deep ruts of the lower road. Awkwardly, he dug into a coat pocket and fished out a match tin and struck one of the parlor matches. The small stick flared, then settled into a tiny flame that lit the small area beneath the canvas tarp. In the glare of the flame, he examined the ore and the gray, cubic crystals infused within each broken piece of rock. "Galena," he muttered.

* * *

The following day, Mitchell sat in a willow chair in the boarding house parlor. The broken windows were boarded up, the shattered glass removed both inside and out, and a new door hung where battered wood had dangled by a single hinge not long before.

Across the room, Mike Deagan sat stiffly in the only chair that had not been torn to shreds by the explosion. "You want me to run Barrett's mining operation?" He asked incredulously.

"You've had experience in all the underground work, haven't you?"

Deagan leaned forward a little as though suddenly realizing that Mitchell might not be joking. "I got no experience with business at all. I couldn't handle that part of it. I got no education to speak of. I could run the crews and follow a vein, but I got no geological training."

For a moment, Mitchell studied the ceiling, considering Deagan's arguments.

"The business side can be handled by the Barrett girl and her aunt," he said finally. "If we run into geological problems or need expert advice, we can send for someone from Salt Lake, or Denver at the School of Mines.

"Your job would be to oversee the three claims and coordinate the work. We'll find a foreman to run each of the sites, and they will report to you and the Barrett girl."

Deagan nodded in agreement. "I could do that," he agreed. "But what about Miss Barrett and her aunt? You're partners, but they own the mines, don't they? How are you going to convince them to let a fellow like me run their mining operation? Besides, I heard Forestall and Gromley offered to buy them out just this morning."

Mitchell leaned forward in his chair and looked directly into Deagan's eyes. "That's not going to happen," he said bluntly. "Barrett's partners have the first shot at a buyout, and I guarantee they will take up the option before they let it go to Forestall and Gromley."

"Then I'll do it," Deagan agreed. "She can always fire me if she ain't happy with my work."

Mitchell stood and picked up the chair. "I'm going out in the shade," he advised. "It's gettin' too hot in here."

Deagan followed him out and the two men dropped into chairs and tipped back against the wall where the side of the house blocked the morning sun. For a long while, they sat quietly and watched as the county deputy trotted his horse down the road and into the yard. Simmons reined in his horse and slid from the saddle.

"You look like you've been roasted like a pig on a spit," Mitchell called from the side of the house.

"I've been riding over to Granite Peak," Simmons replied unhappily. "We rode all over the mountain searching for Taggart's body. Finally found him... just where you said."

"And?"

"And I ought to arrest you for killin' him. But then how am I going to prove anything when all I've got is your word. And you say it was self-defense. The way I see it, I pretty much got nothing."

"Any sign of the fellows who were shooting at us out there?" Mitchell asked.

"I followed some horse tracks for a mile or two," Simmons admitted. "Might have been the fellows you're talking about, but I lost 'em just south of where we found

Taggart's body... can't be sure where they went after that."

Mitchell scowled and looked out into the yard where the morning heat had descended on the world like an invisible cloud. "I have a feeling those fellows are around here somewhere," he concluded unhappily.

Across the road, a stray dog trotted past a sun-bleached building and turned down a shaded alley. The motley colored animal turned to face Mitchell and flopped full length in the cool weeds that grew against a faded wall and lay panting and staring at Mitchell.

"I've been wondering about Williams," he confessed.

"I've been wondering about a lot of things," Simmons countered. "Like why you folks are here at all... and what you think you accomplish by tryin' to do my job."

Mitchell scowled. "First off, we're not trying to do your job," he answered testily. "And we're here because we have an interest in James Barrett's mining operations. Back in October, Daniel Pratt and I put up the money for some equipment Barrett needed. For that, Barrett gave us each a twenty-four percent partnership in his mining claims. Now, we want to know what happened to Barrett and our money.

"I think Barrett is dead. He didn't strike me as the sort that would take our money and run off with it. That's why we're here, and if something fishy is going on, it seems likely that folks like Taggart are going to come crawlin' out of the woodpile like a bunch of weasels. And if they shoot at me, I'm sure as hell going to shoot back."

For a long while, Simmons was silent. "Is that what happened to those fellows down on the express road?" he asked finally.

"That's exactly what happened to those fellows," Mitchell advised. "They chased two kids off the mountain and hunted them down like a couple of varmints. They murdered Allingham's little girl and were hunting Tommy Hawkins when my wife found him and tried to get him away. They shot my horse. And they were about to shoot Sarah when I found them. They were already on the way to Hell. So, I gave them a nudge through the gate."

Simmons looked out across the road. "That dog seems to follow you a lot," he observed.

"She just likes jerky," Mitchell replied.

"I think you're right about Williams," Simmons said, his eyes still focused on the dog resting in the shade. "His nose was broken, like you said. And we found an empty bottle tossed in the brush behind his shack. It still had a little mercury in it."

* * *

Susan Flitton Mitchell raised a brush and stroked the dust from the dun's shoulder. Mort watched closely as the animal shifted his weight, easing his hind hoof from the ground.

"That's a nasty wound," the old man said quietly.

"It seems to be healing well enough," Susan replied.

The old man looked closely at the two raw-looking wounds where the bullet had punched through the animal's rump. "Lucky it come out where it did…came right close to hittin' Sarah, I'd say. Don't see any signs of infection though," he confessed as he replaced the bandaging on the animal's rump.

"I think he'll be fine," Susan answered. "Collin thinks he'll be good as new in a month or two, until then he's the baby of the family."

"How's Sarah taking it?"

"Sarah puts on a good show, but she's shaken, Mort. I can see it in the way she sits so quietly sometimes."

"Can't say I blame her," the old man responded. "It's only been a couple of days."

He finished plastering the bandage on the dun's hind quarter and wiped his hands on a rag.

"You gals are something special," he said quietly. "Like Damascus steel... pretty as all get-out, but sharp... mighty sharp."

Susan took three slow passes of the brush across the dun's shoulder. "I'm not sure how to take that, Mort. Was that a complement?"

"Yes ma'am..."

"Hmmm... Damascus steel..."

"Yes ma'am... they take two or three bars of steel and heat it up red hot... then they hammer 'em out and twist 'em hundreds of times.... When everything is finished, they've got a blade for a knife that's all full of twisty colors like the grain in the wood of that fancy new table you've got... some of the best steel a fellow could want."

"Sounds like a lot of work to make such a blade," Susan suggested.

"Yes ma'am...but it's been through the fire, and beaten, and it's tough and beautiful all the same..."

Susan turned her eyes to the dun's shoulder, feeling embarrassed at the man's praise. For a moment, she said nothing.

"I've been looking at a horse," she said at last. "I saw him a few days ago, but decided just yesterday to buy him."

"A horse?"

Susan brushed the dun's side and looked at the animal's injured rump. "This fellow is going to need some rest," She pointed out. "I thought Collin might need another while this one mends enough to ride again."

The old man shrugged. "He's got that pigeon-toed critter."

"There's a buckskin out back, in the Hawkins' corral," Susan explained. "Mr. Hawkins is willing to sell him. They've had him since last fall when they found him wandering the express road. They think he must have broken loose and the owners were unable to find him. The Sheriff has made inquiries, but no one has claimed the animal. So the sheriff finally sent papers to Mr. Hawkins giving him ownership of abandoned property."

"And you want to buy him," the old man concluded.

Susan stepped away from the dun and worked her way out of the stall. "Come with me, Mort. Come take a look at this horse. He looks like a well-bred animal, and Collin has been looking for another since the grulla was killed last fall."

"Fine," the old man conceded. "Lead the way."

When they reached the corrals near the Hawkins' house, Susan walked up to the rail fence and pointed to one of the four animals that stood near a far corner.

"He looks like a fine one to me," the old man admitted.

"Do you think Collin will like him?"

The old man was silent for a moment. He looked at the animal as though searching for some reason to reject it. "I think he'll do just fine," he admitted finally. "Although I think Mitchell's going to take back that pigeon-toed roan."

"That horse is yours," Susan replied. "If the dun is too crippled to ride, Collin can put him out to pasture and ride the buckskin."

"I reckon…."

They stood quietly for a moment. The four animals ignored them, and the sun bore down on them with a frightening glare that left Susan feeling dried out and ready to blow away with the first breath of wind. She was relieved when the door of the Hawkins' house opened and Nathan Hawkins strode across the barren ground of the yard.

"So, you've come back," he observed congenially.

"I have," Susan confessed. "And I want to buy that buckskin."

Hawkins frowned unhappily and shook his head. "I'm sorry," he replied gruffly. "That animal ain't for sale."

"But we talked just the other day," Susan objected. "You were willing to sell then."

"I changed my mind."

Susan turned away from the corral, her lower lip caught between her teeth. She was too surprised to be angry. Still, it seemed unfair that Hawkins had changed his mind for no apparent reason.

"I thought we had agreed on forty dollars," she said at last. "I brought the money with me."

Nathan Hawkins frowned and shook his head stubbornly. "Can't do it," he concluded. "Not after what happened the other day... I'm giving that horse to you. My boy is home safe because of you folks."

"But we made a deal for the forty dollars," Susan insisted.

"I won't take your money," Hawkins argued. "I paid nothing for the animal anyway. Like I said before, I found him last fall down at Willow Springs. He was in pretty sad shape. His saddle was all twisted around underneath him, and he could hardly move. I cut the rig loose and brought him home. Now that's all I've done, except feed him right along with the other stock. So don't begrudge me a chance to show how grateful I am to have Tom back. His ma and me love him more than anything."

For a long while, Susan looked into the man's face. She saw sincerity there...

"Mr. Hawkins," she said at last, "I'll be happy to accept."

Hawkins grinned and shoved a hand into his pocket. "Good! I got the papers for you... the ones from the sheriff to say I own the critter and one saying I'm giving him to you."

Susan took the proffered pages, holding them tight in her fist. "I don't know what to say..."

"Say nothing. I'd give you the saddle too, but it's a wreck. Sad thing too... looked to be a nice rig, but the critter must have rolled on it, and tried to get free of it by rubbing up against anything he could find. I kept the thing, but I don't reckon there's enough left to repair."

Susan looked across the rails of the corral and watched the buckskin wander away from the other animals.

"Brother Mitchell has a good saddle," she answered quietly. "You needn't worry about that. In fact, I think he's gone over to the Emma mine, so his tack will be gone. Do you have a hackamore I could borrow for a while? I'd like to walk the buckskin down to the boarding house and surprise Collin when he comes back from the mine."

"I think I've got a hack somewhere around here," Hawkins replied. "I think your husband will be pleased," he added. "I've ridden that animal a couple of times a week to keep him in shape. He's a good animal."

Minutes later, the buckskin was ready. Susan held the lead in her hand and was about to leave when Nathan Hawkins carried a dusty rig from a back room and dumped it unceremoniously on a table near the open doors of the stable. Sunlight poured through the doorway as Hawkins pushed odds and ends to one side and splayed stirrups and chinch leather to either side.

"I thought I'd take another look at the thing," he explained. "I haven't looked it over since last fall. Sort of wrote it off as good for nothing but the parts I might scavenge from it."

Susan paused and watched as Hawkins lifted, twisted, poked, and prodded the beat-up rig.

"It looks pretty bad," she admitted.

"I reckon so," Hawkins agreed. "Still, I might be able to strip it down a bit and replace the stuff that's ruined."

"It looks as though it was well made to begin with," Susan observed.

"Sure does," Hawkins agreed. "I looked for a maker's mark, but couldn't find anything. There's a number of sorts stamped on one corner of the skirt, but it looks as though it's been dragged across something rough... looks like a number though... a six and a one maybe. I got no idea what that might mean. Simmons thought it might be something put there by the fellow that made it, but I guess he had no luck figuring it out."

Susan rubbed the tip of her finger across the surface of the skirt, feeling the smoothness of finished leather blend into a roughened surface that felt as though it had been dragged across ragged stone.

"The year it was made?" she suggested thoughtfully.

"Maybe," Hawkins replied. "Maybe not...."

Chapter 18

Utah Territory
Deep Creek Mountains—June 1869

The descent down the main shaft of the Emma mine was like a ride into the depths of Hell, and Mitchell hated every moment of the trip. The platform on which he stood was no larger than a good sized kitchen table, and though more sturdily built, it groaned under their weight, creaked ominously, and scraped unhappily against the walls of the shaft in a slow, foot-by-foot crawl into the blackness below.

Light from their lamps flickered. The platform rocked and swayed, and a death-like grip on the platform's metal frame soon left Mitchell's hand cramped and aching.

"You seem tense," Gromley observed.

"Never liked mines," Mitchell responded unhappily.

"Rather odd that you should own several," Gromley concluded. "Haunting the bowels of the earth would seem to be an occupational hazard, although I found it difficult myself when I first came here."

Mitchell looked down at the platform, imagining the untold depths of the abyss beneath their feet.

"How far down?" he asked.

Gromley shrugged. "About two-hundred eighty feet," he replied. "Don't worry about the lift," he added. "Everything is solid. We raise at least a ton of ore four or five times a shift. We never have any trouble with the lift handling the weight. Henry says they had some trouble getting the mules down, but since then things have gone smoothly."

"The mules acclimated to the lift?" Mitchell suggested.

Gromley was quiet for a moment. "Acclimated…," he parroted. "Now there's a word I haven't heard in a long while… No, the mules didn't acclimate to the lift. The mules never come up," he explained. "Once they're down, they stay down. We keep eight of them down here… two pairs for each tunnel. The grade on either tunnel is pretty low right now. About three-hundred feet along the main tunnel, the number one drift has a forty foot vertical drop, so we have another lift at that point, and another pair of mules at the bottom.

"The mules walk through the platform to the opposite side. They're unhitched with the cart parked on the platform. The full cart goes up; an empty cart comes down. The mules don't get much of a break, but neither do the men."

Mitchell listened to the sound of the creaking pulleys on the framework above their heads and wished for daylight and open space. He knew it was a trip he had to make, but he could think of nothing that could make him enjoy any part of it.

When they reached the bottom of the shaft, Gromley opened the gate and stepped out onto the foot wall. "Watch your head," he advised, pointing upward toward the ceiling of the tunnel. "Hanging wall," he instructed. "Foot wall," he added, pointing at the floor. "The hanging wall can have some ragged edges, and a fellow can bang his head pretty good. I've done it a time or two… bled like a stuck pig… hurt like blazes too."

Mitchell, raised his lamp and peered down the tunnel to where the light simply disappeared into the blackness beyond its reach. "How far?" he asked stoically.

"Not far," Gromley replied. "Quarter of a mile… maybe a little more."

"Anyone working the face right now?" Mitchell asked.

"Two drillers and couple of muckers loading the ore carts. We're between shots, so we're okay for now. We'll make two more shots before Ramsay sends in a crew to set timbers in place to shore up everything."

Gromley led the way with Mitchell close on his heels, counting their steps. At six hundred and fifty three paces, the passageway split—one fork bearing to the right and dipping sharply downward, the other angling ten degrees to the left and maintaining a level grade as far as Mitchell's light could penetrate.

"We'll take the left hand," Gromley advised.

"I counted about six-hundred and fifty paces," Mitchell said. "Short paces though… I figure about thirteen-hundred feet."

"And another eight-hundred to the face," Gromley added.

"And the other tunnel?"

Gromley shrugged. "Another twelve-hundred feet to the face… give or take some. It runs deeper because that's the vein we've been following since Henry bought the claim a little over a year ago. Henry hired Ramsay last fall—just before I bought in. Ramsay was the one who spotted this vein. We started following it last November. It's been producing small but steady amounts of gold for several months now."

Gromley moved on, following the passageway for another six-hundred feet before he stopped. "This is it," he announced.

Mitchell held his lamp at arm's length, examining the walls and the new timbers supporting the hanging wall. "You're sure this is the place?"

"Pretty much… Deputy Simmons took a pick to the wall just there," Gromley said pointing to a crudely shaped *X* pecked into a flat surface with the pointed tip of a pick.

"He wanted it marked just in case he had to come back down and look at the place again. Can't say it looks anything like it did then. The face was just about here... and the pocket was about where you're standing."

Mitchell looked down at his feet and the damp muck clinging to his boots. Overhead, the dampness collected on the fractured rocks, seeped down onto the supporting cross beams and dripped slowly to the floor.

"That's some nasty smelling water," he observed.

"Probably the sulfides in the rock," Gromley suggested.

"Smells like horse piss," Mitchell muttered as he brushed stray droplets from the back of his hand and stepped away from the dripping liquid.

"Do you get a lot of water down here?"

Gromley shrugged. "We've been lucky... no water... no battles to pump the stuff out."

Once again, Mitchell lifted the kerosene lamp and examined walls, floor, and ceiling.

"Not much to see," Gromley suggested quietly.

"Not much," Mitchell agreed. "How do you think they did it?" he asked.

Gromley shook his head. "You mean Deagan and Williams?"

"Who else could have done it?" Mitchell countered.

"Maybe the muckers were in on it," Gromley suggested. "They could have hidden the body in an empty cart. Deagan and Williams could have done the rest."

"They might have," Mitchell conceded, "except for one thing."

"What's that?"

"Deputy Simmons says the body was nothing but bones wrapped in some rotted clothing. The whole thing came to pieces as soon as they tried to move it. I don't see how Deagan and Williams or the muckers could have moved it anywhere and kept it all in one piece."

Gromley shook his head. "Well, it didn't just pop out of nowhere like a rabbit out of a damned hat!" He barked. "*Someone* put it there!"

"But that raises another kind of problem," Mitchell countered.

"What kind of problem?"

"No one could have known that face shot would open up that little pocket... not even Deagan and Williams. Williams is dead, but Deagan swears up and down that they had nothing to do with it. If that's true, I don't see how anyone could have brought the body in without someone taking notice. Deagan claims no one else came near the face before or after the shot. So, unless the body was hidden near the face and was somehow sucked into the pocket by the force of the shots, I'm out of ideas."

Gromley shook his head. "The force of the shots throws everything out away from the face," he replied. "I doubt anything was *sucked* back into the pocket."

Mitchell shrugged. "Just a thought," he confessed.

Gromley lifted his lamp until his knuckles touched the ragged surface of the hanging wall. "Are we finished here?" he asked irritably.

"I'd like to see how they drill the face," Mitchell responded.

"That's another two-hundred feet," Gromley advised. "Are you feeling up to it, or do you still have the jitters?"

"Still jittery, but I think I should take a look anyway."

"Fine.... Just remember if you start acting strange, I'll have one of the muckers knock you on the head and haul you out on one of the carts."

Gromley turned and led the way down the passage. Mitchell followed the shorter man who waddled along in the dimness, his tin lamp thrust forward at arm's length, casting a shadowy parody of the man on the walls of the tunnel.

Thirty paces... The smell of damp earth faded and the smell of burnt powder grew heavier.

Forty paces... Gromley transformed into a silhouette veiled in a glowing haze of smoke.

Sixty paces.... The smoke cleared, and the four men near the face of the tunnel turned and faced Gromley. Gromley raised his lamp to one side and examined four dust-coated faces. "Morning men," he greeted. "Are we making good progress?"

The oldest of the four glared into the brightness cast by the two lamps and shrugged. "Well enough," he replied sullenly. "The kid here is learnin' quick, but he slows us down a bit. Takes time to build up a fellow's arm for swingin' a jack."

"I expect so," Gromley agreed. "Think you're up to the challenge, young man?"

The miner in question stepped out of the shadows and looked directly at Mitchell. "Not exactly what I expected," the Pratt kid confessed. "Quiet... like a tomb... except for the racket *we* make drillin' and blastin'."

"You're new to this kind of work?" Mitchell inquired casually.

"Just this morning," the Pratt kid responded. "Ain't sure I'm suited for it though. Pretty tight quarters down here. A fellow can't hardly move without crowdin' his neighbor... and the shadows...."

"Now don't start that," growled the older miner.

"Shadows?" Mitchell parroted.

"The kid's got the jitters," the older man answered. "Happens to a lot of new fellows. They get scared of the dark an' start seein' things what ain't there... shadows an' stuff whisperin'..."

"Ghosts," muttered the Pratt kid.

"Jitters," the miner argued.

"Too constricted for me," Mitchell confessed. "Makes me edgy. I can understand how a fellow's imagination could take hold and run away."

The Pratt kid frowned and shook his head silently.

"It'll pass," Gromley chuckled. "You seen everything you came to see?" he asked Mitchell.

Mitchell raised his lamp and let his eyes scan the chamber beyond the miners and the half-filled ore cart.

"It's called a stope," Gromley volunteered. "Just a chamber that's larger than the tunnel itself."

"A natural chamber?" Mitchell asked.

"Sometimes," Gromley replied. "Sometimes we create one ourselves, because the surrounding rock is shattered, and can't be shored up easily. We expand the area until we find more stable rock for the timbers. Sometimes we get lucky and the vein we're following branches out. Then we open things up a bit, so we don't miss anything."

Suddenly, Mitchell felt an icy chill, as though the frozen breath of glacial wind stabbed through his jacket, biting at his flesh. "I think I've seen enough," he said quietly.

* * *

"How was your trip to the Emma mine?" Susan asked.

"Not much to see," Mitchell admitted. "The mine goes straight down for about two-hundred feet. They have a head-frame and a hoist that will handle the weight of an ore cart and a couple of men, if you crowd them on the platform. At the bottom, they've opened up a good sized chamber with several short cross-cuts they're using as stalls for the mules that pull the ore carts....

"We followed the main tunnel for about five-hundred feet before we came to a drift on the left. We turned off and followed that one. The drift ran downward at about twenty degree angle at that point.... One place was nearly thirty degrees.... looked like they had to use block and tackle there to help the mules get the loaded carts up or down the grade.

"We were probably twelve-hundred feet from the main shaft when Gromley claimed we were at the exact spot where they found the body. Of course they had gone on following whatever vein they were chasing, and the face of the drift was somewhere farther along."

"Was there anything helpful there?" Susan asked.

"No. Solid walls...roof...floor...timbers in all the usual places...a little water on the floor. I asked about the water. I wondered if they were having any trouble with water, because I had heard that the Comstock mines were having a lot of trouble trying to pump water fast enough to keep operating.

"Gromley says they haven't had any trouble yet... a little seepage in places, but nothing invasive. Anyway, it all looked like you would expect, and I couldn't see any way Williams and Deagan could have taken the body down there unnoticed and faked its discovery. They might have slipped it into an empty ore cart, but there were two other miners with them from the time they rode the hoist down until the time they had drilled the face and were ready to shoot."

Susan raised an eyebrow. "It doesn't sound as though you think they did it."

Mitchell shrugged. "I don't know how they could have done it," he admitted. "I really need to talk with Deagan again and find out what he thinks. I asked Gromley about Deagan. Ramsay fired Deagan and had two other fellows working the face. I asked them a couple of questions, but it was pretty obvious they knew little that was helpful. They didn't even know why they were working the face instead of Deagan and Williams.

"They did vouch for them... claimed they were both fellows you could trust... argued there was no way Deagan and Williams could get anything like a body in or out of the Emma."

"Do you believe them?"

"I think I have to. The place is like a fortress…guards everywhere. Guards at the gate check everyone in and out. Guards at the head-frame check everyone going down or coming up out of the mine. There were no guards down in the mine itself. I guess they figure they have guards enough up above. But there were too many men down below…It would be nearly impossible to move a dead body around unless there were others in on the deal."

Susan smiled. "Nearly impossible?"

"They might have found a way to get the body down to the face, but they could never get it past the guards at the head-frame… unless the guards were in on it."

"Do you think they were in on it?"

Mitchell frowned and shook his head. "I doubt it… I really doubt it."

Chapter 19

Utah Territory Deep Creek Mountains—June 1869

The morning sun was a cold, white flare cutting across the tops of the Onaqui Mountains and bathing the Deep Creek Range in a dim contrast of shadow and light. Mitchell sat quietly, feeling the chill of the morning air seep through his jacket until his skin grew cold and his body shuddered as it fought to regain the warmth that had vanished so suddenly.

His cheeks prickled; his toes felt stiff and frozen, and his thumbs had turned to thick unfeeling stubs. At the moment, he wanted nothing more than to climb back into the saddle and ride home. It had been bitterly cold when he left the boarding house in the hours just before daylight. He had worn a heavier coat and ridden from town directly up the road leading to the Emma mine. He had intended to question Gromley about the wagons, but that idea had fizzled and died when wagons from the Emma had turned up the mountain towards Barrett's claims. Now his coat was tied to the buckskin's saddle, and the animal was hitched in the clearing near Barrett's Lost Crow mine. The wind had grown cold suddenly, and though his fleece-lined jacket kept out most of the chill, it was no barrier against the icy wind rolling across the ridge-tops. Cold and uncomfortable, he waited and watched the men toiling on the rocky slopes below.

The men moved quickly, making numerous trips from the base of the cliffs to the two wagons waiting on the trail below. There was no doubt as to what these men were up to, and Mitchell was more than a little angry as each of the men entered the mouth of the mine below and returned bearing heavily laden burlap sacks and loaded them into the wagons. The process was quickly done, and in less than thirty minutes, the job was finished and the men gathered near the wagons, talking, rolling cigarettes, and watching the road as though waiting for someone.

Quietly, Mitchell waited, watching the men and studying the cliff and the open mouth of what could only be Barrett's Polecat claim—the claim Mitchell had not yet taken the time to investigate.

The cliffs were small, less than twenty feet high and no more than a hundred feet across—a wall of dark stone streaked with the rust-colored stains of iron oxide and thrusting up out of the pinion covered mountainside.

Mitchell had no doubt that these men had jumped Barrett's claim and were even now hauling away more than a ton of ore. He had no idea how often this had occurred, but the swiftness of the process and the smoothness of its execution made it certain that this was not the first time.

Mitchell took a deep breath, inhaling the sharp scent of the pines and exhaling ever-so-slowly in the way Sarah insisted he breathe when he felt a hot anger burning within—three deep breaths—with the focus of his thoughts turned to something other than the thing that had angered him. When he was finished, he looked down on the wagons with a different view.

The wagons belonged to the Desert Range Mining Company, and that company was owned by Forestall and Gromley. According to Susan, Forestall had offered the Barrett girl five-thousand dollars for a seventy-five percent share in the Barrett claims. Forestall had also revealed Gromley's intent to file on Barrett's lapsed claims. Now, Desert Range employees were openly mining the Polecat claim. Mitchell knew that none of the claims had lapsed. Barrett's annual assessment work had been up-to-date at the time of his disappearance, so there was no possibility that Desert Range had any legal right to take ore out of the mine. Yet they were here, and they had been taking ore out of the mine for some time.

"Looks like they're stealin' your gold."

Mitchell flinched. "Dangit, Mort! You gotta stop doin' that!"

"Can't help it," the old man grumbled. "You took my horse... put me on foot. I always was a quiet walker."

"You've got another horse," Mitchell argued.'

"Well she's a quiet walker too."

The old man hunkered down beside Mitchell, snapped off a twig of sagebrush and stuck the twig in his mouth. "You gonna collect them fellers?" he asked thoughtfully.

"You're the collector here," Mitchell responded coldly. "Ain't my calling."

"You could run 'em off," the old man suggested casually.

"I could," Mitchell agreed, "but then I'd have no hope of discovering what Gromley and Forestall are up to."

"They're after stealing your gold," the old man insisted.

"They're after more than that," Mitchell countered.

"You figure they killed Barrett?" The old man asked.

Mitchell glared down on the wagons. "I don't know... maybe...."

"I don't see no horses," the old man said thoughtfully.

"They have them tied in a clearing just below us," Mitchell explained.

The old man frowned. "So when them fellers leave, they're gonna come right over this way."

"And we'll be over the ridge and gone before they ever get near us," Mitchell argued.

"Sounds like a piss-poor plan to me."

"Make a better suggestion," Mitchell growled.

"Too late," the old man grumbled. "Looks like someone's comin' up the trail."

Mitchell watched as the rider slowly approached. The men at the wagon waited, yet seemed tense as the man drew near, and one of them slipped a pistol from a coat pocket and held it at his side where the rider could not see it. Fifty feet from the miners, the rider stopped and removed his hat.

Mitchell strained to see the man's face, but the distance was too great.

"Looks familiar, but I can't see good enough to tell who he is," he complained. "I'll have to get closer."

"Don't be stupid," the old man growled. "You start movin' around, and they're gonna see you plain as day. And them fellers ain't gonna react well when they find you been watchin' 'em."

"I'll be real careful about it," Mitchell argued.

"Not a good idea," the old man countered. "Where's them field glasses I seen you packin' around?"

"Up in my saddle-bags."

"Well ain't that a right handy place for 'em!"

"Didn't figure I needed them when I came down here," Mitchell objected.

"Seems to me you'll live longer if you go get them glasses."

For a moment, Mitchell considered his options. There was a good chance that he could get close enough to see the rider, but there was an even greater chance that he would be seen. And with nearly a dozen men near the wagon, his chances of survival were slim.

Quietly, he abandoned his hideout and turned away from the mine, working his way from one pinion to the next until he reached a point where his movements were no longer visible to the men below. Near the crest of the ridge, he turned onto a narrow game trail and followed it all the way to the clearing where he had left the roan tied to the broken-off stub of a dead pine.

The roan stood patiently as Mitchell rummaged through the saddle-bags, searching for the leather case that held his field glasses. His fingers had hardly touched the leather when something smashed him from behind, slamming him into the roan's side and hammering his face against the thick leather of the saddle's skirt and the hard metal curve of the rear rigging ring. For an instant, the world fell into blackness as he slammed down hard against the stone covered ground.

Reality twisted.

"Kill him," demanded a distant voice.

Pain stabbed through his shoulder as a boot heel stomped hard on his shoulder.

"No shooting!" roared the voice. "Beat him senseless, and throw him off the cliff where Barrett dumped his tailings. We don't want that damn deputy snooping around. Make it look like he fell off the cliff and into the rocks."

Through the haze, Mitchell felt a boot connect with his ribs. Pain shot through his side. He fought the darkness and rolled beneath the roan and away from his assailants. His mind sluggish, he struggled for clarity.

Three of them…

The thought was dull, barely comprehensible.

Get away…

He struggled to his knees… and came face to face with an attacker.

With the bulk of the roan above them, Mitchell grabbed at the stirrup and slapped the animal's flank. Already agitated, Milo twisted away from the striking hand, jerking at the reins and stomping wildly. The man on the ground cried out as a hoof came down hard, grinding against the stony ground, crushing flesh and bone into a mangled semblance of a hand.

The roan reared back. A branch snapped, and the reins came free of the stump. The roan twisted away from Mitchell, slamming the remaining attackers and sending them staggering away towards the rim of the cliffs. Stubbornly, Mitchell clung to the stirrup, and when the roan eased its stomping dance, he dragged himself into the saddle and kicked the animal into a run.

A shot from behind exploded in the brush, hurling bits of wood and bark into the roan's face. The animal leaped forward, plowing through a tangle of oak brush and down the ridge, out of range and out of sight.

Chapter 20

Utah Territory
Deep Creek Mountains—June 1869

Susan touched her boot heels to the mare's sides, urging the animal up the steep talus covered slope behind the town. From the first, the narrow trail winding up the hillside had been rugged, yet they had struggled in only the worst places—places where the trail simply disappeared and the mare was forced to cross hard, uneven ground with barely a hoof's breadth of level ground.

There were no trees. The hillside was barren of all vegetation, and far below, she could see the weathered buildings of the town and the tiny figures standing on the boardwalks watching her progress towards the ridgetop. Now and then, a finger stabbed pointedly in her direction or a hat removed from a head, shading the eyes that probed for a better view of her precarious ascent.

Her own eyes were much busier, as they flashed from the thin ribbon of trail to her horse's feet and back again, instantly assessing each step the animal made and hunting for better ground. When better ground came, Susan Flitton Mitchell was a nervous wreck.

"That was the stupidest thing you have ever done!" she hissed angrily. "Why ever did you come this way when you knew there was a perfectly good trail running past the Forestall house?"

She knew the answer to that question, and despite her anxiety over the more dangerous route, she was reluctant to have either Forestall or Gromley aware of her destination. For reasons she could not explain, she had no trust for either man, and when she crossed the rim of the ridge, she felt a measure of relief. She was invisible to the town now—invisible to curious eyes that watched, lost to minds that meddled, mute to lips that spread the word. Now the windmill lay ahead on a flat spot below the ridge.

The dirty canvas vanes, rounded and stiff in a light breeze, turned lazily with the soft low clatter of wooden gears, and the mountain was quiet, save for the sound of the gears and steel-shod hooves plodding the rocky trail to the mill. No one was in sight. There was nowhere for riders to hide, unless they and their horses were all hidden inside the rock structure that housed the milling equipment. If they hid in the pinions, they were well out of sight and lost to her view.

The fact that the place was deserted was certainly true to Henry Forestall's description of the place, but Forestall could not be telling the truth, if Miranda Barrett was correct in her opinion that the mill ran at least twice a week.

But why would Forestall lie?

The windmill seemed innocuous enough. And why would riders chase two children off of the mountain and all the way into the foothills. And why kill them? The whole incident made no sense.

The mill was a strange conglomeration of wood and stone, thrown together in a manner that made it plain that the builders had worked with the materials at hand, creating a box-like structure of stone and mortar topped by a tall tower of interlocked timbers supporting the frame work of four canvas vanes.

The tower itself was reminiscent of the gun towers Susan had seen scattered up and down the valley from

Provo to Manti—towers constructed as defensive fortifications against the Ute chief Antonga Black Hawk and his raiders. Many of those towers were gone now, their stone and wood scavenged for better uses when an ailing Black Hawk had finally made peace.

The tall vanes of the mill turned slowly, growing larger and taller as she approached, until the top-most point was more than thirty feet above her head when she finally dismounted and stood at the heavily chained door of the box-like structure.

"Why the chain and the lock?" She wondered aloud.

Forestall's claim that they locked the place to keep children out felt untrue, and the fact that Tommy Hawkins and Debbie Allingham had wandered up here in no way supported Forestall's claim. In fact, she found it difficult to imagine that children were of much concern for the owners of the Desert Range Mining Company.

Slowly, she circled the building. She found four windows, all of them set too high for easy access, though they were large enough for her to squeeze through had she been inclined to do such a thing. But there were two doors.

Thoughtfully, she turned her mount back to the rear of the building. Something was different here. The stone construction was the same, yet the base of the tower did not extend to the roof of this part of the structure, and the mortar between the stonework looked newer, as if this shed-like extension had been added at a later time. And there were two chimneys.

"Two chimneys," She muttered. "Why two chimneys?"

Surely the one attached to the main structure would be used to heat the mill while it was in use in the cold of winter. But the second chimney was attached to a side wall of the extension, while an oddly sized door stood near the back corner of the opposite wall. Intrigued, Susan stepped close to inspect the heavy panels of the door.

The planks were thick and roughly sawn, with each plank still bearing the striations created by the circular blade that had cut them. The door, abnormally wide and barely as high as her shoulders hung from heavy iron hinges and was secured by a wrought iron latch-bar and catch. There was no lock.

For an instant, she felt anxious. No one was around, and she wanted desperately to lift the bar and see what lay beyond the rough-hewn door. Yet she held back, halted by a vague uneasiness that made her hair stand on end. It was as though something unseen watched and waited for her to open the door.

Quickly, she turned away from the door, gathered up the reins, and led her mount into the thickest of the nearby pinions. She was hardly out of sight when three men rode up out of the gully to the west. Two of them dismounted and went to the locked door of the mill.

The taller of the pair—an unshaven fellow in a sweat-stained hat and a faded green shirt—produced a key, opened the lock, and stripped the chain from the heavy iron latch.

"Gather up all the moulds and the dies," he told his companion. "We'll take them down to the house and stash them there for now."

Ten minutes later, the men were gone, retreating down the mountain in the direction from which they had come. Susan waited impatiently in the trees, fidgeting, but forcing herself to wait just a few more minutes to ensure that the men were truly gone and not hidden, unseen in the trees, waiting for her to emerge from concealment.

She had no patience for this kind of game. Her nature was to act—sometimes impulsively and too swiftly for

Sarah's liking, but she had never broken the habit and found a waiting game almost intolerable. Quietly, she stroked her horse's neck.

"I'd rather have a bee sting," she told the animal.

The animal ignored her complaint and pressed its muzzle to her shoulder. Half-heartedly, she shoved the animal away.

"Stop that!"

Cautiously, she led the mare from the trees to the front of the mill. There, she found the chain and the lock dumped in the dirt beside the half-open door.

"Now, they leave the place open so just anyone can walk right in." She looked back at the mare. "Like me," she whispered.

Quickly, she slipped inside, stepping into the dimness where the only light illuminating the mill filtered through dirty windows and the door that stood open behind her. Inside, the mill seemed normal to her inexperienced eye. She had heard stories of large circular blades spinning at unbelievable speeds, ripping lengths of huge rough-cut boles, transforming massive trunks into heavy timbers, planks, and smaller lumber. Chips, shavings, and dust covered the floor and the interior of the building fairly reeked with the heady odor of pine. And oddly enough, a faint metallic taste drifting on the air.

"Now what could that be?" She wondered.

Much of the milling equipment was constructed of wood. She saw metal parts here and there... things she knew... things whose function she could guess... gears, pulleys, pins, hooks, the huge blade....

All of these fit her vision of a sawmill. Yet that metallic flavor was odd and fit with nothing she could identify.

Cautiously, she sniffed the air. Nothing... only a faint acrid taste on her tongue.

Slowly, she made her way towards the back of the mill, wondering with each step how the raw timber had been loaded on the conveyor and fed to the huge blade. With walls on every side, it would have been impossible to accomplish the task.

"What are you up to, Mr. Forestall?"

She reached the rear of the building and discovered a partial answer to her questions. Here, the ramp-like conveyor had been dismantled. Parts and pieces lay heaped in one corner, and it was obvious that the conveyor had once extended beyond the wall. What lay beyond the wall she could only guess, and she turned away resolving to discover what lay beyond the heavy outer door at the rear of the newer addition.

As she turned away, her hip bumped a long work table that took up nearly half the length of the back wall—a table lined with more than a dozen small rectangular bowls made of clay.

Overwhelmed with curiosity, she walked the length of the table examining the extent of its contents. What she saw was inexplicable.

Each of the fifteen containers held a murky gray solution, and from each container ran two wires that looped around a long dowel that ran the length of the table above the containers. And like a glittering spider web of metal strands, the wires ran carefully to the wall and a large wooden plaque lined with flat metal levers.

From the levers, like clothes lines ready for hanging the morning wash, two thick wires crossed the room and attached to a mysterious machine. To her untrained eye, the wires resembled the telegraph lines she had seen running here and there about the valley, and for a moment, she wondered why Forestall and Gromley would build their own telegraph.

But there were no telegraph lines strung across the mountain and no logical purpose for a telegraph connection on top of a mountain in the middle of nowhere.

No. This was something else—something altogether different, something new to her experience, something she had never seen before.

The machine was large and cumbersome, taller and wider than her out-stretched arms, and if it had not been built where it stood, it would have taken a freight wagon and many men to set it in place. Its design was alien. Yet in some ways it resembled a smaller version of a riverboat's paddle wheel, only these paddles were constructed not of wood, but of looped and coiled copper wire.

To Susan, the machine made only the vaguest of sense, and she left the mill with her thoughts in a tangle—a tangle that only intensified as she came to the back of the building and passed beyond the rough wooden door and into the blackness of a room filled with coal.

A coal bin…

She had not expected coal. Coal was expensive, and few people considered it worth the cost with good firewood so easily accessible.

Especially in a sawmill!

The thought fairly screamed in her mind. Any sawmill would have an abundance of useable firewood, and coal would be unnecessary… unless….

The idea came suddenly, and she worked her way carefully across the room, shuffling her feet and scuffing stray chunks of the black rock from her path until she reached another door and threw it open, revealing the forge beyond.

Now, she understood the need for coal, and the purpose of the leather belts that fed through the wall from the mill to the bellows now at rest near the cold, unlit forge.

But why have a forge here?

It was too distant from the Emma to be of practical use for any iron-work they might need at the mine. And the town had its own forge and blacksmith.

Cautiously, she moved about the dimly lit room deliberately examining its contents for anything that might explain what Tommy Hawkins and Debbie Allingham had found to cause them so much grief. She was certain they had found something… seen something …. Yet she saw little here that seemed unusual… the forge, a bellows, an anvil, various hammers, tongs, and several cast iron ladles coated with a dull gray substance—a substance she thought she knew.

Thoughtfully, she picked up one of the ladles and dragged a fingernail across the bottom of the cup.

"Lead," she murmured quietly as she considered the scratch left by her fingernail.

She was almost certain the gray substance was lead. She could think of no other metallic substance of that color that could be scratched by a fingernail. Graphite perhaps, but she felt certain that this was not graphite, and silver might tarnish to such a color, but she was uncertain if silver was soft enough to be scratched so easily.

The outer door slammed with a sudden violence that startled her and set her heart to pounding. The narrow shaft of light that had penetrated through both doorways winked out, and she heard the ring of metal on metal as the latch bar slammed home. Then came the clanging of metal hammering metal, and she knew someone had just flattened the iron catch, making it impossible to lift the bar and trapping her within the confines of the forge.

For a long moment, she stood still, letting her eyes adjust to the near blackness of the room and fighting a sudden and uncontrollable terror of being trapped. Her thoughts rushed about in a near panic, yet she stood perfectly still, frozen like a young doe, startled and unable to choose which direction to run.

She wanted to run. More than anything she wanted to be out of this place and into the light. She had never liked the darkness. Her heart had always craved the light of day and the clear blue skies of summer. Quietly, she took a deep breath, letting it out slowly like a deep sigh.

Calmness, or a least something resembling calmness, came down like a warm shawl, enveloping her like Mitchell's protecting arms, and she could almost feel him there behind her, leaning close against her, holding her, his lips close to her ear, whispering that everything would be all right. And there was light. Not the bright light of day. Rather, it was a dim glow that filtered down from the wall behind her—light diffused from the mill through a small opening that had once been a window, where now a leather belt passed through the wall to the mechanism that ran the bellows and back again through the opening and into the mill.

Calmly, she studied the opening. It was small, perhaps less than two feet on a side and easily fifteen feet above the floor. It *was* a way out, if she was willing to do some unladylike squeezing to the other side. But first she needed a way to reach the opening.

A quick search of the forge revealed nothing that would act as a ladder—nothing loose that could be stacked or piled against the wall, giving her away to climb within reach of the opening. The place was simply clear of anything useful to her needs. Only one thing seemed useful, and she had resigned herself to the task of moving and stacking chunks of coal—piece by piece from the coal room to the wall—until she remembered the leather belts—belts that led right to the opening and beyond. All she needed to do was shinny up the belts and through the opening.

Excited at the prospect of escape, she reached up and grasped the lower segment of the belt and lifted her feet from the floor. The belt sagged under her weight; the pulley turned; gears rotated, pumping the bellows and filling the air with powdery gray ash from the forge. Susan drifted downward with the belt until her knees rested upon the floor.

Determinedly, she got to her feet, searching for a way to lock the gears and keep the belt from moving. If she was going to climb the thing like a monkey, the gears had to be immobilized. It took some time, but she finally found what she needed—a hammer and a pinch-point in the gears. Moments later, she jammed the handle of the hammer between the gears, jamming them tightly.

Again, she dangled from the belts. Nothing moved.

"All or nothing…," she muttered anxiously.

Resigned to her plan, she pulled herself upward, wrapped her legs around the belts, and began the upward climb. Immediately, she found the belt was too wide to grip like a rope and too flat for her hands to gain a secure hold. Halfway to the top her hands began to cramp with the unfamiliar chore.

The flat surface of the belt was wide and slick and twisted awkwardly if she did not slide both hands simultaneously and catch the belt perfectly. Carefully she moved upward an arm's length at a time. Three feet from the opening, the belt twisted and she lost her grip.

Suddenly, she found herself hanging head downward, her legs clamped tightly to the belt, her skirts reversed and draped like a bell from her waist to her head.

"That's just dandy!" she exclaimed, realizing how unladylike she must appear at the moment.

"Collin would tease me to death if he saw me like this."

Her legs slipped a little on the belt, and the room swung dizzily. She closed her eyes, blocking her view of the floor twelve feet below. When her awkward swinging ceased, she opened her eyes.

"Now what are you going to do?" She muttered angrily. "You can't hang here like a bat forever."

Unhappily, she started swinging again, rocking back and forth until at last she thrust herself upward, flinging her arms around the belts, hugging them tightly, her arms across the belts, her hands clinging to opposite sides. Stable at last, she crawled up the belts.

Within minutes, she reached the opening and squeezed through to the other side. Ten minutes later, she recovered her horse and rode down the mountain toward Henry Forestall's house.

Chapter 21

Utah Territory
Deep Creek Mountains—June 1869

Susan reined in the mare and looked down on two of the scruffiest looking men she had ever seen. The two were hunched over a bedraggled form on the ground—a form she recognized instantly.

In less than two seconds, she yanked the Smith & Wesson from her handbag and centered its sights on the back of the taller man's head, just a little above the collar of his shirt. The click of the cocking hammer cut through the silence of the lonely canyon.

"Get away from him, or there won't be enough left of your head to bury with your corpse!"

Without hesitation, she shifted the pistol and touched the trigger. Bark exploded from a tree near the man's head. The tall man threw himself backward, away from the tree and flung his hands above his head.

"Good Lord, missy! Don't shoot! We're only tryin' to help this feller!"

"Back away or you'll need more help than he does!"

Franticly, both men scrambled to their feet and backed away as Susan dismounted and hurried to Mitchell's side. She saw the blood on his face, and his clothing looked as though he had been dragged through the dirt.

"He ain't dead ma'am. Olaf and me could see that right away. He looks pretty beat up, but he's breathin' okay."

Susan frowned, examining the pair. Neither looked as though they had been in a fight, and if they had done this to Collin, she was certain they would have been in worse condition than they were.

"You found him this way?" She demanded.

"Just before you rode up. We saw him fall from his horse, right there."

Cautiously, she decocked the revolver. "Give me a hand then."

Both men dropped their hands and came back to kneel beside Mitchell.

"Looks like he's been in a brawl," the tall one observed. "But we've seen him in worse shape and come off okay."

"You know him?"

"Captain Mitchell? Sure... from the Legion. We was with him down to Nine Mile Canyon when the Utes shot him up somethin' fierce." The tall man stuck out his hand. "My name's McDaniel. This is my cousin Olaf Jorgen. He's just come from Sweden, so he don't talk much, but he's an okay fellow."

"The Legion.... You must be Mormons then."

"Yes ma'am, from over Provo way. We work for the telegraph company, checkin' lines and fixin' breaks and such."

Susan took Mitchell's head in her lap and brushed his hair back from his face. "There's a canteen of water on my saddle," she said anxiously. "Would you bring it, please?"

McDaniel turned to his cousin. "Olaf, get the water, will you?"

"There are no telegraph lines out here," Susan pointed out.

"Not many anyways," McDaniel replied. "There's a line out to Gold Hill, I think, but that's about it. Most of our work has been out east of here in the Wasatch Mountains and over into the south slope of the Uintahs—up where the snow gets deep and weighs down the lines.

They break from the weight of the snow and ice, and the telegraph company sends Olaf and me out to fix 'em. We check in at the telegraph office every day, and they tell us if we've got a broken connection.

"Sometimes, we've got nothin' to do for weeks on end. Summertime is real slow, so now and then, we have a couple of youngsters in the family take over for a spell, while Olaf and me do something else to make a living. The telegraph folks know we can't live on such...."

Mitchell groaned and opened his eyes at the cold wet touch of Susan's dampened skirt. She touched the canteen to his lips, and he drank. For a moment, he lay quietly staring at the sky above and the clouds drifting on the wind high overhead.

"I think they cracked a couple of ribs," he said finally.

"Could have cracked your skull," McDaniel replied.

"Looks like you've been in a brawl," Susan observed.

Mitchell sat up slowly, the palm of one hand pressed against the offending ribs. "Pretty much," he affirmed. With his fingers, he probed gently at the damaged ribs. "I found Barrett's Polecat claim. Some fellows have jumped the claim. I watched them for a while from the hillside above the mine, but when I went back to my horse to get my field glasses, three of them jumped me from behind. I was lucky to get away."

"You look a mess," Susan scolded.

"Your horse is around here somewhere," McDaniel said. "Olaf and me will see if we can find him."

"I should have been more careful," Mitchell admitted, when the two men had gone. "Mort warned me I was in a bad spot. I'm not even sure he got out of there."

"I suspect Mort is doing just fine," Susan replied.

Mitchell raised his left arm, rotating his shoulder in all directions. There was pain, but nothing felt torn.

"How did you find me?" he asked.

"That's something I wanted to discuss right away," she replied. "I found something odd at Forestall's sawmill."

"Sawmill?"

"A sawmill. I told you about it. They have one on the mountain above town. I discovered it yesterday when I was out looking for Tommy and the Allingham girl. I went back today because I couldn't understand why anyone would chase two children down the mountain like that, and I could see absolutely no reason to kill either one of them. So, I went back. I thought I might find some explanation there."

Mitchell listened as Susan explained her adventure and escape from the confines of the forge. By the time she had finished her tale, he had forgotten his own pains.

"Do you think Forestall or Gromley discovered what you were up to and sent those men to take care of you?"

Susan shook her head. "I don't know. Anyone could have sent them. At least a dozen people saw me ride up the mountain. And I suppose all of them know there's a sawmill up there. But those men *did* have a key to that lock, and I can't imagine anyone other than Forestall or Gromley giving it to them."

"Not much we can do about it, I suppose," Mitchell grumbled, "unless you see them again."

Susan sighed tiredly. "Even then, we have no proof that the ones I saw are the ones that locked me inside the forge."

Mitchell nodded, letting his mind pick through the odd events Susan had experienced.

"Those wires intrigue me," he admitted. "Something about them seems familiar, as though I should know what they mean. It has to be something electrical though."

"They were a complete mystery to me," Susan admitted. "But I'm certain they are using that forge to melt down lead," she insisted. "Why…? I don't know."

Mitchell scowled at the mountains, letting his eyes follow the trail of torn up ground where Susan's horse had come down the mountain.

"Wouldn't need coal to melt lead" he said at last. "Easy enough with a regular old wood fire. I've seen fellows cast rifle balls over a campfire. You can get a hotter fire using coal and a bellows though… good for iron work or melting down the good stuff like gold or silver."

The sound of horses came from the trees south of the road, and the two of them watched as the telegraph men made their way through trees and brush down to the road.

The men stopped and looked both ways, searching. Mitchell whistled, and when McDaniel finally located them, Mitchell lifted a hand and waved. A hundred yards down the road, McDaniel responded, lifting his hat in the air and walking slowly up the rutted road.

"What are the two of you doing way out here?" Mitchell demanded when the two men came abreast of them.

McDaniel grinned. "Well… the telegraph work has been kind of slow, so Olaf and me have been doin' a little prospectin'. Been huntin' wolves too. What brings you out here Captain? Last time we seen you was over to Nine Mile Canyon, and last I heard, you was startin' a ranch up near the Strawberry River."

Mitchell took the big man's outstretched hand. "I'm glad to see you fellows are alive and well. This is my wife, Susan. Susan, this fellow is Ryan McDaniel, and this other fellow is his cousin Olaf Jorgen. The two of them were with the Legion down in San Pete County last year."

"Nice to meet you ma'am," McDaniel greeted.

Susan smiled and offered her hand. "I'm sorry I shot at you…"

"Did the Captain teach you to shoot ma'am?"

"Yes, he did."

"Well then! No need to apologize! 'Cause you wasn't shootin' at us at all. If you had, I'd be like that headless horseman fellow the Captain told us about… the one over to Sleepy Hollow."

McDaniel handed over Milo's reins and looked up the road towards the canyon where Barrett's Polecat claim lay hidden. "Olaf and me tried goin' up that canyon a few weeks ago. We got shot at and never went back."

Mitchell frowned, remembering the man with a pistol waiting for the rider who had been coming up the trail to the mine. "I watched them from the ridge east of the mine," he admitted. "They were too far away to recognize anyone."

"Don't know who was up there today," McDaniel confessed, "but I'm certain that fellow Ramsay was there the day *we* were shot at. Him and a fellow I've seen hangin' around down in town."

"Another fellow?"

"Dark haired sort…walks with a bit of a limp."

For a moment, Mitchell was quiet, his mind roaming the town trying to visualize every person he had seen. He hadn't met everyone in town, of that he was certain, and no picture of this man came to mind now.

"I don't remember anyone like that," he admitted finally.

Susan, who had been performing the same mental exercise, shook her head.

"Henry Forestall seems to rely on that cane of his," she pointed out, "but I don't think he limps at all."

McDaniel shook his head. "Naw... We've been around that town a little. It ain't Forestall. I'm sure the fellow who was shootin' at us was stayin' at that boarding house until a few days ago."

Mitchell frowned, and McDaniel took a step backward.

"I seen that scary face before," he complained.

"This fellow with the limp was in charge?" Mitchell demanded.

"Sure looked like it."

Thoughtfully, Mitchell examined their surroundings, and when he found the place he needed, he crossed the hard ground to a place where the earth was free of rocks and covered with deep layers of old leaves and needles. There, he sat and leaned back against the thick bole of a tree.

"Ribs are hurting," he admitted.

"It's a wonder you can stand at all," Susan muttered. "We should get you back to the boardinghouse. You could get some rest there."

Mitchell grunted. "Unless someone blows it up again..."

For a long while, Mitchell was silent. Something prodded at his memory... a paint horse and a rider... seen only from a distance, yet somehow familiar....

"A paint horse...," he blurted out suddenly. "Does he ride a paint horse?"

"One of them splotchy brown and white animals?" McDaniel asked.

"That's the breed," Mitchell replied.

"Can't be certain," McDaniel answered, "but I think he might."

"I've seen a fellow riding a paint," Mitchell confessed. "Up at the Emma mine... the first time I rode up there. I never got a good look at him, but somehow, he seemed familiar."

Susan took Milo's reins and dangled them in front of Mitchell's face.

"Can you ride?" She asked. "Or should I send one of these fellows to fetch the buggy?"

Mitchell struggled to his feet and took the reins. "I think we'll ride," he responded. "That buggy ain't very comfortable."

* * *

An hour later, Sarah looked into Mitchell's scowling face and removed her probing fingers from his ribs. "Stop that!" she scolded. "You're curdling the milk in the kitchen."

"You're breaking my ribs, woman... You can't expect me to smile after jabbing me with your crowbar fingers."

"Your ribs are not broken, although they certainly ought to be… It's a pity you were so careless… Especially after Mort warned you to be careful."

"I was not careless," Mitchell argued defensively. He got to his feet wishing he *had* been more careful. If nothing else, he might have avoided a tongue lashing, though he knew Sarah was not truly angry with him.

"And you!" Sarah turned on her sister and glared into Susan's green eyes. "You wander off without telling anyone and get trapped where no one would find you for days."

"I was not trapped," Susan replied calmly, "and there was nothing there to merit the attempt."

"Nothing you recognized," Sarah argued.

"Moulds and dies…" Susan admitted. "That's all they were after."

"Why lock you up, if they took away the things they didn't want you to find?" Sarah demanded.

"I don't know…. Maybe they forgot something…."

Mitchell stood and pulled on his shirt. For the moment he felt lucky that Sarah's ire had been redirected temporarily, although he knew he would hear more about the subject later.

"Maybe they couldn't take everything away," he suggested. "Maybe they were afraid you had seen something that would give away their secret—something that would tell us why they would chase down a little girl and kill her."

"I found lead," Susan offered sullenly.

"In a ladle," Mitchell added. "If you melt down lead, you generally mold it into some other shape."

"Why would anyone be concerned about molding lead?" Susan argued.

"I don't think they were worried about the lead," Mitchell responded. "I think it was the dynamo."

Chapter 22

Utah Territory
Deep Creek Mountains—June 1869

Allingham's store rocked with a rumbling concussion that sent dust drifting down from the rafters and rattled glassware on every shelf. Mitchell grabbed at a large glass bottle, sweeping it back from the edge of the main counter.

Beth O'Neill's eyes followed the falling dust until it lay like a thin gray blanket on every expose surface.

"That was strange!" she squawked excitedly.

Mitchell shoved the bottle farther back on the counter. "Something wrong?" he asked.

"Wrong...." The woman groaned. "Something has gone wrong up at the Emma mine. We feel the face shots all the time, but those are just little thumps. This was too big. I can't imagine what happened, but something has gone terribly wrong!"

The dark haired woman hurried to the front window, pressing her face to the glass panes, then rushed nervously to the doorway and out onto the creaking planks of the boardwalk.

Mitchell stepped out beside the woman and scowled unhappily. "Your son works at the Emma," he concluded suddenly.

The O'Neill woman turned on Mitchell, wringing her hands frantically "He's a mucker at the Emma... down in the number two tunnel. Mostly, I don't worry much.... He's always back at the lower shaft when the face shots go off, so he's safe enough. But that was no face shot. That was bigger, much bigger."

Mitchell looked down Main Street to where it curved to the West and snaked its way up the mountain to the Emma.

"I think your right," he admitted grimly. "Something feels wrong...."

The feeling of wrongness increased, like the dark clouds of a thunderstorm rolling in, enveloping everything in its path. Mitchell shuddered as a powerful bleakness welled up, turning his thoughts black as a starless sky.

"Four men," he muttered under his breath, the thought burning darkly in his mind. "I'll ride up to the Emma and look for your son," he told the woman.

Tears slid down the woman's cheeks. "He's dead," she groaned. "I know he's dead...."

Mitchell strode down the boardwalk and onto the street. He was near the stables when two men raced around the curve of the road and charged up the street—one heading towards half-a-dozen people crowded around the front of the store, the other making a beeline straight at Mitchell.

"Accident!" The miner blurted out between sucking gasps of air. "They blew up tunnel number two!"

"Anyone hurt?" Mitchell demanded.

"Four men buried... probably all dead!"

"How far down?" Mitchell asked harshly.

The miner looked into Mitchell's face and took a step backward, as though seeing the gunman for the first time.

"Some . . . somewhere near the face..." he stammered.

"How near?" Mitchell demanded.

"I don't know ... We was sent to round up the second shift and bring back every man we can find."

The miner stepped around Mitchell and sprinted up the street to Allingham's store.

The news traveled quickly. People fairly popped out of the buildings lining both sides of the street, questioning one another, searching for someone who could reveal what had happened. Everyone seemed to know that something had gone wrong at the mine, but no one knew the cause of the explosion or the extent of the damage done to the miners working its depths.

What began as a strident clamor for information sank to a grim murmur of disbelief and finally ended in a morbid excitement as men dashed to their homes and tool sheds, snatched up picks and shovels, and returned like soldiers armed for battle. Nearly thirty men were thus armed and marching down the dusty road to the Emma mine by the time Mitchell had Milo saddled and out of the corral behind the stables. Mitchell had a foot in the stirrup when a hand grabbed the back of his belt and held him down.

"You are not going down in that mine, *Brother* Mitchell."

Sarah's voice was sharper than an obsidian blade and as inflexible as Mitchell had ever heard it, and the *Brother Mitchell* tagged on the end of that one sentence killed any thought he might have entertained about going into the Emma mine.

"Daniel was down there," he argued.

"I love that boy like a son," Sarah responded, "but you are not going into the Emma again. I don't care if Brother Brigham himself is down there. I've had a couple of awful dreams in the last day or so. Mostly about men dying of suffocation in a place so pitch black they couldn't see their hands in front of their faces."

"How would that change, if I stay away from the Emma?" Mitchell countered. "Seems like they need plenty of help."

"Don't go down," Sarah begged.

Mitchell glanced toward the mountains and felt a deadness in the air. He had no desire to go down into the confining depths of the Emma. Every fiber of his being rebelled against the idea, yet something compelled him, and he felt jittery, as though he had left something undone.

"I need to do something," he objected.

"Then do something… But don't go down in the Emma. You're no miner anyway. You would only get in their way."

"Fine," Mitchell muttered sullenly. "I'll go out and see what the situation is. I won't go into the mine."

For a moment, Sarah was silent. "Let God show you what to do, Collin," she counseled. "He knows what can be done, even if we don't."

Fifteen minutes later, Mitchell heard the sounds of a galloping horse coming up the road from town. He edged Milo behind a cluster of pinion and waited until the rider came abreast of his hideout.

"I see you found another horse," he called out.

The old man reined in a sorrel colored mare, and let his eyes probe the trees, searching for Mitchell.

"Found her wanderin' down by the Express trail," the old man confessed. "Prevoius owner seems to have met his maker. I figured someone ought to take care of the poor old girl."

"Last owner was too handy with a shotgun," Mitchell answered grimly. "That little girl was all the Allingham's cared about, and Tommy Hawkins is pretty banged up from being chased down the mountain. Sarah was next on their list. Seems to me both of those men were overdue for a good look at the gates of hell."

The old man leaned back in the saddle and scanned the road leading up to the mine where twenty men marched quickly towards the open gate—a gate with no guards.

"No guards," the old man offered.

Mitchell turned Milo back onto the road and led the way through the barbed wire gates and up to the small offices where he had first met Jack Ramsay. Henry Forestall came out of the office and stood on the porch as Mitchell dismounted.

"Guess you heard the explosion," Forestall suggested tiredly. He turned and led the way back into the office where a map of the mine covered the surface of a large table.

"What happened?" Mitchell asked.

"I have no idea," Forestall answered. "The miners tell me that the explosion was five or six times greater than one of the face shots. But no one knows why that much blasting powder would be down there all at once. Other mines do it, but we've had a policy that lets only two shots near the face at any given time. We keep the powder and fuse stored in the bunker out back of the office here.

"We have things worked out so that they have enough powder to shoot the face, but powder for the next shot comes down with the muckers and the empty carts. We have it organized pretty well, and there's never been a problem before."

Mitchell scowled and looked at the map spread out on the table.

"Anyone hurt?" he asked tightly.

"We're not sure," Forestall replied unhappily

"No one was hurt on this side of the collapsed area, but we had two men working the face and two muckers unaccounted for. The two men at the face might be alive, but I suspect the muckers were caught where the hanging wall collapsed. They had the empty ore carts and the explosives for the next face shot."

"How close to the face was the explosion," Mitchell asked.

"Our best calculations put our side of the roof collapse three hundred feet from the face. I'm told that an explosion that large could have brought down the hanging wall all the way to the face."

"So there was no safe place for them? What about air?"

"There was a place where the footwall hit a section of shattered rock and the muckers cleared out a stope twenty feet in diameter. That's where they were working when you and Gromley went down for a look. The face wasn't far beyond that."

"The place I looked at the other day?" Mitchell asked.

"More or less...," Forestall admitted. "They cleared it out right after you left. We're forty feet deeper than we were when you and Frank went down."

"About a hundred feet or so from where that body was found?"

"Thereabouts," Forestall admitted.

Mitchell leaned over the table and studied the map.

"How many men do you have down there now?" he asked.

Forestall frowned. "Ten," he answered. "There's no room for more. We have four breaking up the loose rock, four loading two carts, and two men moving the carts back and forth. It's pretty crowded down there, and they're working as fast as they can. "I've got them on four hour shifts, and I've got four crews now.

Mitchell tapped the map where Forestall had marked the probable extent of the collapse.

"How long?" He demanded.

Forestall glanced from the face of the scowling gunman to the finger tapping the plans of the mine. Sweat came suddenly to his forehead, and his voice shook. "There's no way to know for sure," he responded defensively.

Mitchell looked up from the map and glared into Forestall terrified eyes. "Where is Gromley?"

"I don't know. He should be here, but no one has seen him since you came back to town with that Hawkins kid."

Fifteen minutes later, Mitchell turned the pigeon-toed Milo at the gate and rode down towards the road. His thoughts and feelings were in turmoil. His first instincts demanded that he go straight down into the Emma and hammer at the shattered rock of her innards until she coughed up every one of the four men trapped in her craw. But Sarah was right, he had no experience or skill as a miner, and his best efforts would only interfere with those who were more able to get the job done. Still, he had the nagging feeling that there was something he *could* do—something he *should* do—something he *must* do.

Mitchell reined the roan to a stop, and let his eyes rove the mountainside. Oddly, he was nowhere near town. With his thoughts occupied, he had simply let Milo choose his own path, and the animal had turned away from town, plodding its way up the wagon track, deep into the mountains, until the road had dwindled into a pair of narrow ruts winding up the ridge to Barrett's Lost Crow mine.

Dry Creek was a thin ribbon of icy melt water running down from somewhere high in the ragged peaks above, and despite the summer heat, Mitchell felt a sudden chill that made his skin prickle with a sense of dark foreboding.

The roan dropped into a walk. The dark feeling eased a bit, as though the animal's movement pushed back the dark feelings of uselessness and defeat. The roan plodded on.

"Where are you going Milo?"

The roan flicked his ears at the sound of his name and kept moving, following the faint trace of wagon wheels wending their way between the pinions, moving steadily up the ridge.

"Nothing up here but the Lost Crow," Mitchell told the animal. "We oughtta head back to town and see what we can do to help."

But the animal ignored Mitchell and plodded onward through the trees and up the mountain. Barrett's claim was not far, and they reached the clearing in less than half-an-hour.

The clearing was quiet when Mitchell dismounted and walked past the open mouth of the mine. But soon, more than a dozen crows strutted about the grassy meadow, hunting bugs, pecking at twigs, and poking at bits of Barrett's ruined equipment in search of food. A dozen more perched in the trees, squawking and calling to one another, watching every move that Mitchell made.

"Shoulda listened to the old man," Mitchell grumbled.

The birds on the ground halted and stood with heads cocked to one side, staring at the human.

"I ain't feedin' you," Mitchell growled.

Ignoring the birds, he followed Barrett's narrow gage tracks to the edge of the cliffs and looked down on the fan-like pile of shattered, stone tailings that Barrett had dumped from the top of the cliffs. The pile stretched for hundreds of feet in all directions.

Looking down on the tailings, Mitchell could roughly estimate the extent of Barrett's work on the claim. The results surprised him. Everything he had heard about the claim suggested that Barrett had stopped work on the claim soon after his talks with Mitchell and his return from Salt Lake. But the pile below suggested that the work had been much more extensive. The heap below was huge.

Several hundred tons at least….

The thought came suddenly as Mitchell realized it had been no small undertaking for two men. Barrett must have worked himself and Taggart like dogs to drill, blast, and claw so much rock from the earth in the few short months he had owned the claims.

Oddly, the crows grew silent. The air was no longer still, and the breeze drifting up from the canyon below was ephemeral, hot, and ripe with the smell of pinion. For a moment, Mitchell stood looking out across the canyon to the slopes on the east and the ridge that hid the workings of the Emma mine.

Close…, he thought.

They were so close. And while the air on the ridge was fresh with the scent of pines, he knew that the air in the Emma mine would soon grow stale and poisonous. If they were still alive, the men trapped in the Emma mine were even now fighting for their lives.

The sudden squawking of the crows and the commotion of slapping wings dragged Mitchell's thoughts back to the clearing and the Lady-dog who dashed hell-bent among the birds on the ground and snapped up the smallest of them like a hungry crocodile.

"Drop it!" Mitchell ordered sharply.

The dog ignored the human and flopped on her belly—her head cradled between her front feet, the wings of the hapless bird projecting from either side of her jaws.

"Drop it!" Mitchell commanded again.

The dog ignored him and sucked on the bird like a child with its mouth stuffed with store-bought rock candy.

Mitchell stepped away from the cliff, edging toward the disobedient animal. "Give me the bird, and I'll give you a piece of the good jerky," he offered, waving a piece of the *good stuff* in the air.

The dog sat up and stared at the offered treat.

"Drop the bird," Mitchell demanded.

For a moment, the dog stared at the meat. Slowly, as though reluctant, she opened her jaws and let the bird fall to the ground. Stunned, the bird lay quivering and spent.

"Good girl," Mitchell praised, tossing the treat across the clearing, away from the birds.

The Lady-dog was gone in an instant, bounding like a crazed jackrabbit, racing after the meat. As the dog raced away, Mitchell looked down at the crow, watching as it staggered to its feet and took a few disoriented steps.

From the corner of his eye, Mitchell saw the dog leap onto the wooden platform that had supported the head-frame over the shaft, and he watched dumbfounded as the animal skidded across the weathered surface and dropped into the open mouth of the shaft. With half its body down the hole, the animal scrambled, yelping and clawing the air with its hind feet and clinging to the platform with its front claws hooked in the seam between two rough-cut boards.

Startled by the dog's sudden yelping, the crows took flight. Mitchell rushed to the platform and snagged the struggling animal by the scruff of its neck. The dog cried out as Mitchell's fist clamped down hard on a handful of hide and dragged the animal from the hole.

The platform sagged. A plank groaned in protest, snapping in two. Mitchell's foot fell away beneath him, and for an instant he lost balance and teetered on the edge of the hole. Fighting momentum, he thrust out a hand, grabbing for anything that might stop his fall into the abyss.

For a moment, his grasping fingers found nothing... then there was fur and a stiff legged dog growling and holding back against his weight.

"Dumb mutt!" Mitchell growled as he extracted his foot from the hole in the broken platform. "I could have dragged you down with me."

The dog dropped down on her belly and watched as Mitchell laid down on the platform and stared at the sky. Absently, he reached out and stroked the back of her neck. The animal quivered as though half-afraid of his touch.

"Barrett told me that hole is six-hundred feet deep," he told the animal. "That's a long drop for either one of us."

The dog twisted around, thrust her nose at Mitchell's face and licked at his cheek. Mitchell laughed and roughed up the animal's ears.

"Look at 'em," he said pointing to the trees surrounding the clearing and the crows perched on nearly every branch. "They hang around begging for food and won't even lift a wing when we need help. I've got half a mind to send 'em all packin'."

The dog made no reply except to drop her head on Mitchell's shoulder.

Suddenly, Mitchell sat up, pushing the dog away. For a long moment, he studied the hole in the platform and the mud clinging to one boot.

"Damn," he muttered, looking down into the blackness of the shaft. "Let's get out of here. This place stinks like stale horse piss."

Chapter 23

Utah Territory
Deep Creek Mountains—June 1869

Sarah stood at the mouth of the Barrett shaft and peered down into the blackness. The light was gone and with its removal, she felt as though her heart had turned to stone. She had watched the shrinking light from the kerosene lantern until it had dwindled to a mere speck and disappeared in the depths of the mine. Now, she felt as though she might weep over its loss.

"Come away from that hole," Susan scolded anxiously. "Those planks are rotten. They'll break and you'll fall in."

I'm tied to this rope," Sarah defended as she stepped away from the shaft, whipping the rope from side to side like a sidewinder skimming across the ground.

"You're making me nervous anyway," Susan argued. "It's bad enough that Collin is down there. And I don't care how well they say that head-frame is built, or how strong the cables are. The whole business makes me nervous."

Sarah walked carefully across the creaking boards of the platform and stepped down onto solid ground before removing the rope she had fastened around her waist. She had no desire to fall into that hole and feared the possibility more than Susan would ever know.

"It took a long time for their light to disappear," she observed.

"They probably reached the next level and moved over to the other platform," Susan suggested. "Collin told me they scavenged cables and pulleys from the Emma mine, but they set up two stages for the hoist, because the cables weren't long enough to reach the bottom in one stage. I guess some of Mr. Barrett's old equipment was still in place too. They made use of anything that was still safe to use."

"And when did you learn all this?"

"When Collin and Mr. Deagan were discussing how to set the explosive charges. I happened to be near the wagon when they were explaining to Mr. Allingham."

Sarah frowned. "You were eavesdropping," she accused. "But at least you know what they're up to. I still have no idea what they're trying to accomplish. Collin didn't take the time to explain."

Susan eased herself down until she sat on the edge of the weather-beaten platform, her back to the mouth of the shaft. "Something dangerous," she replied unhappily. "Otherwise, he would have told us."

* * *

Mitchell stepped onto the lower platform and took hold of the ropes securing the box to cables running through the pulleys above. He gripped the ropes tightly, knowing what had to be done, yet wishing for some other solution. But it was a job for two men, and Mitchell had been reluctant to ask anyone else to risk it.

Deagan had been willing enough to go down into the mine, and he had jumped into his new job with an enthusiasm that Mitchell could not fathom. Deagan had already inspected the mine several times, running up and down the shaft, checking for problems. What he had found was unnerving.

"We've got three levels," Deagan explained as they moved downward on the third stage. "Everything is stable enough until we get to about fifty feet from the bottom. That's where Barrett must have left off cleaning up the shaft. The bottom drops out into a kidney shaped crevasse about thirty feet long and ten or twelve feet wide.

"Now right where the shaft drops out, there's a big nob of rock hangin' out over the place you want to do your blasting."

"Is it a problem?" Mitchell asked.

"Only if our charge breaks it loose. If we had time, I'd say we blow the nob and clear out the rubble before we even start drilling the footwall. That's the good part.

"I can see why Barrett shut it down. All the rock down here is fractured bad—real bad. It needs to be shored up real good before we set off any explosives. We could have a lot of trouble if we ain't real careful."

Deagan looked at Mitchell through the dimness. "So, I need to know what you really want to do down here. Any vein Barrett was following has disappeared, and it ain't likely we'll find it without a lot of work... maybe never."

Mitchell looked at the heavy rope sliding along beside the platform. "I want to save four men," he answered quietly.

"The fellows trapped in the Emma?"

"Those are the ones."

Deagan shook his head in disbelief. "I don't see how anything we do here can help those fellows."

Mitchell glanced at the tools and explosives piled at the center of the platform. "Tell me how a man can disappear as though he never existed and then magically reappear in a tomb of solid rock?"

"I never understood that," Deagan confessed. "It just ain't possible."

"Exactly," Mitchell replied coldly.

* * *

"I think we're going to run out of water!" Kate Pendleton waved an empty dipper in Sarah's general direction.

Sarah went to the wagon where the frustrated Kate stuck the dipper into the water barrel and banged it around to demonstrate the barrel's lack of cooperation.

"The damn thing leaks!" She protested as Sarah came to her side and peered down into the offending object.

"Someone will have to go down and bring up another," Sarah concluded.

"I think you are elected," Kate replied. "You or your sister… I'd go myself, but someone has to keep Janet busy or she'll cry herself sick again."

"I can't imagine how she feels," Sarah admitted.

Kate glanced toward Janet Allingham and dropped her voice to a conspiratorial whisper. "Debbie was their only daughter," she confided. "They've got the two older boys, but Debbie was their baby. They both doted on her."

Sarah stared at the barrel. "My heart wants to break for them," she said unhappily.

"Mine too," Kate admitted, "but now is not the time. They need us up and doing for them, so they can mourn for their little girl. So, you'll have to go for the water. Take a horse and have one of the Allingham boys bring up a wagon with another barrel and some blankets. I have this odd feeling that we'll need them."

Sarah looked across the clearing to where Mort sat with his back against a tree, his hat pulled down over his eyes as though he slept. She watched as Tommy Hawkins sidled up to the tree and planted himself on the ground beside the old man.

"Tell me about the angels, Mr. Mort. Tell me about Mouriel."

"You know that name, do you? Some folks call him *Uriel.*"

The boy shrugged and leaned back against the tree, imitating the old man's reclined posture.

"He's my friend..."

The old man grunted. "You don't say... an archangel for a friend.... Where's your mom and pop?"

"Pop's helping on the hoist thing," the boy answered, pointing to the makeshift pulley system connected to the head-frame at the mouth of the shaft. "Mom's at the wagon makin' dinner."

The old man gazed into the fire, and for a moment, he sat silently gathering his thoughts as though at a loss as to what he might say. Finally, he looked up at the three women and the boy and began his story.

"Once," he said, "A long time ago, there was a war—a great war fought for honor and power. Some folks wanted to be able to make their own choices, and there were folks that wanted things easy; they wanted someone else to make the choices and take all the blame when things went wrong. They turned away from everything they knew and tried to change things. Other folks didn't agree... they tried to convince the rebels to give up, but the rebels wouldn't listen, and they started a war so bad it's hard to imagine."

Sarah shuddered at the thought of so much hate and destruction. "They say tens of thousands died in the War Between the States," she suggested.

The old man shook his head. "It weren't that kind of war darlin'. It was a war over power so great it's hard to imagine—a war where a word was power—a war where a fellow might speak, and the world would tremble to its core. But those folks wanted power they hadn't earned and didn't deserve, and all they cared about was destroyin' everything that had gone before. They wanted to rebuild everything in the image of what they thought was right.

"They had a twisted logic and persuasive arguments. I was nearly taken in by their promises. I would have been lost. But my brother convinced me that the rebels were wrong, and I followed *him* into the war." The old man shrugged. "I owe him everything, so I keep an eye on him and the rest of my family – try to help where I can."

"You never mention your family," Sarah said reprovingly.

The old man laughed. "Never had much reason to speak of 'em," he admitted. "My cousins… pretty gals… I love 'em like sisters… Analiel and Araliel…. and my brother Mouriel."

* * *

Mitchell held the lamp higher, shedding light across the footwall where a large chunk of rock nestled down, filling a depression the size of a wagon bed.

"You think we can do it?"

Deagan shrugged, but shook his head. "Sure, we can do it," he responded, "but we'll be takin' a big chance. We could bring the whole thing right down on top of us. That big knob is the worst of it."

Mitchell stomped a boot heel beside the big rock. "I just want a man-sized hole right there," he instructed. "I don't think it will take a big charge … just enough to loosen things for a couple of feet down."

"Just two or three feet?"

Mitchell frowned. "I don't know. I'm taking a wild-ass guess here."

Deagan shook his head. "Well… I suppose we could clear it out and shoot again if it doesn't do the trick."

Mitchell scowled in the dimness, wishing they had more time. But if he was right, they were already pushing the limits. The men trapped in the Emma needed air. Every minute counted, and he knew that even now they might be too late. "We can't afford the extra time it would take to bring down that cornice and shore this place up," he reasoned. "Those fellows could be out of air right now."

Deagan glanced overhead, studying the spur of rock hanging above their heads. "We better get started then," he said finally.

The next hour dragged like a dog gnawing at a bone. Mitchell held the long shaft of the drill steady as Deagan swung the eight-pound double jack time and again, driving the bit inch by inch into the rock. Mitchell flinched each time the face of the jack slammed the head of the steel rod and prayed that Deagan was skilled enough not to miss.

"Stinks down here," Deagan grumbled as he laid the jack on the floor and pulled a large bandanna from his pocket and wiped the sweat from the back of his neck.

Barrett must have had mules down here," Mitchell suggested. "There's a bit of track and he must have had an ore cart down here before the vein disappeared. Some of the track is still there, but he must have moved everything else to his other claims."

"Wish he had moved the stink," Deagan grumbled as he took up the jack and began a steady pounding on the head of the steel rod.

The head of the double jack slashed downward in a shadowy blur that moved so quickly Mitchell had no time to shift the long drill if he had wanted to. And when the face of the eight pound sledge slammed the head of the rod, the sound of steel against steel filled the shaft with an ear shattering *ping*.

"You're tippin' the rod away from you," Deagan complained sharply. "Keep it straight or this jack is gonna slip off and make a mess of your hands."

Mitchell pulled the steel back to a vertical position and gave it a quick twist as Deagan raised the jack again.

"Once we get the hole a little deeper, things will go easier. The rock will help keep the steel steady. It's the first three or four inches that's the worst."

The jack pounded the steel, and Mitchell twisted the rod again. Time and again the jack struck, until finally Mitchell fell into the rhythm. He stared at the rod, keeping it steady, twisting the shank with each strike of the jack. Yet, his mind drifted away, churning through the things they had learned since coming to this place.

Barrett must have returned to his claims and found the Lost Crow a bust, and with two more promising claims nearby, he had shifted his efforts to the claim Sarah had found higher up the mountain. Taggart had certainly helped in the removal of the equipment from the Lost Crow and its relocation to the claim under the cliffs.

Yet, someone had wanted Barrett's claims badly enough to kill for them. At least it seemed likely Barrett had been killed because he wouldn't sell.

"You awake?"

Mitchell came out of the fog of thought.

"Just thinking," he answered.

"That's okay, but it's probably better to stay focused on what you're doing here. You're holding that steel good and solid, but it ain't good to let your mind wander too much. Better to concentrate while you're learning to keep the steel steady, and you sure as hell can't drift off like that if you're ever swingin' the jack."

Mitchell nodded. "I'll remember," he conceded. "I was just wondering who might have killed Barrett."

"Miranda's old man?"

"Yup...."

"Thought he just disappeared?"

"Ellen Wells says that body you and Williams uncovered in the Emma mine was her brother."

"I never heard that," Deagan admitted. "That fellow had been shot right between the eyes."

"You think Taggart might have done it?" Mitchell asked.

"Taggart? I doubt it... The old man was pretty good to Taggart."

"Anyone else who might have done it?"

For a moment, Deagan was silent. "Maybe," he said at last.

"Forestall?" Mitchell asked.

"Maybe ... Gromley maybe...Ramsay... All of 'em maybe..."

"Desert Range?"

"I heard they wanted in on something Barrett had going," Deagan offered.

"But why?" Mitchell countered. "If the Emma is producing and making a profit...Why would Forestall or Gromley resort to killing Barrett?"

Deagan wiped the sweat from his forehead and lifted the double jack. "Don't know. I heard Miranda's aunt hired a fellow to run things for them. That fellow is the one that scares me," he confessed. "The one that rides that paint horse. He's just plain mean. He rides all over the mountain up behind town.... hangs around up at that old windmill.... something fishy goin' on up there if you ask me."

"How so?"

"Wagons comin' and goin'...clangin' noises all the time...."

"Wagons? Loaded with lumber from the mill?"

"Nope. I got a look one time, when no one was payin' attention. Looked like a load of lead bars... seemed mighty strange... Why bring them bars all the way back here?"

Deagan raised the jack into the air. "Hold steady now. We got drillin' to do."

Mitchell dropped to one knee and steadied the drill, and the shaft soon reverberated with the incessant ring of steel against steel.

Half-an-hour later, the blast shook the mountain, and for long minutes the cavern groaned and dust clogged the air like a thick fog. Mitchell clutched a damp bandana tightly to his face and hunkered down against the ragged stone of the cavern wall. Beside him, Deagan pushed up tight against his own section of the wall with his face buried in the front of his shirt.

"We're still alive," Mitchell announced.

"Unless that chunk of rock cuts loose and squashes us like a couple of stink bugs," Deagan protested.

"That rock ain't gonna fall," Mitchell argued. He pushed to his feet and wiped the dust from his face. "Let's see what kind of damage we've done."

When they reached the hole, both men dropped to their knees, examining the results of their efforts.

"There's a hole punched through at the bottom," Deagan reported.

With the handle of a shovel he poked around in the bottom of the larger bowl created by the explosion until the handle plunged downward into the chamber below.

"That's it!" Deagan exclaimed. "It's only about the size of my fist, but it goes though…"

"What next?" Mitchell asked.

"A couple of small shots down near the bottom," Deagan replied, "just enough to blow out the bottom."

"How long?"

"An hour if we're quick with the drillin'."

"Nothing we can do to make it go faster?"

"Maybe," Deagan answered. "We'll try a single shot on that section right there," he said pointing to one side of the hole. "There's some fracturing there that might let us take out a big enough area to let a fellow get through, if he ain't a big old fellow…."

Mitchell nodded and took up the long steel rod of the drill. "Let's get at it then."

Half an hour later, the single charge went off with a muffled thump. And when the two men looked into the hole they saw a man-sized opening and the reflection of light on the steel tracks below.

"Beats me how you figured to come out on top of the Emma tunnel that way," Deagan admitted. "What made you think of it?"

Mitchell eased himself down into the hole until both legs dangled into the tunnel below.

"Horse piss," he answered as he dropped into the darkness below.

Lamplight flickered dimly from the narrow gage rails pinned to the floor of the Emma tunnel, and for a moment, Mitchell paused, listening for any sound that might indicate the condition of the Pratt kid and his fellows. For a long while, he heard nothing—nothing but the low groaning of the surrounding rock as the earth shifted and finally settled into its new conformation. The minutes passed… finally, he heard them… low voices and the clatter of loose rock as they shuffled through the wrecked tunnel.

"Pratt!"

Mitchell's call echoed down through the darkness.

"Here!" came the answer.

Chapter 24

Utah Territory
Deep Creek Mountains—June 1869

The team crawled down a rutted trail illuminated by the pale light of a waxing gibbous moon. The evening sky was awash with stars, and the Milky Way arched across the vault of heaven like a glittering white fog. The evening was quiet, and only the rattling of harness, the sharp *clack* of hooves striking rock, and the creaking of the battered old wagon encroached upon the ear then fled into the dark expanse of the night.

There was a chill on the air, and Sarah pulled her jacket close about her throat, wishing she had thought to bring her heavier woolen coat. She had left the warmth of the fire and the hectic activity at the Lost Crow mine, reluctantly returning to town for water, not knowing if Collin was safe... knowing only that he was deep in the bowels of the earth. She had no idea what Collin was up to, and she was half-a-mile from the Lost Crow when the explosion rumbled through the earth, and the sound had rolled down the canyon like the echoing thunder of a cannon.

It had taken every pitiful stitch of her willpower to keep from turning the team and flying back to the mine. But somehow, she had stayed the course and continued down the road towards town and the water Kate Pendleton was so certain they would need. Now the wagon thumped and bumped over rocks and half-exposed roots, and the lights of Silver City glowed just a mile ahead on the curving shoulder of the mountain.

Slowly, she passed the Forestall house, its tall clapboard structure standing dark and foreboding against a starlit sky, like a castle bathed in pale moonlight. The house was eerie in its solitude, far from the road and surrounded by trees.

Gromley's house was nearest. It was a quarter-of-a-mile farther on, and it too was a lonely place, isolated from the road and nearly invisible in the shadows. It was a ghostly place, run down, unpainted and worn at the edges like rock ground down by wind and water.

Silently, the windows of the house watched like square, black eyes as the wagon rolled closer on the bumpy road. A breeze rocked the tops of the trees, waving the branches of the clustered junipers like the arms of a ghostly crowd clamoring silently for her attention. Sarah fought the sudden urge to slap the reins on the backs of the team and run the horses for town. She fought the feeling that something watched her walk the team through the glow of pale moonlight. She was abreast the house when the soft glow of lamplight drifted across a darkened window, and the sharp crack of a pistol-shot ravaged the silence of the night. Bravely, she stopped the horses in the middle of the road and climbed from the wagon.

The path to the house was covered in shadows as she made her way slowly across the rutted ground. Unseen rocks battered her shoes. Brush tore at her skirts. But she forced her way through the overgrown yard, and finally, after fifty long paces, she reached the window. Beyond the grime covered glass a light shifted fitfully, as though held aloft by an unseen hand. Cautiously, she peered inside. In the dimness, a lamp drifted across the room, held high in the hand of a woman who moved quickly from place to place, tossing books from shelves, dragging drawers from a large wooden desk, and peeling the corners of a large rug from the floor as though hunting for something that evaded her swift yet probing search. Dim light touched the woman's face, and Sarah knew instantly that this was Henry Forestall's wife—a woman she had known before—a murderous woman—Eliza Richards.

Long moments passed before Sarah realized that the woman was not alone. A second person occupied the room—a person who sagged limply in an overstuffed chair less than two feet from where Sarah stood peering through the window. The man was dead, and his open eyes stared blindly at Sarah through the dirty glass.

* * *

When Mitchell came out of the mine, the clearing was filled with noise. More than two dozen men and women stood in a tightly packed group, talking loudly and pressing closely upon the four men who sat tiredly on the bole of a fallen tree. All four were wrapped in woolen blankets and said little in reply to the unending questions fired from the crowd.

Mitchell pushed his way through the crowd until he stood near the Pratt kid. The Campbell girl was already at the kid's side, clinging tightly to one arm.

"Glad you dropped in when you did," the kid confessed. "It was getting hard to breathe, and I was worried about O'Neil… he's got a busted arm."

"It's a wonder none of you are dead," Mitchell replied. "Forestall told me the explosion was much bigger than a normal face shot."

"It was pretty big," the kid agreed, "and a couple of us would have been caught in the blast except something mighty strange happened."

"Something strange?"

The Pratt kid shook his head and stared at the ground. "It was all pretty strange," he said finally. "After you and Gromley left, Kevin O'Neil came down with an empty cart. We were loading it and talking about Deagan and Williams... O'Neil was one of the muckers who worked that tunnel most of the time.... I never thought much about what he was telling me.... It was just talk about some stuff Art Williams had been telling him a while back.... Thing is; I had the strangest feeling we were being watched. I even walked up the tunnel a ways, but I never saw anyone.

"Later on, O'Neil brought down another cart. I got the feeling we were being watched again, so I started back up the tunnel. All of a sudden, I see this fellow runnin' towards me a wavin' his arms and yellin' 'run!' So I turned around and ran for the stope. Then the place blew up..."

"What happened to the fellow who warned you?"

"That's the strange part. It was that ghost I been seein' down there."

* * *

Frank Gromley's hand shook uncontrollably as he raised a kerchief to his forehead and mopped at perspiration that seemed to almost pour from his flesh, running in crooked rivulets down his face and neck, soaking his collar to a dark, wet blue.

Mitchell scowled at the trembling mine owner and pointed to Forestall's body and the blood-spattered room.

"You're lucky Sarah heard that shot and got here quick enough to see that woman tearing the place apart."

Sarah trembled slightly, and held tightly to Mitchell's arm. "I'm glad you came back to the mine for me," he told her quietly.

"Why would she do it?" Gromley moaned. "I never did anything to her, and Henry gave her everything she wanted."

"Forestall was broke," Mitchell argued. "But you knew that, didn't you?"

"I thought so," Gromley countered, "but Henry told me everything was just fine and showed me the money he had locked up in the safe. He had thirty or forty thousand dollars in gold hidden away in there."

Quietly, Mitchell studied the room. It was not a large room. The floor was composed of thick lumber and looked as though it had come from the sawmill in the hills above town, with the curving marks of the rotating saw blade still easily discernible in the rough-cut surface of each pine board. A sofa, covered in a material of mixed lime and forest green, stood against one wall, while on the opposite wall, near the room's only window, stood the over-stuffed chair that held the body of Henry Forestall. The room was drably plain and gave Mitchell the impression that the home was little cared for, except for a multitude of framed pen-and-ink drawings hung on every wall.

"Your work?" Mitchell asked, nodding toward the drawings.

"I like to draw," Gromley answered. "It's been a hobby of mine since I was a child."

"Quite good," Mitchell concluded, looking closely at the drawings, and wondering what it was that intrigued him about such a seemingly simple form of art. "A couple of them may be ruined," he observed, noting how flecks of blood had dampened the ink, causing dark blotches among the finely sketched lines.

Sarah stood at the doorway, her back stoically turned to the body and the blood-spattered wall.

"Why did she destroy this room?" She asked quietly. "If she was only trying to make it look as though you killed her husband, there was no need to rip this room apart."

"Perhaps she was searching for the safe and the gold," Gromley offered. "I thought Frank was very secretive about the whole business. It's possible he didn't trust her and never told her where the safe or the money was hidden."

"And did she find it?" Mitchell asked.

"I believe so," Gromley admitted. "The safe is in the floor behind that chair," he said, pointing to Forestall's body.

Mitchell crossed the room and looked down on several pieces of flooring that lay discarded against the wall and a crumpled rug that had once concealed the safe.

"Looks empty to me," he observed quietly. "She must have known the combination," he added thoughtfully.

"She must have gotten it from Henry," Gromley concluded. "I never told anyone."

"Why was the safe here, in your house?" Mitchell wondered aloud.

"It's not my house," Gromley explained. "The house belongs to Henry… at least it did… He lived here, up until four months ago. He built the big house after they were married, because Eliza thought this one was unsuitable."

Mitchell scowled at the room, wondering what had prompted the sudden killing of Henry Forestall.

"Just what was going on here?" he wondered aloud.

Gromley turned away from the empty safe, and when he spoke, his voice was as dismal as their surroundings. "What do you mean?" he asked.

"Something made them change their plans," Mitchell explained. "I can't believe their only objective was to steal the money from that safe. They could have done *that* months ago. They had to be up to something else—something more elaborate."

"I don't understand," Gromley complained. "There was a very large sum of money in that safe. They could have lived for years on that kind of cash. That's probably all they wanted."

Mitchell shook his head. "I don't think so," he replied. "I keep thinking about that sawmill," he added.

Gromley threw his hands up in frustration. "Henry had a crew cutting timbers for the mine whenever a load was late coming from the mills in Provo. Other than that, the place is locked up to keep kids out of it."

"Can we go?" Sarah asked suddenly. "My nerves are on edge and standing here discussing Mr. Forestall while his body is sitting in that chair is just a little too much for me right now."

Mitchell shot a quick glance at the body and hurried across the room to where Sarah stood in the open doorway. "I'm sorry," he said quietly, taking her by the arm. "Gromley, we're leaving. If Simmons asks about us, tell him we'll be at the boarding house."

Gromley looked at the body and nodded. "I'll tell him," he replied.

When they were away from the house, Mitchell took Sarah by the hand and led her down the path to the road and the waiting wagon.

"There is something odd about that man," she insisted as Mitchell helped her climb into the wagon's seat.

"How so?" he prompted.

Sarah shook her head as though uncertain how to explain. "Did you see how his eyes kept darting about the room?" she asked finally.

Mitchell slapped the reins against the backs of the team, starting the animals down the moonlit trail towards town. "Looking for something?" he suggested.

Sarah shook her head again. "I'm not sure... It was more like he was looking at the walls."

"The walls?"

"Probably nothing... I'm probably making too much of the whole thing," she said quietly.

"Maybe not," Mitchell answered, remembering the drawings hanging from every wall. "There was something that struck me odd about those drawings... what it was though.... And I wonder what has become of our Mrs. Forestall and the money from the safe?"

"We're a long way from any town she'll want to settle in for long," Sarah concluded. "She's not the type for small towns and dirt roads."

A quarter of a mile from town, Mitchell stopped the team and dropped to the ground. At the back of the wagon, he unhitched the roan and climbed into the saddle.

"I'm going back to Gromley's place," he explained quietly. "I should have taken a closer look at those drawings while we were there. Something about them is nagging at me."

Sarah looked over her shoulder, into the darkness beyond the eerie realm of the moonlit road.

"Be careful," she advised. "I don't trust Mr. Gromley... and try not to be gone all night."

Mitchell turned the roan and rode away, leaving Sarah on her own. He disliked leaving her there, but the need to return to the house weighed on him, pushing him to ride back. Within minutes, the wagon had disappeared and Gromley's house had grown from a shadow-like blot on the hillside to a glimmering, dreamlike silhouette shrouded in the embrace of tall, somber junipers.

The roan walked the path to the house with the muffled sound of hooves on dust—dust that grabbed at the low, plodding thumps and sucked them into the earth, leaving the air void and silent. At the front of the house, the evening was silent. Nothing moved save a light breeze tugging at the junipers, waving their branches like the arms of a shadowy choir caught up in the rapture of a wind-blown hymn. There were no lights in the house, only the moonlight glowing on darkened windows.

In five steps, Mitchell was at the front door, rapping sharply with his knuckles. For a long while, he waited. But Gromley did not come. He rapped again, and again Gromley made no reply. Finally, he snatched the Smith & Wesson from its holster and kicked in the door.

Frank Gromley was gone. The house was dark and empty. The drawings had been stripped from the walls, and the only indication that anything was amiss was the body of Henry Forestall still slumped in his chair like a puppet whose strings had been cut.

Chapter 25

Utah Territory
Deep Creek Mountains—June 1869

At first, no one noticed the fire. If they noticed anything, it might have been a brighter radiance of flickering yellow light filling the doorway of the stables and spilling out into the street. But for several minutes, no one took notice of the growing flames or the small form that lay broken against the doorpost. Nor did they notice the crumpled body of the little boy lying at the edge of the flames near the crushed shell of a kerosene lantern.

For nearly five minutes, the flames ate at the interior of the building, roaring among the stalls, gorging on straw and hay, devouring the bone dry skeleton of the stables. Finally, smoke boiled from the doorway and into the street.

The smell of smoke brought exhausted men to their doors, peering up and down the street, searching in all directions until they discovered the source and sounded the alarm. Abruptly, the smoky street filled with bucket toting forms that dipped buckets in horse troughs and scrambled towards the stables. Someone doused the unconscious boy with water and dragged him away from the raging building.

At the boarding house, a rough looking character stood at the edge of the porch and spat his *chew* out into the yard. "Just the stables," he grunted harshly. "Let the damn thing burn, I say."

Ellen Wells shot an angry look at the man.

"You wouldn't feel that way, if it was your place burning down while some jackass stood around and said 'let it burn'," she growled. "You help put out that fire, Dave Isakson, or you can find another place to stay. And that goes for the lot of you!" Angrily, she glared at each of the men who stood in the yard watching the flames. Within minutes the men were gone from the yard, running toward the general store where Charles Allingham tossed new buckets from his store into the street.

When Sarah and Susan reached the fire, the bucket line stretched more than a hundred feet. Buckets dangled and sloshed from hand to hand until the remaining water was thrown frantically at the burning building.

"We're going to lose the stable," Allingham yelled above the roar of the flames and the noise of useless instructions called back and forth down the line. "We have to stop it from spreading to the grass or the other buildings!" he bellowed.

"How can we do that?" Susan yelled over the din as they filtered into the crowd and began passing buckets in both directions along the line.

Sarah glanced toward the nearest water trough where empty buckets were being dipped and filled repeatedly. She was amazed that the trough was not already drained of every ounce.

"We must be nearly out of water!" She exclaimed.

Allingham shook his head. "Two of these troughs are fed by a pipeline that connects to a storage tank on the hill behind my store. There's a small spring and a well that feed the tank. It's not much… we could empty the tank. If that happens, the whole mountain could burn down, not just the town."

"Then we should let the stable go and concentrate on keeping the fire contained!" Susan shouted.

"I hate to say it, but that's what has to be done," Allingham agreed. "Hawkins will hate me for it, but the stable is too far gone. We've got a hundred feet or more between the stable and my place, and there is nothing much on the other three sides. If we can scatter folks around the stable they can chase down anything that catches in the grass or the out buildings and put it out.

"But we can't let another building start up, especially my place. If my place takes off, the whole west side of town will burn. Everything is just too dry."

Allingham turned away and ran quickly down the line, calling out instructions. Within moments, the bucket line was reorganized and people scattered to more distant locations on the fringes surrounding the conflagration that had once been a stable. Here, the men and women of the small town stood with buckets full and ready to attack any new flames on the ground. Others hurried from place to place, shoveling a quick spade-full of dirt onto stray sparks, conserving water for more stubborn areas that flared into life.

Near Allingham's store, the ground soon turned to mud as someone dropped a pump into the nearest trough and started water flowing through the town's only fire hose. When the stables finally collapsed, the Hawkins' house and Allingham's store were thoroughly soaked. The inferno of the stables had dwindled to a bonfire, and the town's water supply was again focused on the blackened remains of the Hawkins' livelihood.

The moon was low and bright, balanced on the tips of the mountains like a pocket medallion on a chain of glittering stars. It had been dark for less than an hour, and the five women made the walk from the burnt-out rubble of the stable to the boarding house under the light of a gibbous moon. Each of them was silent, thinking their own thoughts and exhausted from the effort of fighting the fire. No one felt like talking when they reached the boarding house, yet none of them wanted to be alone.

"Tommy Hawkins has been hurt pretty badly," Sarah reported unhappily. "Collin will be upset."

Susan eased herself into one of the parlor chairs and let out an exhausted sigh. "What happened? How was he hurt?"

Sarah dropped into a chair of her own, and dabbed at her blackened face with a damp kerchief.

"I talked with several people," she confessed. "Only one saw anything. She told me that just before the fire, she saw a wagon race down the street. The driver veered very close to the stable doors for no apparent reason then raced out of town toward the express road."

"She said she saw nothing unusual at the stables, so she went back inside and thought nothing more of the incident."

"They ran him down deliberately!" Susan exclaimed angrily. "Did she recognize the driver?"

Sarah frowned. "She said it was the fellow who rides a paint horse."

"Grady Cannon!" Ellen Wells exclaimed. "Grady Cannon would never do such a thing! I've never met a kinder man!"

Sarah shrugged. "It was Kate Pendleton who saw it.... I can't imagine that she would be mistaken about this. She seemed certain."

Ellen Wells stood and walked to the window, staring out into the darkness. "I don't believe it," she murmured unhappily. "Grady has helped us more than anyone. He's gone out nearly every day to keep watch on the Lost

Crow until we could hire a crew to re-open the mine. We hired a crew just a few weeks ago, and Grady put them to work. The men worked for a couple of days and quit without a word. Grady paid them out of his own pocket, because he knew we were strapped for cash. We haven't been able to hire a single soul since then. Grady says the miners who quit have been telling everyone the mine is too dangerous."

Sarah stared at the woman. "You had a crew working up there two weeks ago?"

"Yes."

"And they walked off the job because the mine was unsafe."

"Yes, they did."

For a long while, no one spoke, and the silence became oppressive.

Sarah's thoughts raced, and she could see Susan shaking her head in disbelief. "I feel restless..." she said at last. "Dog tired, but restless...."

"I feel it too," Susan answered.

"I can't stop thinking about Tommy Hawkins," Sarah confessed.

Susan looked up from where she sat in an old rocking chair near the ruined wall of the kitchen. "We should go up to the Hawkins' place," she suggested wearily. "I don't think we'll have any peace until we see Tommy."

* * *

The smell of smoke was heavy on the air and had been for more than an hour when Mitchell came down from the mountain. He was tired and moved slowly and carefully. The road back to town was nothing more than a rock-strewn track, lit by a moon now lost in the milky radiance of cotton-white clouds. The roan moved easily enough on the edge of the deeply rutted path, but Mitchell took his time, walking the animal step by step down the mountain, his eyes searching for good ground, while his thoughts raced as he struggled to unravel a situation that seemed more tangled each day.

The Pratt kid and his fellows were safely extracted from the depths of the Emma mine, but the entire situation seemed tangled beyond comprehension; and what had first appeared to be a simple case of greed and murder had now metamorphosed into something more complicated—something that made little sense.

Barrett was dead; that much was certain. He had been killed in the Lost Crow Mine or dumped there, and his killer had set off a charge that had dropped a large chunk of the hanging wall on Barrett's tiny little tomb. Since then, a number of people had shown an unusual degree of interest in Barrett's affairs, and almost certainly, one of them had done the deed.

Ellen Wells had nothing to gain from her brother's death. In fact, Barrett had supported her and kept the boarding house from going under when the income from the house had been too small to meet the debt that had accumulated. Ellen Wells owned the place now and might make a go of it, but her brother had made that possible, and Ellen Wells had loved the man for it.

Miranda Barrett inherited the mines and the money. She was flighty and immature, but Mitchell saw nothing in the girl that made him believe she could have killed her own father. Yet, the woman's blouse they had found at Williams' shack could not be ignored, and it was of a size that would easily fit Miranda Barrett.

If Miranda Barrett and her aunt were removed from suspicion, the list of people who might have wanted Barrett out of the way grew more manageable. In

Mitchell's mind, the most likely suspect was Henry Forestall. His money was gone, and Barrett's refusal of a partnership would have left Forestall in a difficult position. Forestall had, in fact, already shown his willingness to jump Barrett's claims by working the Polecat claim under cover of darkness, knowing full well he had no right to any of the ore they were taking from the mine.

Frank Gromley was high on the list as well. The money he had invested in the Emma mine might never be recovered, and though he had been in town only a few weeks when Barrett disappeared, he could have easily discovered the financial difficulties of the Desert Range Mining Company and tried to make his own deal with Barrett.

And there were others.

Brandon Taggart must have had multiple opportunities to kill Barrett, and given the right motivation, the job would have been easy. Money had motivated him quickly enough when Forestall wanted the location of Barrett's gold producing claim.

Jack Ramsay was hardnosed and arrogant. That had been obvious from their first meeting. And Mitchell was certain that Ramsay had been employed at the Emma long enough to know where the skeletons were hidden, and Ramsay was not the type to sit idly while his livelihood disintegrated. Allingham seemed to think the man was honest enough, and no different than anyone else caught in the same circumstances. Allingham seemed a good enough judge of character, but Mitchell had seen enough of the world to know that people were not always what they seemed.

When the town came into view, it was shrouded in moonlight and the smell of smoke. The stables were gone.

Nothing remained but a pile of burnt out rubble. He turned towards the boarding house, but someone stopped him on the street just south of the post office.

"We've been watching for you," Allingham said in voice hoarse from smoke and yelling. "Up at the Hawkins' place. Their boy has been hurt, and he's asking for you."

The walk to the Hawkins' place was not far...a hundred yards uphill beyond the burnt stables, but it seemed like miles before Mitchell was ushered into Tommy Hawkins' small upstairs bedroom. The lamps were dim, and the atmosphere melancholy. Mitchell went to the bedside and knelt beside his friend.

For a moment, the little boy looked up into Mitchell's eyes. He smiled and pulled on Mitchell's sleeve. "The angels are here," he whispered.

"I'm sure they are...," Mitchell agreed.

"In the corner," the boy insisted. "I asked mom to see if they would come. I knew *you* would come if they did."

Mitchell glanced to the corner where Sarah and Susan stood quietly watching.

"A mighty good pair of angels...." he whispered.

"They keep the dark away," the boy replied. "I never seen lights so bright... 'cept yours."

"I ain't very bright," Mitchell answered.

"I kept this for you." The boy pressed his hand into Mitchell's and dropped a heavy coin. "Debbie found it up at the sawmill. She gave it to me 'cause she likes me. But the *shadow man* wanted it. That's why he shot her. My cat's dead too; the man with the pretty horse done it. My mom gave me Cat. Why'd he hurt my cat?"

Mitchell was silent, searching for something to say.

"Mr. Mort says Mouriel can take the *shadow man* away...." The little boy took a shallow breath. "Will you take me home first?"

"I'll take you home," Mitchell said softly. "Then Mouriel will take the *shadow man* away forever."

An hour later, Mitchell stood in the coolness of the boarding house yard and gazed up at a sky lit by a billion stars—stars that flooded the sky with glittering light—stars that reminded him of Tommy Hawkins. Sarah and Susan stood beside him, waiting for him to gather his thoughts and tell them what he had discovered.

"Gromley was gone..." he said finally, "all the drawings too. I don't think he even waited for us to reach the road before he started pulling them down."

"You didn't pass him on the road?" Sarah asked in surprise.

"He must have gone south, through the foothills," Mitchell concluded.

"He might have gone up the canyon," Sarah suggested. "The road goes back quite a ways, and I've heard there's a good trail all the way to a small basin at the head of the canyon."

Mitchell shook his head. "If he went that way, it might be impossible to track him down. That's rough country up there."

"What made you go back?" Susan asked. She found a willow chair, eased down onto the seat, and pulled a knitted shawl about her shoulders.

"The drawings," Mitchell replied.

"The missing drawings?"

"The same... something bothered me about those drawings from the start, but I couldn't get a handle on it. So I went back for a better look."

"And now they're gone," Susan concluded.

"They're gone," Mitchell admitted. "But I think I know what was wrong with them."

"What?" both women demanded in unison.

"They were pen and ink engravings."

Chapter 26

Utah Territory
Deep Creek Mountains—June 1869

It was early morning when Mitchell reached the windmill. The sun was just broaching the eastern peaks of the Onaquis, and the mountains were awash in the flames of a red-orange sunrise. A cold wind rushed down from the mountains above, tugged at the dirty canvas sails of the windmill then raced down the mountain and onto the broken flats of a salt encrusted desert.

Gromley was nearby. Mitchell could sense it like the touch of ants crawling across his flesh. It was an unpleasant feeling that made him pause at the open doorway of the mill, his hand dropping to the butt of the pistol at his hip.

Cautiously, he eased through the opening, moving carefully to avoid alerting the man he hunted. Two quiet steps and the light fled. A dark gloominess gripped the interior of the building, shrouding everything in shadows. Four more steps, and he could see the dark opening of the doorway leading into the forge.

Everything was as Susan had described it… the tall wooden structure of the milling platform running the length of the building… the large, circular blades with their offset, ripping teeth… the long leather belts running through wooden pulleys as tall as a man… everything as Susan had described it… everything as it should be… except the dynamo and the canvas sacks that lay bulging upon a long workbench that stood jammed tightly against the back wall.

Gromley was nowhere to be seen, yet the mill was filled with shadows that could easily hide ten men. Cautiously, Mitchell made his way past the tall framework of the cutting table, past the gears and belts of the mechanism that drove the man-sized blades, past the dynamo, following the length of the outer wall until he came to the bench and the door leading into the forge. There, he waited.

When Gromley came through the doorway, he came quickly and purposefully, a heavy sack dangling from each fist.

"Shit…"

"Not expecting company?" Mitchell asked quietly.

"You just surprised me. What are you doing here?"

"You thought you could just ride away?" Mitchell asked coldly.

"What do you want?" Gromley demanded.

"I came for you," Mitchell replied.

"You came for me?"

"It took a while for me to put it all together," Mitchell explained. "Killing Barrett wasn't even the beginning, was it?"

"I haven't a clue what you're talking about," Gromley snarled. "I hardly knew the man."

"Oh, you killed him," Mitchell replied. "Then you kept Cannon busy hunting the vein in the Lost Crow long after you knew it was hopeless. It kept him busy and out of your way."

"And why would I have anything to do with Grady Cannon. He's nothing more than a small-time confidence man."

"It was Cannon that brought you here," Mitchell accused. "Canfield is his real name… and he wanted your help in a big-time scheme he had cooked up."

Gromley dropped the heavy sacks on the workbench and shifted a step to Mitchell's left and into the deeper shadows at one corner of the milling platform.

"I came here as Henry Forestall's partner," he countered. "Henry asked me to come out and see the operation before I put any more of my money into the partnership."

"That's not quite true," Mitchell answered. "Forestall did have a deal going with Frank Gromley; but you're not Frank Gromley. At least that's what your drawings tell me."

"My drawings..."

"Pen and ink engravings actually," Mitchell asserted. "I've seen that kind of work before... meticulous kind of work... every line perfectly placed... the kind of drawing a professional engraver would do. But not something Frank Gromley would do."

"The signature..." Gromley hissed.

"Owen Lachner," Mitchell replied.

Lachner moved again and was swallowed in the shadows. "I should have left those drawings packed away," he growled from the shadows. "I never let anyone into that room... but that stupid woman had to kill Forestall right there. I told Canfield she was trouble." Lachner's voice changed in volume, growing quieter as the man slipped farther away.

Something clattered near the doorway. Four quick strides brought the door back into view, but Lachner was still hidden by the bulk of the milling platform. Mitchell eased the leather loop from the Smith & Wesson's hammer and stepped closer to the heavy timbers of the platform.

Gromley was lost in the shadows, moving silently, like a cat on a carpet of sawdust and wood chips, his movements hidden by the early morning sounds of the mill itself… the soft crack of expanding wood as the heat of the morning sun touched the building… the brush of a tree branch against an outer wall… the erratic tapping of a wire draped across a wall and touched by an errant current of air sweeping in from the open doorway….

It was nearly silent, yet not.

"You shouldn't have killed that little girl!" Mitchell called into the silence of the mill.

For a moment, the silence continued. Then Mitchell felt the hair on the back of his neck stand on end.

"Don't move." Lachner's voice came from somewhere above… somewhere on the upper deck of the milling platform.

"Everything was going smoothly," he said coldly. "But when I saw the girl playing with that coin, she had to go. They both had to go. The boy ain't right in the head, but once they started talking about finding gold coins up here, everyone in town would wonder what was going on. I put a lot of effort into this deal, and I couldn't let a couple of kids screw it up. But that idiot stable boy got away, and everything started to come apart."

Sunlight touched the doorway. A cool breeze drifted across the floor, stirring the sawdust and the smaller debris littering the floor. A voice whispered, and Mitchell turned to face the muzzle of Lachner's pistol.

"You shouldn't have killed that little girl," he said coldly. "Now it's time for the *shadow man* to come home."

Mitchell threw himself to one side. Gromley's pistol roared in the confines of the mill, reverberating from the walls and showering dust from the rafters twenty feet above the floor. Gromley stabbed the pistol downward through the white smoke of burnt powder, searching for a target, but finding none. Angrily, he leaned over the platform railing, but Mitchell was gone.

Like a snake, Mitchell squirmed beneath the structure of the platform, forcing his way between the unmoving posts and cross braces that held the platform together. It was a dark and painful route, but it had been his only chance, and for the moment, he was happy to worm his way between the heavy timbers that supported the platform, working his way towards the open doorway and the beckoning light of the outside world.

Without hesitation, Mitchell thrust himself between the last of the beams supporting the platform and hurled himself through the open doorway. Two steps… he twisted around the door frame. Lachner's pistol bellowed behind him, but Mitchell was clear of the opening when the Remington's .36 caliber ball ripped through the door frame, flinging splinters into the clearing beyond the door.

Lachner was at the door in an instant. His revolver boomed three times in quick succession, belching smoke in Mitchell's direction, spitting lead wildly into the pinions beyond the clearing. For a moment, Lachner was hidden in a roiling cloud of sulfurous smoke. The mountain reverberated as the sound of the gunshots rolled outward in all directions, down the mountain and into the town where people stopped for a moment and looked upward toward the unseen sails of the mill.

Then the .44 American roared twice.

Chapter 27

Utah Territory
Snake Valley—June 1869

The sun was high, and the ground threw off waves of heat that shimmered across the air, twisting and stretching the desert into a dreamscape of unreality. Mitchell eased the pigeon-toed Milo to a walk.

There was no hurry now. Owen Lachner was dead and waiting for buzzards on the mountain behind Silver City, and Grady Cannon was not far ahead.

Cannon had missed the turn-off for the old express road at Willow Springs and followed the road south into Snake Valley. There, the road had quickly turned into a dust covered trail of rocks—rocks that beat at the lightweight chassis of Cannon's buggy and threatened to rip the wheels from the axles.

A mile south of the springs, Cannon slowed his team to a walk, as though searching for the express road, and turned southeast, out of the rutted trail, weaving between clumps of shadscale and rocks, searching for smoother ground but finding only more of the same unforgiving terrain. But Cannon drove on; heedless of the battering to the buggy, searching for a road that was ten miles farther north. And Mitchell followed, past the cutoff and into the desert, tracing the buggy's trail of crushed and broken shadscale, dislodged rocks, and sporadic wheel marks. Fifteen miles from the springs and far from the old express road the trail ended, and Mitchell paused to study the dry earth.

Snake Valley, like most of the desert in the territory, was not barren of life. In fact, life was abundant, if a fellow took the time to observe. The hard-packed ground was unforgiving and dry enough to choke the life from most plants, but the things that lived here had adapted to the bone dry earth and the orb that blazed overhead, sucking the moisture from everything that had neither the sense nor the ability to find shade or water.

Across the flats grew a scattering of shadscale, salt grass, and stunted sagebrush that punched through shattered bits of stone and rock-hard mud that had been alternately soaked by rain and baked by the sun for thousands of years. It was an ancient place—a place avoided by most men, but home to thousands of rodents, jackrabbits, coyotes and snakes. It was a place that cared nothing for those who wandered there, whether by accident or by choice. It was a place that simply existed; brushed by the winds, beaten by the rains, and baked by the sun.

"Tracks just disappear," the Pratt kid observed.

Thoughtfully, Mitchell dismounted and walked the roan between patchy clusters of plant life.

"Now where did they go?" he muttered unhappily.

To his left, several small up-thrusts of ragged stone stabbed upward out of the valley floor like small mountain peaks. At the base of each, fan-like flows of shattered rock spread outward onto the flats in a hard-packed layer that would easily hide the tracks of the buggy and its team.

For a moment, Mitchell felt miniscule. Like an ant staring out into the depths of the universe, the depth and breadth of the wilderness flooded his senses with a deep sense of how tiny and vulnerable he really was.

For a long while, Mitchell scanned the rocks. Nothing moved, but he knew Cannon could even now be hiding in the rocks, watching.

"Something ain't right," he told the kid.

Deliberately, he turned and walked back the way they had come. In less than a hundred yards, he found it—a melon-sized stone half-buried in the ground and the telltale mark of a wheel, veering off to the west and into a deep arroyo. Mitchell drew the Smith & Wesson and walked slowly to the edge of the gully.

The team was gone. The broken-down buggy lay on its side, one wheel smashed beyond repair, with parts of it strewn along the bed of the arroyo. All was silent. Nothing moved.

For a long while, Mitchell stood at the edge of the gully, letting his eyes rove the arroyo and the surrounding landscape. Finally, his gaze caught and held. Twenty yards away, on the opposite wall of the arroyo, and darker patch of soil lay exposed—soil disturbed by the passage of more than one large animal.

"Horse tracks," he said quietly.

Minutes later, the roan lunged up the side of the gully and onto the flats beyond. It was there they found Eliza Richards sprawled face down and half-concealed within the embrace of a cluster of shadscale. Grimly, Mitchell brought the roan to a halt and dismounted near the bedraggled form of the woman. The woman made no sound, nor did she move. And long before Mitchell reached her, he knew Eliza Richards was dead.

The ground was splashed with her blood, and when Mitchell rolled her body from the salt bush, the woman's eyes were open wide and her throat slashed from ear-to-ear.

The Pratt kid stepped back as the body rolled over. "Damn!"

Mitchell swallowed hard at the sight of the woman who had caused so much trouble—a woman who had hired at least a dozen men to kill the entire Mitchell household. More than a dozen people had died because of her greed, and Mitchell had disliked the woman immensely. In his mind, she had surely earned her demise. Still, it bothered Mitchell that the woman had gone to her maker bearing such a heavy load of misdeeds.

Grimly, he set about the task of burying the body. He had no tools, but the gully was there, and with his knife, he cut lose a section of the buggy's black canvas top and wrapped the body tightly. Thirty minutes later, the bank of the arroyo slid downward, covering the remains of Eliza Richards. For a moment, Mitchell looked up into the blue vault overhead.

"Lord," he said quietly. "You know I didn't like this woman. She seemed like a bad one to me. But *you* know us all, and she's in your hands now. So keep this place safe until I can send someone to give her a decent resting place."

For a moment, Mitchell stood near the makeshift grave. The smell of freshly turned soil hung faintly in the air. It was the smell of damp earth, the musty smell of age, the smell of time and stability.

Thoughtfully, Mitchell paused. Something had changed. The world felt different. The light seemed brighter. The air smelled clean and cool like it did after rainstorm. And on the periphery of his vision, something moved.

He could almost see her. She stood at the edge of the arroyo like the specter of a lost little girl, staring down at the dark hump of soil. Frantically, she looked from side to side, as though unable to comprehend her situation.

Mitchell could feel the sudden panic that seized the ghostly figure. Yet beneath the panic, he felt something else, and for an instant, he thought he understood the woman.

"Don't be afraid," he said quietly.

The eyes of the wraith turned and riveted on Mitchell's face, and panic turned to terror.

"It's time to go home," Mitchell added soothingly. "And that old fellow behind you has come to show you the way."

The wraith turned and stared at the old man who stood quietly waiting. A moment later, both were gone as though they had never existed.

The sun beat down unmercifully on Mitchell's shoulders, dragging him back to a sense of his own time and place. The day was hot. The sky was clear. And the air was filled with the smell of sage and the sound of the wind brushing across the ground with the soft clatter of leaves jostling one another.

"That fellow has three horses now," Mitchell told the kid. "I guess he figured that gal would just slow him down."

Bleakly, Mitchell climbed into the saddle and spurred the roan out of the gully. The animal took the side of the arroyo in two lunging jumps and came out on the flats above with all four feet planted and his forward momentum exhausted. For a long while, they stood on the brink of the gully as Mitchell scanned the area for signs of Cannon's passage. But Cannon had vanished.

Mitchell dismounted and carefully walked the ground in sweeping arcs, searching for traces of the killer. Thirty minutes later, he stopped and massaged the stiff muscles at the back of his neck.

"Nothing," he muttered crossly.

The roan stood quietly, nipping at the sparse grass, and in the distance, miles to the southeast, the dark shapes of crows whirled and dived in aerial chaos.

For a moment, Mitchell watched the birds, and pondered their odd behavior. They seemed much too far from their normal haunts.

"What now?" asked the Pratt kid.

Mitchell shook his head. "I've lost the trail," he admitted. "The ground's so hard he's not leaving any marks."

"We could circle a bit... he's probably still headed south," the kid offered. The kid was silent for a moment. "You know... that was that Richards woman that caused so much trouble in Ogden last fall."

Mitchell nodded. "It was... and this Cannon fellow... I'm sure he's her husband, Jason Canfield. He's a bad lot, and it looks like he decided she wasn't worth taking along. He'll be moving fast now, and I hate to waste time just looking for a place to start."

For a moment, Mitchell stood quietly. "We need a dog," he said suddenly.

Thoughtfully, he reached into his shirt pocket and retrieved his stash of jerky. He focused his attention on the nearest cluster of saltbush.

"I see you," he called out to the bush. "Come out of there and make yourself useful."

For a moment, nothing happened, only the wind moved, rattling the leaves.

"If you don't come out, I'll let those crows have it all," he threatened.

Slowly, the dog rose to its feet and looked out through the leaves of the shadscale. Mitchell flipped a piece of the jerky across the gap between them, and the dog lunged forward to snap up the treat.

"Guess you got a dog," the Pratt kid muttered.

"Let's see if she has a nose on her," Mitchell suggested.

For more than an hour, they followed the sniffing, barking dog as she dashed ahead, twisting and turning among the salt brush. The ground had changed, and Mitchell had no trouble following the trail himself, but the dog ran eagerly now, running ahead then turning back to bark at Mitchell, as though urging him to greater speed, then rushing ahead again following the trail.

The dog found the horse, and the paint horse was dead. Canfield had ridden the animal hard and fast, until a lather of sweat had covered its neck and shoulders, and the animal had dropped in its tracks.

"That was unnecessary," Mitchell growled.

"Looks like he stripped it and rode off on one of the others," the Pratt kid offered.

"What did he gain by that?" Mitchell complained. "With three horses, he could ride practically day and night. We'd never catch up."

"They'll all be tired now," the kid observed. "He'll have to stop."

Mitchell let his eyes scan their surroundings. Canfield was nowhere in sight, but the tracks of his horses led eastward into a narrow canyon where sandstone cliffs rose steeply into the sky.

Mitchell felt the hair prickle on the back of his neck. Canfield could be anywhere.

"I don't like this," he told the kid. "We're sittin' ducks."

The words were hardly out of his mouth when Daniel's horse stiffened, and the roar of a gunshot thundered down the canyon. The horse dropped. The Pratt kid had no time to kick loose of the stirrups and was dragged to the ground with the dying animal. The animal rose up, instinctively struggling for life, but the bullet had struck the saddle just ahead of the Pratt kid's left knee, driving through the thick leather and puncturing the animal's lungs.

With one foot free, the Pratt kid forced his knee against the saddle's seat and pushed. Again, the animal struggled to rise, and the Pratt kid slid from beneath the animal and snatched his rifle from its scabbard.

In an instant, the Pratt kid disappeared into the brush covering the slopes at the mouth of the canyon, and only the sharp *crack* of breaking branches gave any indication of his progress as he forced his way toward the dry riverbed at the bottom of the ravine.

Mitchell scowled and jumped the roan onto a narrow trail leading up the mountainside into the junipers. Finally, when they were lost in the thick of the trees, he dismounted and tied the roan. He had no idea what the Pratt kid intended, but for the moment, the kid was unharmed and out of sight. The shot had come from somewhere high in the cliffs on the south face of the canyon walls, and Mitchell knew that Canfield could easily follow their movements unless they could stay hidden in the thickest stands of brush and trees.

Slowly, Mitchell eased his way through the trees. For two-hundred yards, he moved like a cat stalking a bird, until finally, he stopped beneath the protective cover of several closely spaced junipers. Quietly, he opened the Smith & Wesson and added a round to the chamber beneath the hammer. Only then did he continue working his way through the trees, moving from one thick stand to the next, avoiding every clearing that might reveal his position.

It was a trick of the mountain that worked against him now. Like every hunter, he was well aware that a high position on an opposite ridge could open up a view that exposed anything that moved, and he knew his only hope of crossing to the opposite side of the canyon was to move slowly and deliberately and stay hidden beneath the canopy of the trees.

For a long while Mitchell stood quietly in the depths of the junipers. Carefully, he scanned the cliffs, searching for any sign of Canfield. From where he stood, the mountain sloped downward for several hundred feet then dropped vertically into the bottom of the canyon. The opposite side of the canyon, however, was a steep climb from the dry streambed across loose fans of rubble to the base of a cliff that loomed like a gigantic sandstone wall, towering more than three-hundred feet above the dusty canyon floor. It seemed impossible that the shot that had killed the Pratt kid's horse could have come from the cliffs, yet there was no other possibility. Only the cliffs offered a place with a view clear enough for that kind of shot. Carefully, Mitchell studied the cliffs, imagining the most likely path of the bullet, until at last he found the place where Canfield must surely be hidden.

It was a well protected spot, set high above the canyon floor, nearly invisible beneath an outward bulge of the cliff, blending into the colors of the sandstone mountain as though it belonged there. Yet, it was a man-made thing, built from scraps of the mountain itself and wedged into an angular hollow eroded from the face of the cliff.

Mitchell had seen its like only once before, and he marveled at the engineering that had allowed those ancient men to build their homes in the face of a cliff. It was an ancient place—a place of shadows—a place where hot winds gusted upward from the desert floor, sucking the dust and debris of lost millennia into a windborne cloud that surged in fits and starts through the winding canyon to the heights of the mountains above. The ruins were old. Even the dust smelled of age, and Mitchell felt as though he had been thrown into a time that had died a thousand years before his own ancestors had set foot on the continent.

The world was silent; the birds said nothing; no animals moved. And the mountain waited as Mitchell stood on a carpet of fallen needles, listened to the silence, breathed the smell of the junipers and tasted the sandstone dust.

Ten minutes later, Mitchell eased himself along a narrow path, testing each step before committing his full weight to the fractured surface of the ledge. For the most part, the sandstone path was strong enough to bear his weight, and foot by foot he shuffled forward until at last, he stepped onto the wider surface of the ancient alcove and stood among structures more than a thousand years old.

For a moment, the feeling of age weighed down upon him. His lungs grew heavy with the breath of ancient air, and the shadows thickened in the expanses beyond crumbling doorways and broken walls. Cautiously, Mitchell slipped from sunlight into the shadows cast by the vanishing disc of a fiery crimson sun.

The ruin breathed in a hot breath, lifting red sandstone dust in tiny swirls that spun fitfully between crumbling walls. The shadows whispered, and Mitchell shivered at the sound of a voice at the fringe of his perception. He felt the hair rise on his arms and for the hundredth time prayed that his mind was not lost on a path to insanity—a path where voices clamored for attention and reality vanished in a dream of continual war and devastation.

The dreams were the worst of it. And when they came, it was as if his soul dangled from a pendulum that rocked between alternate realities and left him clinging to a barely rational sense of self. He was himself, and yet he was not. And it was that other self that gave him pause and filled him with a feeling of infinite age and purpose.

With infinite care, Mitchell worked his way closer to the ancient stone wall and eased himself to a place where the stonework had broken away and tumbled to the floor of the alcove. It was a natural lookout, for it stood at the brink of the cliff, yet a little above the other structures crowded towards the back the huge expanse of the hollow and afforded a view into the shadowy rooms of the apartment-like complex. Yet his hiding place guarded the path leading from the cliff, making it a stronghold against any force attempting to enter the complex by means of that narrow ledge. For a long while, he stood beside the wall, watching and listening. When the sound came, it was the sound of a footstep—a boot crunching softly in the eroded gravel that had collected at the foot of nearly every wall.

Quickly, he took a step toward the sound, and his boot came down on a rock. It was not a large rock—hardly as big as an apricot, but it was large enough, and when the heel of his boot came down on its rounded surface, it rolled, twisting his ankle outward. Arms flailing, he stumbled violently, his body lurching clumsily toward the edge of the alcove floor and a sudden plunge into the canyon below.

Suddenly, he was down on one knee and sliding toward the edge. The edge was mere feet away, and there was no time to think. His reaction was instinct alone as he stabbed the barrel of the Henry rifle point first into the hard surface of the sandstone ledge, dragging it like a brake until his momentum slowed and he came to a stop.

Less than a foot from the edge, he stared into the depths below.

He saw it there—in the bottom of the canyon where water had once filled the streambed and flowed down into the valley. It was a sinkhole larger than any he had ever seen. It was dark and deep, and its grinning mouth spanned the entire width of the canyon bottom, sneering at the heavens like the fanged jaws of a medieval gargoyle, sucking moisture from the mountain into the abyss below.

"That's a dang big hole."

Mitchell flinched at the sound of the old man's voice.

"You're gonna get yourself shot," he hissed angrily. "I thought you were back at that tower."

The old man inched his way to a spot beside Mitchell and peered into the abysmal depths below.

"Thought I'd tag along…you always this clumsy?"

"I stepped on a danged rock."

"Hell of a drop."

"You think?"

Carefully, Mitchell eased himself back from the edge, not trusting his footing on the rounded slope that had nearly taken him into the depths below. When he had regained more level ground, he moved closer to the ancient structures.

"Them old folks must have been built like mountain goats," the old man muttered.

"They must not have been scared of heights," Mitchell offered as he searched the complex.

In the fading light, the shadows grew longer and deeper, until finally, in the fading glow of sunset, he glimpsed a flicker of movement—a shadow among shadows, flitting swiftly through the arch of an open doorway.

"That has to be Canfield," he told the old man who had joined him silently and now stood at his shoulder. "Now we know where he is, we can work our way down there and catch him between us.

"Reckon not," the old man responded. "I ain't here to collect that fellow, bad as he is."

"Then why are you here?" Mitchell demanded.

"To watch your back—like I always done."

Thoughtfully, Mitchell stared at the crimson sky flowing over the mountains and flooding the valley. There was a familiarity in the glow of the evening sky, and in his mind's eye, he saw a swirling pattern of lights gathering behind him like a cloud of brilliant white sparks—sparks that followed like the chisel-shaped point of an arrow as he pierced the angry crimson heart of the enemy.

"Mortiel," he whispered.

"I'm here," the old man responded. "Until you're done with this world and take back this calling."

The fiery disc of the sun dropped lower on the ragged tops of the Deep Creek range. Shadows grew darker, lengthening across the faces of the ancient buildings. Mitchell glanced quickly around the eroded corner of a crumbling structure, searching for any sign of movement. When nothing moved, he hurried across a narrow alleyway to the next building.

Only moments before, he had seen the telltale whisper of dust curling across the ground, and he knew that Canfield had slipped unseen into one of the crumbling structures, disappearing into the depths of the complex. All was quiet. Mitchell slipped past a crumbling wall, intent on the spot where the dust had moved. The shadows whispered with movement, and he cocked the forty-four.

Canfield lunged out of the shadows with an explosion of violence and hatred that caught Mitchell by surprise. The knife in his fist slashed downward, slicing through cloth and flesh, sliding across bone.... It was only the whisper of a voice on the wind that saved Mitchell... a whisper that urged him to turn in the instant Canfield lashed out.

Mitchell went down hard on the rough surface of the alcove floor, his left arm ablaze with pain. Canfield came down on top, and the blade slashed again, smashing against the trigger guard of the Smith & Wesson in a blow that sent both weapons spinning across the terrace. Mitchell lashed out with a fist and Canfield rolled aside, his nose broken and gushing blood. But the killer came to his feet snatching at the pistol tucked in his belt.

"I'd rather cut your throat and watch you choke to death," he snarled. "But you've been a burr under my saddle way too long. And it don't really matter how I kill you, long as the job gets done."

Mitchell said nothing, but got slowly to his feet, his right arm cradling his damaged left across his chest. Canfield watched closely, shifting his pistol and centering the bore on the base of Mitchell's throat.

"I thought you was dead," he snarled. "When Jack Kelton was killed back in fifty-seven, some folks said it was you that done it. I didn't believe it though; because I knew we left you dead in that ravine up on the mountain. Then you showed up in Ogden last year...."

Slowly, Mitchell worked his fingers into the pocket of his shirt and fished out a piece of jerky.

"Mort found me and pulled me out of that ravine," he replied. "So I guess you didn't do a very good job of killing me."

"I'll do it right this time," Canfield snapped.

"Why did you kill that little boy?" Mitchell demanded suddenly.

Canfield cocked the pistol. "Those kids took a coin from the sawmill," he replied. "We couldn't have them showin' everyone what they found... too many questions. We caught up with them, but the girl didn't have it, and the boy run off. The others caught up with the boy, and I heard shootin' down by the road, but they never come back. I could never get near the kid after that, and I knew he'd show it around. Sooner or later someone would realize it was a fake and start askin' questions. So, Eliza and me figured it was time to get out. I got the little brat though."

"And then you killed Eliza... what was that all about?"

"She thought she should rule the roost. I finally got tired of all her crap. Same as I'm sick of you and those women of yours. The one stabbed me with a damned hatpin you know. I got an infection from that... damn near crippled me."

"Too bad it didn't do worse," Mitchell growled.

"Shut your mouth!" Canfield waved the pistol. "I'll take care of that one.... And we'll see how *she* likes hatpins."

For a moment, Mitchell was silent. Dark shadows darted across the ground, and he felt an anger rise up from somewhere deep inside—anger that this man took no thought for the lives he ruined.

"I think not," he said coldly.

"You ain't even got a gun," Canfield hissed. "And I've had about enough of you and that crazy old man, and your women too. Nobody's gonna save your ass now!"

"Maybe... maybe not," Mitchell said quietly and flipped the jerky across the gap between them.

Suddenly, the shadows scrambled madly, and like leaves caught in the tangle of a whirlwind, the crows dropped in a chaotic, squawking mass, clawing and tearing at the prize. Canfield staggered backward with the assault, throwing his hands up and firing wildly into the flapping black cloud.

Another step....

Suddenly, the killer was down and sliding....

A moment later, he was over the edge and gone.

Cautiously, half afraid of sliding into the abyss, Mitchell worked his way to the edge of the cliff and looked down into the black depths of the sinkhole. But Canfield was gone, and the world felt cleaner for it.

Something moved behind him, and quietly, Mitchell looked over his shoulder as the old man shuffled down from the ruins above.

"Them birds... now that was tricky," the old man muttered. He arched himself awkwardly and looked down into the pit. "Well, he's down that hole like an egg suckin' snake," he growled. "And good riddance."

Silently, Mitchell looked up at the sky where the stars were beginning to light up the heavens. A warm wind surged up from the valley below, and he felt a sudden calmness, as though a healing balm had touched a wound that had festered for much too long.

"You done good," the old man said softly. "I can feel it on the air... The war ain't over, but every bit makes a difference... The stars are weeping for a brother gone bad, but they're smiling 'cause that feller ain't gonna hurt no one again."

Chapter 28

Utah Territory
Fish Springs—July 1869

Twenty miles southeast of Silver Creek, between the shimmering waters of Fish Springs and the old Express Road, a campfire flickered with yellow and orange flames and filled the night with the smell of smoke and the crackling snap of burning pinion. Sparks drifted around the flames, rising slowly and burning out quickly in the stillness of the evening air.

The night was silent save for the crackling of the fire and the endless chirping of a billion crickets. And the travelers, exhausted from the day's journey sat close to the flames, savoring the warmth and listening to the singing of the insects.

"What made you think the Emma was connected to the Lost Crow?" Sarah asked quietly. "No one else suspected they were anywhere near one another."

"It was the smell," Mitchell confessed. "Down in the Emma, Gromley took me to the place where Deagan and Williams blasted open that little pocket and found Barrett's body. Deagan and Williams had already worked well beyond that spot, and the new crew had gone even deeper. So, I was able to take a good look around. Everything had been shored up… the hanging wall, everything. There were so many timbers supporting the area that it all looked pretty solid.

"But the thing that intrigued me was the water. It was only a small amount, but it was seeping down from the headwall. And it smelled bad. At first, I thought it was just the smell of mules from a puddle on the floor, but I could still smell it after we left the mine. It turned out some of that water had dripped on the sleeve of my shirt. And that's what got me thinking about Barrett and mules, and how Barrett might have ended up in the Emma mine. And that's when I suddenly realized that Barrett was never in the Emma at all."

"I'm not sure I follow you," Sarah confessed. "What did the water have to do with any of this? And whose body did Deagan and Williams discover?"

"I was a little confused myself," Mitchell admitted. "When I rode down from the Emma, nothing was making any sense. I wasn't paying attention, and the roan turned up the road towards Barrett's claim. Once I realized where we were headed, I decided to look around a bit. Someone had destroyed the head-frame and the work shack, but I didn't think it was Barrett.

Barrett had talked about working the Lost Crow again, so it seemed unlikely that he would take down the only means of getting down into the mine. That meant someone else must have been there and put the hoist out of commission. And I wondered, *why*? There was no reason for it, unless someone was trying to hide something."

"You thought there was something hidden there?" Susan asked.

"Definitely...but I didn't know what.... So, I sat down on the platform to think about it. I started teasing the dog with a bit of jerky, and she nearly went down the shaft chasing it. That's when I noticed that horse urine had saturated the ground beneath the platform. I think that's when I realized where the water in the Emma was coming from. And I knew how Barrett had ended up wedged in that little pocket of solid rock."

"The Lost Crow!" Sarah exclaimed suddenly. "Barrett was in the Lost Crow, not the Emma!"

"Exactly," Mitchell agreed. "Everyone assumed it was a pocket set in solid rock, but Barrett was killed down in the bottom of the Lost Crow, and Barrett's killer had set off a charge that ripped loose a big chunk of the hanging wall in the Lost Crow's lowest tunnel. That big hunk of rock dropped right on top of Barrett's little tomb and plugged it like a cork in a bottle.

Deagan and Williams had no idea that they had cut into the bottom of the Lost Crow. Fractures in the hanging wall are not uncommon. So Deagan, Williams, and everyone else had no reason to think anything of it. The plug was big; it spanned the entire width of the Emma tunnel. And with a few timbers, every indication that they had cut through the bottom of the Lost Crow disappeared."

"So there was nothing to show any connection between the two mines, and only the killer knew what had happened to Barrett," Susan concluded.

"That's right," Mitchell replied.

"Forestall wanted a partnership in Barrett's operation," Mitchell explained. "He knew Barrett had a claim producing a little gold, and Forestall needed it badly. The Emma had been producing galena in good amounts for about a year, but with the war over, the market for lead had nearly dried up, and the Emma was playing out.

"In September, Grady Cannon came to town. Eliza Richards was not far behind, and for a while Forestall forgot his problems with the mine. But he couldn't ignore them for long. So he went to Barrett and tried to make a deal. When Barrett refused his offer, Forestall was in a panic. Gromley's money was gone, and Gromley was already in Ogden and on his way to Silver Creek.

"But Gromley was a strange fellow. When he finally arrived in October, he seemed almost clueless when it came to business. He wandered around town, but paid little attention to the mine, and when folks asked him how things were going at the mine, he told them he could see loaded ore carts coming out of the mine every day, and for him, that meant the Emma was making money.

"Then Barrett disappeared, and Forestall saw a new opportunity to take over Barrett's claims and get some cash flowing. He made an offer to Ellen Wells, but she refused. So, he paid Taggart to show him where Barrett was getting his gold, and about three months ago, Forestall started taking a wagon load of ore out of the Polecat mine every night. All he had to do was wait. When he could show Barrett had abandoned the claims, he could file on them and take over."

Sarah frowned. "I'm surprised Mr. Gromley was so lackadaisical about his money.... Most investors would be expecting a return on their money."

Mitchell nodded. "Gromley was not as innocent as he seemed. In fact, Frank Gromley was dead."

"Dead!" Susan hissed. "How could he be dead?"

"That was a little hard to figure out," Mitchell replied. "It had to do with Grady Cannon though."

"Grady Cannon killed Mr. Gromley?" Susan asked.

"In a way.... Grady Cannon and Eliza Richards were partners for years," Mitchell explained. "They must have come here shortly after our dealings with them in Ogden last fall. I can't be certain, but I think they planned on taking over the Emma mine long before they went after Barrett's claims. Eliza Richards married Forestall last November, so I'm sure they were both up to no good before Barrett disappeared. Ellen Wells said Forestall had been ill for several months.

"I think his new wife started poisoning him as soon as they were married, and I think she was using mercury so it would look like Forestall had been exposed to it by accident. I don't know how she was doing it... putting it in his food maybe... I don't know... but it was killing him slowly, and eventually Eliza Forestall would own the Emma or at least half of it."

Sarah shook her head. "But the Emma was producing only a little galena and very little silver. There was no money to be made from the mine," she reasoned.

"That's true," Mitchell agreed. "But by the time they realized the Emma was a failing lead mine, they were in too far. So, Cannon came up with a revised plan—a plan that became more complicated than they expected."

"Something to do with the windmill?" Susan asked.

"Yes," Mitchell admitted. "Cannon had another partner… a counterfeiter named Owen Lachner. Cannon sent a telegram telling this fellow to come at once. Lachner was a skilled fellow, and he had engraved a set of stamping dies that he claimed could stamp out perfect twenty dollar gold Eagles. It was Lachner who met Gromley on the express road. Gromley must have told Lachner where he was headed and that all his dealings with Forestall had been through a lawyer. When Lachner realized Forestall and Gromley had never met, he saw an opportunity he wasn't going to pass up. So, he killed him."

"Then he came into town and pretended to be Gromley," Susan added.

"He did," Mitchell agreed. "But they had a problem… no gold…. And not enough silver in the Emma to spit at. But Barrett had gold, and everyone knew it.

"So, Lachner found Barrett at the Lost Crow and tried to cut a deal with him, but Barrett wanted nothing to do with it. So, Lachner killed him. Things should have been set after that, but they couldn't find the gold, and all they needed was a little....

"Cannon spent weeks going over every inch of the Lost Crow hunting for the vein. He never found it because Barrett had lost the vein at a shear-fault down on the lowest level. Some kind of geological movement had let one side of the fault drop and literally cut the vein in half. Last fall, Barrett told me his only hope was to drop a shaft straight down and try to find the vein at a lower level. That was going to take more money and equipment, and Barrett had neither. That's why he came to us for money. He sold us a partnership in all three claims to offset the possibility that he would never find that gold vein again.

"Cannon knew nothing about the fault, so he wasted a lot of time searching the mine, but found nothing. He was getting desperate when he finally spotted Forestall's men hauling ore from the Polecat claim after dark. He thought something fishy was going on, so he told Lachner, and Lachner started diverting all the high-grade ore to the windmill."

Sarah was silent, her mind rushing through the possibilities. "The dynamo!" She exclaimed. "They used the electricity from the dynamo to plate the lead coins with gold!"

Mitchell smiled. "They shipped galena ore from the Emma to the stamping mills near Tooele. Most of the lead was sold and the money used to cover the cost of running the Emma. That kept Forestall from suspecting anything, but they brought back some of the ore in lead ingots. They built a forge on the back of the mill and started melting the ingots down into coin-sized slugs. They ran the slugs through the stamping dies, making a rather good copy of a gold Eagle. The dynamo provided the electric current and they plated the slugs with the gold they took from Barrett's mine."

"Mort was telling me about dynamos and electric current just the other day," Susan admitted. "I had forgotten all about it."

"The coins were pretty good imitations," Mitchell confessed. "I found about five-thousand of them stashed in an old cliff ruin out in Snake Valley. It was hard to tell the difference between the counterfeits and the real thing. The fakes were a little lighter in weight, and the engravings on the real ones were just a little cleaner. Lachner was a real artist."

"He seemed so different from what he really was," Susan remarked, "so affable. But that's why you went back to his house.... You saw his signature on those drawings."

"I did. And when I got back to the house, the drawings were gone. I knew then something was fishy."

"What about Art Williams? Why was *he* killed?"

"That puzzled me for quite a while," Mitchell replied. "At first, I thought it had something to do with finding Barrett's body. But no one bothered Mike Deagan, and he saw everything Williams saw. The two of them were together every minute."

Sarah leaned forward and poked a stick into the fire, stirring the white hot coals in the bottom of the shallow pit. "He must have discovered something—something only he knew."

Mitchell shook his head. "Mike Deagan knew. But he never said anything. Deagan gave money to Williams, and Williams took samples from the Emma's number two tunnel to the assay office. When the results came back, he told Deagan what they meant. But Deagan had never been concerned about the assay or the results. He put in his money because Williams was his friend, and Williams couldn't let go of the idea they were digging a tunnel to nowhere. The assay proved him right. There was no ore coming from that tunnel, only rock... and no money being made from all their work."

"And who killed him?" Susan asked.

"Eliza Forestall. She was outside the assay office when Williams picked up the results of the assay, and she overheard him muttering about the results and how the Emma mine was a fraud. She knew people would question the purpose of a tunnel that produced no ore. So she followed Williams back to his shack and killed him."

"But why would she kill Henry Forestall?" Sarah asked. "The Emma was hardly worth it."

"He must have realized what she was up to," Susan suggested.

"It was the money," Mitchell answered. "For her, it was always the money. She knew the safe held all the legitimate money the company had. Forestall kept the company profits hidden there. And Eliza knew there were no counterfeits it that stash. It was the money paid to Desert Range for the ore they sent to the stamping mill near Tooele.

"Forestall knew nothing of the counterfeiting, but he knew that some of the ore they were sending to the mills came from Barrett's mine. Money from the galena operation barely paid the bills, and it was the money from Barrett's mine he kept hidden in that safe.

"Eliza knew how to look out for herself," Mitchell concluded. "All she had to do was get that stash, and she could live well for a long time. And no counterfeits to worry about."

Sarah sighed unhappily. "So she killed Forestall and took the money."

"All while Cannon and the others were trying to get away with the counterfeits," Mitchell added. "And they might have gotten away with it if Tommy Hawkins and Debbie Allingham hadn't gone poking around the sawmill and found one of their coins," Mitchell suggested. "After that everything went wrong."

Suddenly, Mitchell got to his feet and walked to where he had left the roan tied to the wagon. The animal stood patiently, saddled and ready to fly in an instant. But the quiet of the evening had done its job, and Mitchell felt at ease, as though the earth itself had breathed out a healing sigh.

Fifty yards away, in the shadows cast by a small cluster of cattails, Mortiel sat watching as Mitchell stripped the saddle from the pigeon-toed horse and began brushing the dust from the animal's back. The roan dropped its head like a big dog and leaned into the brush.

The old man sighed and looked upward, and in the vault of a darkening sky, he saw the first star of the evening smiling down on a brother he loved more than life itself. A brother whose calling he shared....

The old man smiled.

"Mouriel..." he whispered softly.

Author's Note

This story and its characters are fictional. It is a mingling of three genres, historical, mystery, and western. The historical facts are as accurate as I could make them and still allow enough flexibility for a very limited interaction between historical individuals and fictional characters.

Many of the scenes in this story unfold in settings that have changed greatly in the last one-hundred and fifty years. The town of Silver Creek did not exist. It is a fictional place, set at the mouth of Goshute Canyon in the Deep Creek Mountain range of Western Utah.

Susan and Sarah Flitton were real Mormon pioneers, although neither was ever involved in plural marriage or any gunfight that I am aware of. They were, however, part of the inspiration for this story, and I have taken the liberty of using their names for two of my main characters.

Susan Flitton was my 2nd great grandmother, and Sarah was her sister. Susan lived into her nineties, and in 1949, the State of Utah awarded Susan a bronze medal for being the oldest living Utah pioneer.

Any Latter-day Saint doctrines mentioned in this work are expressed in the context of a fictional character's interpretation, and may not represent *true* LDS thought on the subject.

Mouriel is a fictional character whom I have yet to meet.

We hope you enjoyed this book.
Please look for other books by J.T. Fleming at
Amazon.com – Barnes and Nobel
and other booksellers.
Available in trade paperback & E-book.

Your review at amazon.com
or
barnesandnobel.com
will be greatly appreciated.

Thank you!
Fortress Publishing LLC
fortresspublishingllc@gmail.com

About the Author

J.T. Fleming is a *Magna Cum Laude* graduate of Weber State University with a B.S. in English as well as a B.S. in Anthropology. Mr. Fleming works as a technical writer for an international manufacturing company and has published numerous stories as a community news correspondent with the Standard-Examiner in Ogden, Utah.

Mr. Fleming has written three books in the Collin Mitchell series: *Tracks of a Pigeon-toed Horse, The Obsidian Serpent, & Mouriel.*

Born and raised in Utah, Mr. Fleming is a member of the LDS church and has hunted deer, elk, and gold in the mountains and deserts of Utah and Colorado. With his wife and family, he lives west of the Wasatch Mountains, near the Great Salt Lake.

www.ingramcontent.com/pod-product-compliance
Lightning Source LLC
LaVergne TN
LVHW091021080826
845145LV00002B/321